ENGULFED BY NIGHT

Sometime around midnight, when all the lights in the Graham house were out, Mary awakened with a shudder. Again, she thought she was hearing the sound of hoofbeats.

She padded barefoot across the floor to the window and peered from behind the lace curtain at the dark midnight world just in time to see the ancient drawn coach. Pulled by four gigantic horses, it plunged precariously down the avenue and turned swiftly in the direction of the great woods. She wasn't able to see the coachman or the passengers. Even the horses were engulfed by nightshadows. The immense creatures' beating hooves clattered eerily in the silence of the town. There was a distant whinny, and they were gone. . . .

READ THESE HORRIFYING BEST SELLERS!

THE WITCHING (746, $2.75)
by Fritzen Ravenswood
A spine-tingling story of witchcraft and Satanism unfolds as a powerful coven seeks unrelenting revenge!

MOONDEATH (702, $2.75)
by Rick Hautala
A peaceful New England town is stalked by a blood-thirsty were-wolf. *"One of the best horror novels I've ever read . . ."*—Stephen King.

THE UNHOLY SMILE (796, $2.50)
by Gregory A. Douglas
Unblemished virgins, stone altars, human sacrifice . . . it sounded like an ancient sect. But the screams were too real, the blood too red, the horror too evil. And with each sacrifice, the satanic cult craved more . . .

DEATH-COACH
by J.N. Williamson (805, $2.95)
While the town of Thesaly slept, the sound of hoofbeats echoed in the night. An ancient, bloodthirsty vampire flew above the town, seeking the next hapless victim to be borne away by her DEATH-COACH . . .

CHERRON (700, $2.50)
by Sharon Combes
A young girl, taunted and teased for her physical imperfections, uses her telekinetic powers to wreak bloody vengeance on her tormentors—body and soul!

Available wherever paperbacks are sold, or order direct from the Publisher. Send cover price plus 50¢ per copy for mailing and handling to Zebra Books, 475 Park Avenue South, New York, N.Y. 10016. DO NOT SEND CASH.

DEATH-COACH
BY J. N. WILLIAMSON

ZEBRA BOOKS
KENSINGTON PUBLISHING CORP.

ZEBRA BOOKS

are published by

KENSINGTON PUBLISHING CORP.
475 Park Avenue South
New York, N.Y. 10016

Copyright © 1981 by J.N. Williamson

All rights reserved. No part of this book may be repro-
duced in any form or by any means without the prior written consent of the Publisher, excepting brief quotes used in
reviews.

Printed in the United States of America

Dedication

For Mary, my favorite wife; for Marylynn, Leslie Gelbman and Nancy Parsegian, my favorite sisters; and for my son John, who is everybody's favorite.

DEATH-COACH

But come! now hear how 'twas the sundered Fire
Led into life the germs, erst whelmed in night,
Of men and women, the pitied and bewailed;
For 'tis a tale that sees and knows its mark.
                                    —Empedocles

PROLOGUE

And insofar the lightest at their fall
Do strike together in the blood-streams,
    back-leaping into it.
The heart is nourished, where prevails the power
That man call thought; for lo the blood that stirs
About the heart is man's controlling thought.
                                        —Empedocles

The morgue of Indianapolis's Civic Hospital, despite local beliefs, was not in operation by night. No stygian shadows crept across the floor while moonlight revealed strange doctors doing stranger things.

It closed, most days, at four-thirty. Only the passing of a notable summoned Dr. Anthony Empusa from his comfortable northside home once he'd removed his shoes and devoured one of the Greek meals that Linda had recently learned to cook. He kept business hours; he was no more preoccupied with the dead than his neighbors; and his working quarters were well-illuminated, immaculate, and modern.

Until today.

They brought the body in on a gurney cart shortly after four o'clock and Tony Empusa merely glanced at it at first. There was no hurry. His customers weren't going anywhere and the police did not suspect homicide in this case.

He started to have the corpse transferred to the conveyor that slid decently out of sight into a wall of well-marked freezer compartments, then decided, sighing, to have a quick look. The attendants had already gone home for the day. He'd put the body away later himself.

Tony, at forty-nine, was an M.E. who enjoyed continuity. His outlook was 180 degrees away from that of the man who liked everything finished at the end of the day. Tony didn't *want* to begin fresh in the morning. He'd always preferred a cursory examination that might give him something to think over while he was at home. These days it helped keep him from missing his daughter, who'd got married last year, and his son, who was strung out somewhere on drugs.

It didn't have to be a big deal, that something to think about. Just a little question or nagging doubt that kept him alert, on his toes. Tony felt that it made him stay mentally fresh, ever new to his work.

He tugged the sheet free of the pale white form

and folded his arms across his chest. At this point in the examination Tony never touched them. He saw them, *really saw* them, appraised every visible inch, before lifting an eyelid or moving a bare arm.

Finally he switched on his lab recorder, and without removing his eyes from the *corpus*, spoke offhandedly into the swinging microphone: "Got here a deceased male, Caucasian, age estimate thirty to three-five, prelim report of heart attack as cause of death. No discernible scars or marks. Fingernails cyanotic, degree of rigor apparently normal."

Got here, he thought suddenly as he switched off, a living Caucasian male, age forty-nine, who has to take a leak.

Dr. Empusa retreated hastily from the main lab of the morgue, cursing the extra beer he'd had for lunch.

For awhile it was still as death, as quiet indeed as morgues are reputed to be. Giant ceiling fluorescents bathed the room in persistent, eye-aching brilliance. Equipment shone in readiness. The only motion occurred when the left arm of the deceased male, too close to the edge, toppled. It swung grotesquely until gravity halted the involuntary movement.

Then, *it* was there, the swarthy, umbrageous figure only feet from the corpse.

It would not be accurate to say that it materialized, since it entered the room in the usual way. Sure and silent, it moved quickly to the body on the cart. A flash of steel came from

11

beneath the caller's long, heavy coat and plunged, hastily carving in the region of the abdomen. When the caller straightened, dangling slimy, tubular things from its free hand, it paused only momentarily before dipping its head to drink.

Thirst slaked, mouth smeared scarlet in the insistent fluorescent glow as it oscillated its skull to peer around, it then hastened to the head of the gurney cart and bowed once more, this time to present a tender and meaningful kiss.

Finished, it stalked stealthily across the room to stand, crouching, in the shadow of a filing cabinet, entrails pocketed for later use.

Dr. Anthony Empusa returned, relieved, and found desecration.

Deeply shocked, his skilled fingers trembling as they felt the awful wound, he quickly ascertained that the carving had been done with surgical precision, and turned his head in outrage to scan the room.

That was his worst mistake, but it probably wouldn't have mattered in any case. What he confronted had never been defeated in the memory of man.

Having been returned to life during the bizarre three-thousand-year-old ceremony, the naked corpse sat up, a pale, white claw snaking-out to seize the M.E. from behind.

The caller, seeing the situation well in hand, stepped away from the filing cabinet and bestowed a pleasant smile of greeting.

Before his neck was snapped, Tony Empusa's memory flinched defensively backward to his

I

But come, by every way of knowing see
How each thing is revealed. Nor, having sight,
Trust sight no more than hearing will bear out,
Trust echoing ear but after tasting tongue;
Nor check the proof of all thy members aught:
Note by all ways each thing as 'tis revealed.
—Empedocles

The house was a gift from beyond the grave,
Mary felt—the last thing that Barry Graham
would ever do for her and their children.

That obligated her to keep it and move to
Thessaly, Indiana, and she resented Barry's
typical impulsiveness for the last of countless
times. He had been born a free-thinking, cre-
atively spontaneous creature, lived that way
despite every evidence of increasing poverty, and

17

had spent his secret hoard of cash on this house's down payment even as he was dying of lung cancer. Without telling her a word about it! It must have appealed to his romantically morbid side, what he called his "Poe possession," knowing how astonished she would be to learn she was a lady of property.

What a hopeless, irresponsible dreamer he'd been!

And, God! how she missed him, as she and two of their three children surveyed the unbelievable task before them.

The inexpensive nonunion moving men she'd hired to bring them from the Indianapolis apartment eleven miles to this Thessaly cottage had discharged their duties as casually as possible. Then they'd left Mary and the two kids to sort through the wreckage. Boxes, crates and chipped furniture lurked everywhere in the room like the peculiar stone figures in front of the houses of her neighbors. Thank God that Chuck was strong as an ox or they'd wind up sleeping on beds in the living room.

Pulling herself to her full five-six and pushing back a dark tousle of hair from her forehead, Mary Graham began getting things organized. Chuck, at seventeen, six foot and more than two hundred pounds, automatically got all the heavier assignments. He would be the only male present until Jeanne Lange brought Joey here tomorrow. Ellen, at fourteen, was given instructions to act as Chuck's memory bank, so that they could place things in locations similar to the old apartment

18

layout. As well, being a no-nonsense girl who enjoyed sporadic helpful moments, Ellen began hefting lighter boxes and articles of furniture without being told.

Mary smiled and went out to the kitchen to make sure the refrigerator and other fixtures were functioning properly, and to make lunch. While she was in a grateful mood, she thought, she should thank Heaven that Jeanne had agreed to keep Joey at her place overnight. The nine-year-old was classified "hyperkinetic" by one child psychologist, "emotionally disturbed in a moderate manner" by a second. Whatever terms they chose to describe him, he remained a child who managed to be beautiful despite a harelip scar, and one who managed to be hell-on-wheels despite his good looks. Sometimes Mary referred to her youngest as "Hurricane Graham," a designation everyone considered understatement. It depressed Mary to realize that Barry, the only one who had ever been able to corral Joey, was forever lost to them just days from Joey's tenth birthday.

The bologna sandwiches prepared and the Diet Pepsis divided into three glasses, Mary paused to shiver as she looked out the window at her new backyard. The furnace was running but it seemed so cold in this house. Seeing the range of trees marking the beginning of forty acres of forest only fifty yards from the french doors, the low December sky barely topping the massed spruces and elms, Mary wondered if her decision to move the family here had been just as impetuous as Barry's actually buying the property.

19

Buried only two months now, Barry's startling acquisition of the house had been announced in the reading of a will Mary hadn't known he had. She was sure there had been nothing intentionally secretive about it, nor about the money he had saved. Barry was simply Barry, given to dramatic surprises.

Yet she had felt no desire to see the cottage, at first. They had wanted to own their own house for years, but had never had the chance to lay aside enough money. Having a home only after Barry's death sentence seemed both ironic and hollow. How could she possibly rattle around in a house without him at her side?

The kids had viewed it differently, especially Chuck. "He wanted you to have it, Mom," the teenager reminded her one Sunday afternoon. "I'm sure that he would have told you about saving the money if he hadn't learned first about his sickness. And I'm sure he bought the place because he knew you'd never do it without him."

She knew the boy was right, and within ten days Mary had been talked into driving to Thessaly, "just to take a look." She had planned to appraise the value of the house and hire a real estate agent to dispose of it. Yet within another two weeks she had agreed to occupy the property when the lease on the apartment expired.

She thought now about the first reactions everyone had to Thessaly. The town, incorporated a scant twelve years before, was convenient to Mary's employment and the children's schools in Indianapolis. Ellen liked the fact that it was almost more a community than a town, the sign at the outskirts boasting of a population of 204. She thought that friends could be more readily made here than in the burgeoning city.

Reluctantly, Mary admitted liking the diversity of the town's houses. Although they were scattered east to west over a mile, with three parallel streets and two short intersecting streets, Thessaly had clearly existed as a rural community prior to twelve years ago. One of every three homes seemed to be teetering with age, ancient white frames dotted here and there as if in a forcible reminder of the area's roots. The majority of the other houses seemed to have been built when Thessaly was incorporated, except for a half-dozen or so tri-levels that appeared newer. None, she'd noted with passing surprise, seemed to have been erected for at least five or six years.

They had been curious about the heavy stone pillars, intricately but incomprehensibly carved, which stood before each Thessaly home. They reminded her of totem poles. In the one block offering the town's sole commerce, she had gone with Chuck into Nick's General Store, where they were greeted by an expressionless middle-aged man who said that he was "Nicholas Melas, Prop.," as suggested by the sign on his store.

"Those things are called *agyieus*," Melas answered them with a shrug, when they asked about the stone pillars.

"In what language?" Mary had inquired.

"Greek." Another shrug. "Everyone who lives in Thessaly is Greek, you know."

21

"No, I didn't know." She paused. "We may change that. My husband bought property on Attica Avenue."

He didn't appear surprised. "You moving in?" His question was sharp.

"We aren't sure about that yet." She had touched her son's arm. "Come along, Chuck. We have to get back."

At the door, Nick Melas's slightly strident voice stopped them. "We're hard to know, at first. But if you move in, we'll surely try to make you welcome."

She had turned to face him again. "What are the—the *agyieus* used for, Mr. Melas?"

"Protection. From the gods, an old custom," he'd replied. "To seek favor."

Mary and the children had laughed about it in their aging Granada. Well, it was an interesting place, but it represented too much of a change for them. Or so she'd thought and said until Joey began to cry. "I wanna come here," he'd announced from the back seat. Forcefully enough to make her twist and evaluate the disappointed expression on his well-proportioned little face.

"Why?" she'd asked.

"Daddy *wanted* us to," he wailed. And stopped, abruptly. "Besides, all those terrific woods behind the house—man, I could *always* be good if I have a place like *that* to play in!"

In a certain sense, that had settled it. Oh, she had argued that her youngest would only get lost in the woods or wander through them to distant U.S. 40. But Chuck quickly pointed out that the forest was full of paths that Joey could use and was fully fenced in with barbed wire and No Trespassing signs meant for nonresidents of Thessaly.

She had reminded them that the entire town, commercewise, seemed to be limited to Nick Melas's store, a Wake-Up gas station, one Haag Drug Store, a strange-looking church, a closed Lindner's Ice Cream Parlor, and a one-story house converted into a library. There was, she indicated, no bonafide supermarket, no police department or sheriff's office, no department or hardware store, no doctor's or dentist's office, no clothing stores, no moving picture theatres, and no bank. About where the town conducted its business—where City Hall was located—she had no suggestion to offer.

But pert Ellen quickly reminded her that they were within eleven miles of the sprawling Washington Square shopping center on the far east side of Indianapolis, available via a national highway that made the miles melt away to nothing. And Washington Square seemed to have everything.

"Then you all want to move to Thessaly?" she had asked, at last.

To her surprise, the vote was unanimously in favor of it.

Now, she sighed and turned from the window. Barry had made their bed and she had arranged for them to sleep in it. Whether it was a wise decision or not, here they were.

What was that?

She realized belatedly that she had seen something odd—something that didn't belong—through the window and deep in the woods.

She peered closely at the early winter haze and slowly shook her head. For a moment there she thought she'd seen an old-fashioned carriage pulled by a team of great horses. Mary laughed at her own imagination; she must be more tired than she realized.

Passing the built-in kitchen counter, her hands full of sandwiches, she glanced at an alarm clock she had placed there till they could tack the starburst clock to the wall. Nearly four o'clock. There was only an hour or so of daylight remaining. Hurrying, she turned to back through the pushing door separating the kitchen from the front of the house.

Turning back, she almost dropped the sandwiches.

A lovely, strange woman sat in the single easy chair that was unlittered by boxes. Part of Mary's shock came, she realized in an instant, because of the incredible loveliness of the stranger and her mesmeric eyes. "You must be Mrs. Graham," the woman said politely but without smiling.

"Why, yes." Mary smiled her own welcome although she detected something uncompromisingly steely about the other woman. "You must be one of our new neighbors." She put the saucers with sandwiches on corrugated boxes before Chuck and Ellen, noticing that each was perched in a manner to best see the stranger.

"I am Lamia Zacharius, but I fear that *you* are

the new neighbors," she said. The voice was quite low and well-modulated. There was the trace of an attractive, even enigmatic accent. Apparently near Mary's age of thirty-eight, the caller was tall and raw-boned, with high, prominent cheekbones beneath deep-set, inquisitively-exploring black eyes. The eyes, Mary thought, were the most striking she had ever seen. For a moment they looked almost masculine; then she realized that Lamia Zacharius simply reflected a directness, an adamant determination, rare in her own sex. Wearing a pants suit that looked to have come from a fine New York store, this Zacharius woman was chic, coolly self-controlled, and utterly beautiful. "I live on the next street up, Alexandria Avenue."

"How nice." Mary cursed herself for the idiotic rejoinder and realized how *gauche* she must seem in her own dirt-stained jeans and one of Barry's ancient white shirts. She looked for a place left to sit, fruitlessly, and tried to hide a torn pocket on the shirt. "It's good of you to stop by."

Lamia's enormous, wise eyes studied her with shocking frankness. "I do hope it will prove to have been good that you moved here. In the meanwhile, I wished to offer my tentative welcome." She paused, allowing her words to penetrate. "Tell me, my dear. Is Graham a Greek name or simply a perversion of one?"

"I have no idea of its derivation," Mary said tersely. She felt the short hairs on the back of her neck rise in protest, some of her old independence returning. "We are not particularly concerned with the question of nationality; we're not into the 'roots' thing, if you follow me."

"Oh? Well, that is unfortunate, Mrs. Graham, for *we* are. All of us." Her calculating gaze swept over young Chuck, already unable to keep his eyes from the beautiful visitor, outrageously seeming to seek his support. "A man or a woman is the sum of all his parts—his family heritage. *Nothing* is more important. Or so, at any rate, we of Thessaly believe. Universally."

Mary took a breath. "We don't," she said pointedly.

"*I* have an idea!" The lovely Lamia seemed to have achieved a marvelous revelation. "You might actually *have* a strand of Greek blood without realizing it! Or, since Graham is doubtlessly your married name, perhaps your *maiden* name is—"

"There's no point in continuing with this," Mary interrupted, crossing her arms over her upright bosom. "We are welcome if we're Greek. Otherwise, we are to be ostracized. Well, let me tell *you*—"

"No, no, *no!*" Lamia Zacharius laughed a chain of husky, golden bells, seeming for a moment a Greek Lauren Bacall. "You can be welcomed here in any case, of course! I fear that I have overstated the matter. It was merely a question of first things first."

"Would you care for some coffee or something, Mrs. Zacharius?" Chuck asked, eagerly. His mother shot him a withering glance.

"No, thank you, boy. And it's *Miss*, not Mrs.

Zacharius." She turned her full, blazing attention on the seventeen-year-old, peering at him from beneath a prettily lowered brow. At that instant she might only have been sixteen. "I haven't been a married woman for ages."

Young Ellen laughed and Lamia turned to her, brilliant and equally attentive.

"Oh, don't *laugh*, child." She offered a wide-mouthed smile, suddenly the Welcome Wagon personified. It was an astonishing performance. "It's quite a serious *mat*ter to be single at my advanced age." Then, as if catching herself in an unfashionable *faux pas*, she gave her hostess a look of confused sympathy. "I'm so terribly sorry about the way this has gone. I—I understand you're recently widowed."

"Yes, I am." Mary relaxed slightly, still wary of this exceptional woman. "My husband left this place to me in his will. He wanted us here."

"How very *for*tunate for you!" Lamia sighed theatrically. "He must have been a most considerate American."

Much of the waning daylight had already gone, Mary saw wanly, trying to hide a sigh. "We had a good marriage, I'm happy to say."

"You must not continue to grieve, Mary—*may* I call you that?" She didn't pause for an acknowledgment. "You see, Mary Graham, all that has happened is really just *change*. A subtle shifting of elements."

"But I don't have those elements with me any longer," Mary said sweetly, "Lamia."

"Change is at the very heart of life." The Greek

27

woman spoke just above a whisper, seeming to reveal vital data. "When one must experience her most demanding change, she is actually moving close to that throbbing, pulsing heartbeat of vivification. A vivification that *renews*, gives fresh meaning to life."

"Lamia, I'm sorry; but there's *so* much to do before we can call it a day." Enough was enough. Mary placed a hand on each child's shoulder. "Please do come again when we have more time to become properly acquainted."

A look of surprise, even respect, crossed her visitor's beautiful face.

Then Lamia arose in a single athletic motion, sinuous and swift. She was at least two inches taller than Mary, sleek as a female wolf, and considerably lighter. Yet her smile, just then, appeared genuinely warm. "I fear we're off to quite a shaky start, so I shall take you up on that, Mary, and make amends."

"There's no need." Mary's own smile was frosty.

Lamia touched Chuck's shoulder as Ellen saw her out, startled by her mother's lack of courtesy. When the door had closed behind Lamia, Chuck began giggling.

"Wow, wow, *wow!*" he exclaimed, striking a knee with his open palm. "*Wow!*"

"Wow *what?*"

"Like wow, she is *beautiful!*" His giggle came again, broad shoulders shaking and his crinkly blue eyes aglow with admiration. "That woman is a *gas!*"

28

"Why, yes," Mary said slowly, nodding as she turned; "I suppose she is."

With what was left of daylight the three of them finished arranging their bedrooms and that of the absent Joey Graham. Ellen helped Mary make the beds with crisp, fresh sheets. Finished finally, Mary appraised their efforts and nodded, both with satisfaction and relief. "It's beginning to look more like home," she complimented them happily, and Ellen hugged her.

They ate pork cutlets for dinner on the kitchen table, because the dining room suite was still covered with cartons and boxes. The children were rather subdued. Mary realized that, back at the apartment in Indianapolis, they would probably have gone out or entertained friends for the evening. But she was pleased to see that Chuck's gigantic, teenage appetite hadn't suffered in the least.

Together, they watched a few hours of television, staring at the screen over mountainous tables and chairs, then decided to call it a day. "I believe an early start is indicated in the morning," Mary told the kids, adding—above their groans—that she would settle for an eight o'clock kickoff.

She was in her own room, undressing for bed, when Ellen rapped at the door and then entered without waiting for an invitation. The young girl's eyes were round in disbelief.

"What is it?" Mary asked, curious. "What's going on?"

From behind her back Ellen produced a bottle the size of a magnum. "That woman—Lamia—

just came to the door. To give you this."

Mary hefted the enormous bottle.

It was an excellent brand of champagne.

Mary drank a glass, alone in her bedroom, and found her mind picking at some loose end that she temporarily couldn't grasp.

Then she did. Lamia Zacharius had called her by name from the outset. She had also known that Mary was a widow. How could she possibly know such facts? And what was the purpose of her visit anyway?

Well, the champagne was marvelous. Mary drank a second glass as she read a historical novel, then fell into exhausted, dreamless sleep.

As a rule, the Synod met nightly. Special sessions were called when necessary, even in the early morning or the middle of the night. All were called by the exclusive group of four entitled the Syndic—four, because it is the number of justice, steadiness and endurance—and usually by the Patriarch, himself. The number of meetings had increased of late.

Most of the Synod—which meant the people of Thessaly—attended the meetings because the Syndic controlled their lives, and their deaths. And because they respected the Patriarch more than any being on earth, in Heaven, or in Hades.

A saturnine, swarthy wrath of a man was on his feet. "I think we must learn *exactly* why they are here! Does anyone really believe what Lamia has told us?"

The Patriarch replied mildly, "I've inspected

the legal aspects. What she said appears to be the truth. The man, Barry Graham, purchased the property shortly before he died."

"But how could we have let it get away?" Vrukalakos protested. "It was essential that every piece of property in Thessaly remain in our control until after Commemoration."

"I'm afraid that's my fault," Nicholas Melas responded. His voice was tremulous as he tried to avoid peering into the dark man's mesmeric black eyes. "I named a price that was too much, more than the house was worth." He shrugged meaty shoulders. "But it was the amount Graham had saved and he wrote a check. It was done."

"Spilled milk, spilled milk," murmured the Patriarch with a gesture of dismissal. He brightened. "Tell me," he began, "is there a chance that we can recover the house? Would Mrs. Graham consider selling?"

"I'll see to that!" Vrukalakos snapped.

"You stay out of this!" the Patriarch exclaimed with flashing eyes. "Simply tell Lamia to remain in contact with the family, to make herself a friend of the new people. I may drop by myself. There are more than three months until March . . . and Commemoration. Ample time to do—whatever must be done."

"And *if* they don't want to sell?" Vrukalakos demanded.

The Patriarch's smile was gentle. "There will be a solution contained somewhere in the *Logos*, in the *grimoire*. Now: the other matter. Can we consider disposing of the creature from the

31

hospital on Thursday morning? No one has a use for it between now and then, does he?"

There were no oral replies to his questions. They had really been statements and everyone knew it, knew you didn't question the Patriarch.

Even Vrukalakos.

II

Knowing that all things have their emanations.
—Empedocles

The old G.E. alarm clock, transported from the kitchen to Mary Graham's bedroom, clacked insanely. It was largely missing the bell by now and rattled like children striking tinpans on New Year's Eve.

Lips pressed tight, Mary lifted her dark brownette head resentfully from a crumpled pillow and squinted at the contraption through a half-opened, light green eye.

It tolled dutifully, she observed, for the time she had set it.

"I'd think you could be more understanding after all these years," she told the much-used clock grumpily, sitting up in a rush and depressing the alarm switch.

She yawned at a bedside picture of Barry, his hair swept back from his forehead, his near-sighted eyes cheery behind the thick spectacles. Her mind experienced the old feeling of warmth and she wondered, a little nervously, how long it would be before this good-morning glimpse of her late husband became nothing but routine.

Her bare feet hit the bare floor. Her legs were hard and muscular from years of use in various sporadic employment—in the McDonald's assembly line, at grocery checkout lines, and now as a spotter for a dry cleaning firm—all in a failing effort to keep Barry's ship of commerce afloat. Mary had come to loathe her legs.

She wore only pink panties to bed, the waistband stretched with age so that she needed to adjust them as she padded to the bathroom. Above them were her body's best feature, perfectly round, heavy breasts that, coupled with her five-six and Catholic-reared modesty, obliged her to wear a size sixteen. Barry used to complain that she dressed like an old lady, but Mary felt that she had little, physically, to offer the world.

Often, as Barry's job losses had mounted and his determination to "do something creative" increased in proportion to their debt, she had wondered if she really had anything to offer Barry himself.

She peered with some mild irritation and confusion into the unfamiliar mirror fronting the medicine cabinet. The customary crack was gone.

Instead, the mirror was chipped in the lower right-hand corner and a triangle of black peeped through. The sun streaming through the golden curtain gave her usual olive complexion a slightly jaundiced look, prejudicing her view of herself. A normally amiable face with a pertly upturned Irish nose, emerald-green eyes, uneven and nearly shaggy eyebrows, and a pair of full lips grimaced back at her. Sticking her tongue out at her image, she had no idea that observant, mature men found her wholly beautiful.

"I look forty-five," she muttered distastefully, aloud, moving to the blue-not-green bathtub and hating its alienness. The water, coming in evenly hot at first touch, soothed her somewhat.

In point of fact Mary Graham looked thirty-eight, her age. She had looked thirty-eight when she was twenty-six and would look thirty-eight when she was fifty-five. It was in her genes, but she was bored silly with herself, had been for years.

Nevertheless, age wasn't the first thing that came to the mind of someone meeting Mary. He would be accorded one of a wide range of moods, from studied courtesy to artificial interest to cordial intensity, from austere spinster to deeply-in-love wife to militantly defensive mother, from calculated compassion to nerve-masking social grins to sunny, even hilariously silly good humor. It depended upon who and what the viewer was. If he or she were under twelve, or over sixty-five, he got Mary at perhaps her best.

With the sole exceptions of her late husband

Barry, her children, and her teacher friend Jeanne Lange, Mary tended to be what she was motivated to be at the moment. Her quite effective gift of defense consisted in her being flexible to present company, except that she wasn't always consistent and sometimes guessed wrong about what she was meant to be. Then, only then, was she flustered.

A teacher's child, she had been a serious student unable to supplant a brilliant older brother in her mother's selective regard. As a first girl friend, she was warm, cooperative, and Catholic. As a singer in the chorus of Starlight Musicals, when she was nineteen, she had been a warm, cooperative, serious professional with both Catholic and catholic interests. She had been ready to go to the New York stage if anyone proposed it. No one had, so she had married Barry Graham at twenty and tried, very hard, every day, to be everything he expected of her.

The fact that he had died seemed a measure of eventual failure to her, a yardstick she would soon be obliged to face. Which is not to say that Mary had no mind of her own or was weak-willed. Her largely unutilized IQ was over 150. Rather, Mary suffered, at thirty-eight, from having attempted industriously to get her own way always by dint of her chameleonlike adaptability to what was most expedient, and with Barry's loss, found herself obliged—for the first time, really—to learn the true identity of Mary Graham.

After bathing and brushing her medium-long

hair, she went downstairs to find Ellen still abed, and Chuck frying eggs and an enormous quantity of bacon. She adored watching the children eat— her mother sometimes accused her of being a secretly converted Jewish mama—and stood beside him, her eyes now wide.

"I heard some noises down here," she said in a little girl voice, "an' I thought mebbe m'horsie had finally come."

Chuck smothered a grin, faked a camouflaged stern expression. "You and your damn horsie," he fake-grumbled. "We're all tired of hearing about it. I paid a nickel-ninety-eight for the nag so it's bound t'come, sooner or later."

"But it's been five months!" she wailed, hitting his bicep.

"I sent for it in Wyoming," Chuck asserted loudly, turning his eggs. "It takes time to get to Indiana from Horse Creek, Wyoming."

"*Half* a *year?*" she demanded. The game, one of many she had devised over the years, had helped the kids and Mary to survive since Barry's death. "Golly, if'n I had m'horsie, I could ride him *all* over Thessaly an' people would know I was a real growed-up person."

"Hi, Mom." It was Ellen, unknowingly sexy in her loose flannel nightgown and bare feet. She also struck Chuck's bicep, hard; he made no indication that he'd felt it. "H'lo, ugly," she told him. "Mom going on about her silly horsie again?"

"Ain't she *always?*" he moaned, turning to slide his breakfast onto a plate.

"When is Joey coming, Mom?" Ellen asked as she tugged the half-gallon milk container from the refrigerator.

"Why d'you ask?" Mary inquired, seldom quick in giving answers. You gave away too much when you didn't stall.

"I dunno," Ellen shrugged. "I just wanna be somewhere else when His Royal Majesty gets here. Got any Tang?" She poured milk on a bowl of cereal.

Mary went to the sacks of food she had brought from the apartment and bent to rummage for the orange juice mix. Stooped, her hurt expression went unseen by the other children. They rarely realized—or rarely cared—that she was hurt every time any of the kids was insulted, even by one another.

Not that she could honestly blame Ellen for feeling the way she did. In simple, candid terms, Joey did his best to make life miserable for his sister. To begin with, girls were stupid beasts. When Mary pointed out that *she* had been a girl, Joey only stared as if suggesting that that proved his point. He accused Ellen of staring at him, of telling tales behind his back, of going through and stealing his things. Knowing his big brother's temper matched his bulk, Joey treated Chuck more deferentially—but scarcely so. He merely altered his tactics, resorting to moves of stealth and cleverness that were nearly Machiavellian.

The facts were that Ellen and Chuck seemed to tolerate Joey as best they could, but that they weren't perfect children either. Sometimes Barry would feel that they used Joey as a scapegoat; sometimes Mary felt the same way, and they tried to give the child the benefit of the doubt. Then he would take a completely intolerable step, purposely destroying something valuable in a temper fit, and both parents felt conned, hustled by a little boy.

Perhaps Joey Graham had been doomed from the start, Mary sometimes thought. Born with a harelip, he'd been obliged to stay in the hospital a few weeks to have it repaired, and, nearly ten years later, remained preternaturally self-conscious about the faint scar. An observant child, Joey had seen that rabbits actually *did* have harelips, and he eliminated them—banished the creatures—from his young life. Coloring books and greeting cards with bunnies met instant destruction at his hands. He'd have died before accepting one as a pet. Easter, with rabbits in a thousand diverse forms peering at him everywhere he looked, was especially difficult for Joey.

And when things were hard for him, they became much harder for those around him. Little Joe made sure of that. A hyperactive child under the best of circumstances, breakage was astronomical—much of it intentional, including several holes Joey had put in apartment walls with tiny, fiercely angry fists. She recalled now, with pain, the times Barry had been obliged (and humiliated) to retrieve the boy from trees, rooftops and fire escapes. As a rule, Joey Graham never slowed down from early morning to bedtime and went to sleep only when sudden exhaustion rendered him unconscious.

Mary ruminated over her youngest throughout preparations for breakfast, frying Chuck an extra egg as she fixed hers and Ellen's. Once, Joey had been a lovely baby whom she could barely keep awake. She often found him curled up in surprising places like bookshelves and closets, sound asleep. Until his enormous range of sensitivity—to expressions, intonations of the voice, even casual gestures—became clear for all to see (when she and Barry began to quarrel about his inability to maintain a job), Joey had been a model child. Did he blame himself, perhaps, for the grown-ups' problems, Mary wondered, when it was the other way around? Two psychiatrists had failed to put a finger on it. She also wanted to remember to ask Jeanne Lange, when she brought Joey back, about the nature of changelings.

Even though it was Wednesday, breakfast was a leisurely affair, like one on a weekend. Mary wasn't expected back by Dutch-Touch Cleaners until Friday, Ellen was excused from John Marshall High School, because of their move to Thessaly, until tomorrow, and Chuck had dropped out of school a year ago. She had been nagging the boy since well before Barry's death to get a job, sensing both his essential laziness and an inclination to be led by others. She hoped they would all make some worthwhile new acquaintances in Thessaly.

At midmorning, they had an opportunity. Most of the heavy moving was done and Mary and Ellen were discussing the placement of smaller pieces of furniture with a pinpoint attention to detail that left the masculine Chuck ineffably bored. He was saved by the doorbell.

Mary herself admitted them, the old man and the old lady who introduced themselves as Milo and Velda Traphonius. Mrs. Traphonius was a woman with a mane of creamy white hair and an impressive superstructure encased in a smart blue suit. She led the way into the living room, commenting a mile a minute on "the nice touches you've brought into this house already."

But once they were all seated and Milo was clearly ready to speak, Velda Traphonius lapsed into a silence that appeared totally obedient.

"We shan't stay long," he said in a mellow baritone that belied his years, "because I know how trying it is getting used to a new place. I surely do! But we did want to say hello and see if you're enjoying the champagne."

"I'm adoring it," Mary said, puzzled. "But I thought my daughter said it was Lamia Zacharius who dropped the magnum off last night."

The old man smiled. "It was, I confess. I don't wish to appear ungallant, but it was upon my suggestion and from my cellar." He had a way of sitting forward in his chair, wide palms open on his knees, that compelled attention. "I felt that Lamia might have been a trifle peremptory— *enoi!* she can certainly be so at times!—and Velda and I merely wished you to feel truly welcomed to Thessaly."

"That's very kind, it really is." Mary smiled warmly. "Is Lamia a relative of yours, then? Your

41

daughter perhaps?"

He shook his great head and laughed a little. "No, no *direct* kinship really. But I perceive the source of your confusion. I, dear, I am rather the unofficial mayor of this little town, the old bird the others look to when they've tumbled from their nests."

"I suspect it's our age that makes the others look to us," Velda Traphonius offered with a sidelong glance at her husband.

No, it's more than that, Mary decided. Despite the fact that he had to be seventy, at least, Milo Traphonius was a man who commanded respect. Some six feet tall and still erect, he had a huge head made even more conspicuous by gray hair that totally encircled it and extended out at the sides. While he might never have been theatrically handsome, because of a rather squat nose, his blue eyes twinkled with captivating intelligence and his almost sensuous mouth appeared equally suited to laughter or to solemn address.

"Well, it's very nice to have the blessing of the mayor," Mary smiled, "official or unofficial."

"Is there anything we can do to make you feel more comfortable here?" the old man asked.

"Not really." She brightened. "Perhaps it would be nice to have one of the little protective statues the others have in front of their homes—the *agyieus*, I believe they were called. How could we obtain one?"

"*Dios Kodion!*" Milo exclaimed. "I fear they are reserved for Greeks, my dear." He mastered a smile. "Greek gods for Greek believers, y'know.

42

Tell me, is this a temporary habitation or have you thought of making Thessaly your home?"

Mary frowned. "We're buying it."

"Yes, yes, I know that," he admitted. "But these days, Americans are so transient, are they not? They come and go rapidly."

"We plan to remain, Mr. Traphonius."

"Milo, my dear Mary—call me Milo." Heartiness had replaced his little moment of prying. "And this is Velda. Well, one never knows unless one asks. The shortest distance between two points, and all that."

"I understand," Mary said. It was a lie. She didn't understand this clannishness Thessaly showed at all. Since when did Greeks have ghettos?

As the old couple was departing, Joey Graham came bursting up the lane to the front door, narrowly dodging Milo Traphonius as he completely ignored them all, purposely banging against the front door and then charging like an invader into his new home.

Milo chuckled, waved, took his wife by her arm and climbed into a late-model Oldsmobile.

Behind it, Jeanne Lange had pulled up and was rescuing her relative bulk and shambling toward her old friend. In the teacher's arms were several boxes which Mary would bet contained gifts for Chuck and Ellen, to compensate for the largesse Joey had doubtlessly enjoyed. A woman of average height, approaching forty, Jeanne was elegantly coiffed, her golden hair shimmering in the sunlight, and dressed in what she often called

"the best damn horse blanket money can buy."
While she was less than obese, Jeanne could stand
to lose thirty pounds and good-naturedly ignored
the fact.

"Does the welcoming committee come in a new
Olds these days?" she asked, struggling with her
packages into the house.

Mary laughed lightly. "That was no mere
committee, that was the mayor and his wife.
Impressed? Here, let me help."

The two of them carried the gifts inside where
Joey seemed to have vanished. Jeanne literally
tossed the presents to Ellen and Chuck. "The
candy I got should give you a head start on a
glorious bod like mine," she told the girl, lowering
herself wearily into a chair. "So this is fabled
Thessaly, Indiana," she marveled, "the Athens of
the Midwest."

"Don't be a smart-ass," Mary told her.

"What did you think of our town square?"
Chuck demanded.

"I didn't meet him. Oh," Jeanne corrected
herself, "you mean the shop and the store. How
d'you big city people plan to live without all the
excitement of metropolitan Indianapolis?"

"What excitement?" Ellen sniffed airily. "If
you don't like high school basketball, a smelly
State Fair, the Indiana Pacers, or the 500 Mile
Race, they treat you like an outsider. We've only
been here a day but there's a feeling of tradition
about Thessaly."

"Well, that's one convert," Jeanne counted.

"And I can't wait to explore the woods," Chuck commented.

"Me too, me too!" Joey returned to the downstairs with a thump and a rush, scurrying to his mother with his deep blue eyes wide. He paid no attention to an ashtray he knocked off an end table. "Can I go out now, Mom? Huh? Huh?"

Mary glanced absently at her wristwatch. Only ten-forty-five. "Why don't you wait until after lunch?"

"Aw-w-w," he protested, leaning against the wall to sulk. "Why?"

"You haven't been in the new house five minutes and you're making demands," she said pointedly. "Why don't you just relax awhile, get used to the place? Then Chuck can go with you after lunch."

"I hate it here." He made the announcement with a look of sincere, scathing hatred. "It ain't any better'n the apartment if you have to stay inside alla time."

"Isn't," Ellen put in, raising her eyebrow. "*Isn't* any better."

"You ain't my mother," Joey said, sneering. "Mind your own business."

"Enough!" Mary exclaimed. "Joseph, go wash your face and put your things where they go in your room. Now."

It wasn't exactly now, but he eventually did as he was told—or at least left the room and clumped upstairs.

Mary sighed. She turned to her friend. Jeanne

Lange was not only a grade school teacher with infinite patience but a close student of the paranormal. "Jeanne, what can you tell me about changelings?"

"Changelings?" Jeanne laughed. "You think Joey's one?"

"I don't know, that's why I asked. Honestly, he has us all at wit's end."

Jeanne burrowed her wide buttocks deeper into the chair and adjusted the hornrimmed glasses on her rather thick nose. "There aren't any changelings unless you believe in fairies—and I don't mean the kind with dresses and false eyelashes. There's a myth, Irish in origin, that the wee people sometimes have a need for genuine human babies. Being 'taking folk,' they steal infants and replace them with pigs or artificial babies."

"Artificial?"

Jeanne nodded. "Strange, misshapen babies— or ones that appear normal, even just like the ones that are stolen, until they begin doing bizarre, awful things." A brow raised above one eye. "I have a lot of respect for the occult and I've come to learn that there's so much smoke arising from the supernatural that there's plenty of fire. But Joey's a good kid, at heart."

"You want to keep him another night?" Mary demanded.

Jeanne laughed heartily. "By God, Mare, maybe you're right about him!" She glanced through the interior of the house and out the french doors. "Judging by that forest of yours back there, you may have an entire colony of elves for neighbors."

"Only people like me."

Both women started. The voice had come from the area around the front door, which Mary had left ajar. It was surprisingly warm today for December and the house needed airing.

A head appeared around the edge of the door. "Hello. May I come in?"

It was lovely but difficult Lamia Zacharius, Mary observed with dismay. Did the entire town of Thessaly intend to parade through her house every day? She smiled as warmly as artifice demanded and gestured. "Come on in."

"Thank you." The tall Greek woman slithered fashionably to a chair, clutching a currently modish purse to her high, narrow bosom and taking her seat with exaggerated poise. "Well, well, what a wonderful job of tidying-up you've done, my dear."

"We still have a ways to go. Miss Zacharius, I'd like you to meet a dear friend of mine: Jeanne Lange. Jeanne; Lamia."

"'Lo." It was barely a grunt from Jeanne. Her own gaze hardened appraisingly.

"How good to meet you," Lamia purred.

"She isn't Greek either," Mary put in, unable to resist. Jeanne giggled.

"Now, I thought we were going to try to be good friends," Lamia chided her, offering a tight little smile. The physical contrast between the Greek and Jeanne, mused Mary, was almost ludicrous. A man might not have believed they were of the same sex. But even more than that, Mary

47

continued to sense the power of an incisive, nearly male intellect—male in the sense of ruthlessness, not superiority. "Do you work for a dry cleaning establishment too, Miss Lange?"

How in hell did she know I *did?* Mary wondered, startled.

"No, I'm a teacher," Jeanne replied shortly. Clearly, she was aware of how upstaged she was. Womanlike, she tried to judge how friendly Mary was toward Lamia. She leaned forward two inches. "What do *you* do?"

Lamia laughed. "Not a great deal, I fear. Independent income." She lifted a few fingers from her lap, gesturing. "I do like to sketch and paint, in the forest. There is something marvelously *free* about a woods, don't you feel?" She shuddered theatrically. "I can feel positively wanton there."

"I'll bet," Jeanne murmured, squinting through her thick glasses.

There was a small explosion. "Can we eat lunch now so's I can get outta here?" It was Joey, scurrying into the front room with a scowl marring his fair-skinned features. It looked just the way Mary had seen it last: Unwashed, smudged, angry. "I did what y'told me to, and all, so now it's up t'you to keep your parta the bargain. Right?"

"We have company, Joseph," Mary said, embarrassed for perhaps the thousandth time by him. "This is Miss Zacharius."

Truly noticing the guest for the first time, Joey turned to Lamia. They, too, made a severe contrast: The dark, sleek, poised and brilliant woman and the pale, furious, frantic boy. Mary saw his expression alter, not enough for a stranger to notice, perhaps, but enough for his mother. He had somehow tuned in to the Greek beauty with his uncanny, impressionable child's sensitivity and was reacting to Lamia. But how, just then—in what manner—she could not tell.

"I did not have the fortune to meet you yesterday, Joey," Lamia said in her low, husky voice. She crossed silken, mile-long legs and touched his cheek with electrifying fingers. "You're quite a handsome fellow."

"You're *beautiful*," he gasped.

Mary was astonished. She'd never heard her Joey pay a compliment to anyone before, not ever. Yet even as she was pleased by his childish response to Lamia Zacharius's uncommon beauty, Mary could discern something . . . *more* . . . in the boy's open face. For a moment she didn't recognize it. But when she did, she shivered.

It was fear. Joey was distinctly *afraid* of Lamia.

And Joey was afraid of nothing human.

"How old are you, lad?" Lamia asked, smiling, her head inclined at an almost coquettish angle. It was amazing how genuinely interested she seemed to be in him.

"Nine-goin-on-ten," he blurted.

"Joseph will be ten Christmas Day," Mary expanded, managing a smile. "He was our Christmas present ten years ago."

Obese Jeanne Lange, listening and observing with a practiced perception and keen intuition for which no stranger would have given her credit,

49

saw the Greek beauty's expression just then. Like Joey's, it altered. Mary, absently stroking the boy's blond head, could not see it.

But Jeanne did: A flicker of intense emotion and virtually enthralled fascination suddenly aglow in Lamia Zacharius's ebon eyes. *Now why,* Jeanne mused, *was this goddam rude bitch so excited by Joey Graham?*

"May I ask an impertinent question—even an improper one?" Lamia's deep voice throbbed another octave lower. She had turned to Mary a face of sudden female passion, of vast curiosity. Uncertain of what was to follow, Mary nodded slowly. "That trace of a scar on your little boy's upper lip," Lamia proceeded. "*Was* that . . . a harelip?"

Would this woman's presumptuousness never cease? "Yes, it was," Mary confessed, on the verge of losing her temper. She didn't look at Joey because she knew how hurt he must be by this stranger discerning his darkest personal secret. "But why in the world do you ask such a thing?"

Lamia did not reply. She realized now she'd gone too far. She looked down at her hands, then gathered her suede gloves between long, slim fingers and prepared to depart. "No reason, actually; and I did not mean to be rude. He is . . . a strikingly handsome lad. Perhaps," she continued, her gaze still lowered, "perhaps the gods gave Joey the defect simply to prevent the corruption of absolute perfection. If he had been perfect, you see, he'd have had to proceed directly to Paradise."

She raised her eyes then and there were astounding tears in them. A tender smile—the first thing gentle Mary had seen about the woman—was almost wistful, even sad. It softened her beauty incredibly, yet heightened it.

But Joey Graham no longer stood near his mother. He had sped across the living room in silent haste, seeking his Aunt Jeanne, craving distance from the beautiful visitor. He gripped Jeanne's plump hand tightly, his muscular little form leaned against her arm. Now Mary saw what her friend had seen: Sucking his thumb and casting doubtful glances back at Lamia, he seemed filled with abject fear.

There was nothing more to add just then and in moments Lamia Zacharius left, a lithe, lean shadow of dark loveliness and eternal wisdom who had, for once in her life, been just as startled as the lesser beings whom she had visited.

Jeanne paused heavily at the door beside Mary, confiding in a rough whisper: "I'm not sure what the hell that woman is up to, pal, but I don't like her. I don't like her at all, hurting kids with questions like that. If I were you, I'd meet some other 'Thessalonians.' If they're all like that broad, Mare, hike your ass back to Indy."

Mary closed the door moments later and returned her attention to Joey, deeply concerned.

Before she could speak he was putting on his cloth coat and tugging a knit cap over his blond head. "I just gotta go out and see them woods for awhile, Mom," he said with the ponderous sense of urgency she sometimes noted in his voice.

51

She smiled. Whatever threat Joey had felt, it was gone. She nodded and hugged him. "Be careful," she whispered, kissing thin air as he twisted like a streak and vanished out the french doors to the beckoning forest.

The remainder of the day was uneventful.

That night, Mary slept sporadically, deeply when she could succeed but otherwise awakening suddenly with a lurching sense of imbalance and tentative anxiety. Once, she awoke to reach out on the bed, groping, looking for Barry's reassuring body.

And once, when she awakened so abruptly that she sat bolt upright in bed, she thought that she had heard the sound of hoofbeats speeding past the old cottage, in a night grown suddenly quite chill.

Lamia Zacharius stood trembling in the entrance to Vrukalakos's house. She trembled from the need for fresh sustenance, and she would get no kind of warmth from the saturnine Greek who heard her story.

"So! It is, indeed, a sign—just as you say." Vrukalakos seemed pleased, a sight Lamia rarely witnessed. Not that his implacably hard features altered. It was the shiny, marble quality of the ebon eyes and the sudden, jubilant pacing. "I trust you did not alarm them, in your excitement?"

She ignored the insulting query. "You must not forget that he is merely a child."

"You think so, eh, Lamia?" Vrukalakos smiled but it twisted into a sneer. "A child *now*, possibly. Well, the Patriarch will be filled with happiness. It is clear that the boy is . . . one of us."

She paused, considering shrewdly. "Was it indicated in the *Logos*—the *grimoire?*"

"Do not overstep, woman. So said the Patriarch, so it was written," he replied faithfully.

"You are such a hypocrite. You despise everything the Patriarch stands for." But Lamia smiled, tempering the words with her frosty beauty. She moved across the room, still craving sustenance and warmth, and shivered out of her clothes. Before donning a heavy robe she turned to him, her extraordinary, slender beauty revealed to him. Her small breasts were placed high, the nipples elongated and hard from her internal need, her waist scarcely stretching the handspan of a large man, her black pubic hair a tangled nest in the shadows of the room. But for such a creature as Vrukalakos, her exceptional figure held no magic and she knew it, taunted him with it. "So tell me: How shall we take this Joey Graham?"

She had meant, how should the Synod persuade or procure the child? But the monster misunderstood or preferred his own interpretation. "It does not matter for there is ample time. Seven times seven, from his birthday to the beginning of the last period—and Commemoration." He shrugged and removed his uncaring gaze from her nakedness. "Personally, I believe the boy is quite as good dead as alive. He is prepared now for the change and requires only purification in the sight of Apollo. Thus, woman, it matters not how we take him."

Suddenly an idea gave a glint of emotion to Lamia's shrewd, dark eyes. "Tell the Patriarch that I know a way to obtain this Joey for us. A way preferable to killing." She stretched, the taut breasts lifting. "Tell him to allow Lamia Zacharius to try first."

"Very well. I must go now." He touched her buttocks with icy fingers. "I think they won't wish the Grahams to leave now. When the *thallophoroi* know that the lad has come in time."

III

More will I tell thee too: there is no birth
Of all things mortal, nor end in ruinous death;
But mingling only and interchange of mixed
There is, and birth is but its name with man.
—Empedocles

In the final few moments before dawn on Thursday, the Syndic gathered alone in full force of four, deep in the forest of Thessaly. The reborn Vale of Aphaca shone with a coat of dew that glinted on the immense rocks and single boulder shielding the entrance to the ancient tunnel. Above, a chiaroscuro sky was shot through with slashes of carmine, blood seeping sickly in veins and making the new day's clouds look like so much soaked cotton.

55

It had turned cold for so early in the Indiana winter and the quartet of influential Synod officials had thrown topcoats over the tunics denoting their stations. Despite the coats, their bare legs protruded absurdly beneath; the men shivered spasmodically each time wind gusted through the Vale.

Except, that is, for the iron-willed one whom they called the Patriarch. He stood on the high ground, calf muscles knotted athletically, sandals crunching dead brown leaves and microscopic life. He appeared composed, as well as inordinately pleased, beaming down with equanimity on both the living and the dead.

"The news which Vrukalakos brings us is of supreme magnitude for the entire *akousmatikoi*." He inclined his huge, bearded head in hearty agreement with his own delighted sentiment. "Yes, our youthful benefactor, our blessed guide, has indeed arrived! And well ahead of Commemoration, *Dios Kodion!*" His smile caused him to appear years younger. "Just as the *Logos* foretold in its eternal record."

George Aristides squinted up, troubled by the sun rising behind his *pater familias*. He scrubbed thoughtfully at his bald dome. "There is the essential problem of . . . persuading the lad, Patriarch."

"That is true," remarked Nicholas Melas, fingering the keys to his general store as they jingled in his coat pocket. "All of us will feel better if the boy lives, if his guidance is entirely voluntary."

"Have I led you so long, so far, that I deserve pessimism? Doubt? The boy does not yet even know who he is, or *what* he is. He is young! Come, we shall give Lamia her opportunity, my *phrateres.*" The Patriarch's words were firm, determined. "She has proved herself quite effective indeed over a period of time. We owe her the chance to succeed, especially since she agrees to undergo change once more." He swiveled his great head to peer down at the creature Vrukalakos and the burden slung across his shoulder. "Proceed."

Vrukalakos tossed the body to the ground and pulled the brown blanket away from it. To no one's surprise, dull eyes stared out at them from ruddy and bloated skin. A twisted, quite hideously eager smile moved on its protruding lips. Then the corpse from the hospital morgue sat up as Vrukalakos motioned to it. Even the Syndic's necessary adversary averted his head to avoid the stench of garlic and putrefaction filling the corpse's mouth.

The two dark forms approached the stones of the Vale of Aphaca, and with a single, mighty twist of his powerful arms, Vrukalakos tore away the great boulder. A dark, cavernous mouth opened hungrily, framed by craggy lips, and from inside—deep inside, in its bowels—could be heard the rumble of secret waters gurgling like a damp, lunatic voice. Vrukalakos paused, steeling himself; George Aristides produced a lantern, lit it, and handed it over.

The saturnine keeper of Antipodes peered up at

the Patriarch to muster courage again, his own thin, bloodless lips curved in a terrible grimace of a smile. "It hungers, Patriarch," the keeper said, with something that might have been a laugh, or a sob. "Oh, it hungers for *demetreioi,* for the vivified dead. It is utterly monstrous, all-powerful and unchangeable, is it not?—but I alone, *I,* Vrukalakos, fear it not!"

The bearded father of the Synod looked downward wearily and tactfully withheld the words that had leapt to his incisive mind: *Of course you don't! You, also, dine on carrion!* He kept the remark to himself and bided his time with the creature as he had done for so very long. Aloud, he said: "Go ahead down, now. Take your creature to Aether for the appeasement. It knows not the difference between the truly alive, the truly dead, and the revivified ones."

As Vrukalakos and the other stepped carefully, slowly, into the imposing cavern, smoky vapors twisted and twirled like cotton candy from hell, and, below, *something* heard the two creatures coming and panted its eagerness. Parts of it rustled kittenishly, making a sound of chainmail clashing.

Ellen Graham had stayed up until one to watch Neal Diamond on a talk show and had slept late. Joey had been up three times during the night, wetting his bed and insisting that Mary change the sheets. Now he slept soddenly, his high forehead sparkling with perspiration and his blue eyes moving like small animals beneath tissue-thin lids.

Mary had looked in on him several times, and now, tired by early afternoon, she was finishing her housework.

She had approached the entire moving job as a series of stages, each one being a satisfying "completion" which permitted her to take a break and feel that something had been accomplished. The first stage had been simply getting everything from Indianapolis to Thessaly, and into the house. The second had been getting the large articles put in their proper rooms, and the third was making sure that everything was stationed in its suitable room.

Now, she had finished putting everything away in drawers, cabinets, bookcases, and hutches and had given the entire house a perfunctory dusting. The next-to-last step would be getting everything both neat and clean.

And the final stage would be learning to adjust to this, the different world, one in which presumably well-meaning neighbors dropped by several times a day. That was apparently the price one paid for living in a small community and it might be worth it, she thought, depending on the people themselves. Certainly she was inclined to like Milo and his wife. Besides, she would be back at Dutch-Touch Cleaners tomorrow, Friday, and every weekday thereafter. She might as well enjoy meeting her neighbors now, while there was time to do it properly.

That was why she had decided to work this hard in the kitchen, putting together a buffet. Mary planned to lay it all out on the dining room table, with paper plates, and ask anyone who stopped by to join them for a snack. So far she had a ham cooking in the oven, to be sliced down, and huge bowls of homemade potato salad and bean salad cooling in the fridge. If she was going to draw so much attention, she might as well be likeable about it.

Chuck, meanwhile, had taken his new shotgun and ventured out to the forest in quest of rabbit. He had never shot an animal in his life and had no real confidence about his ability to do so.

But lately, since Dad's death, he had experienced a growing sense of responsibility which both troubled and excited him. Not that he deeply missed Barry Graham. It was Chuck's most shame-ridden secret that he had never truly loved his father, a secret that he believed no one suspected. Dad had never mistreated him, exactly, but had taken the approach that it was fundamentally impossible for him to be wrong or for Chuck to be right. Since Chuck felt fully capable of pointing out dozens of weekly mistakes by the rather independent, romantically creative man who had been his father, he had tended to see the older man, in life, as a bit of a hypocrite. Freethinkers were supposed to wear beards, play guitars, smoke pot, step out on the wife, and look upon the kids as gentle little gifts of a Great White Father. And Dad had been none of those things, done none of those things. Barry had managed to live with a tight set of standards that made him more straitlaced and regulated than most men, by virtue of having allowed himself to think, study, appraise and decide about everything in the world that he wished to. His yearning for independence was expressed through a widely diversified range of opinions that baffled the more down-to-earth, plodding Chuck. Dad had had views, and twenty ways of buttressing them, on subjects which Chuck had never begun to consider.

It was the central distinction between them—Barry's creative and investigative mentality contrasted with Chuck's boyish realism and willing acceptance of what seemed obvious, and it was more than Chuck would be able to forgive until he was much older.

Now it was clear to the seventeen-year-old that there should be a man in the family and no one else seemed to fill the description. Money was hard to get; food cost money; ergo, free rabbit would relieve his sense of new responsibility.

He came upon the Greek woman in a clearing, dappled by sunlight. The morning had been very chilly but the temperature had climbed all day, hovering now around fifty.

Even so, he was surprised to see how comfortable Lamia Zacharius appeared in a simple lightweight dress barely reaching her trim knees. It had a high, scooped bodice that revealed her small breasts to their best and most generous advantage. Incredibly lovely, she sat before her easel, sketching something he could not discern from his own vantage point. Occasionally she raised her artist's pencil at arm's length, prettily, to measure; then she hurled herself furiously into her work for another moment of concerted effort.

It seemed to Chuck, as he hid his wide-shouldered bulk behind an enormous oak, that Lamia looked younger today, even more desirable. Before, she had been unusually gorgeous, but clearly far out of his league, beyond his serious consideration. Though beautiful, she had been the age of his mother. Now he watched as the Greek woman's slender fingers paused. The arms dropped, the fingers nestled in the nadir of her lap. He could not be sure what she was doing yet his own huge hand instinctively fell to his crotch. Gripping, it moved stealthily. Now Lamia's scarlet tongue tipped her lips, darted over them—a red bird tasting. Her deep black eyes were closed and she seemed oblivious to all but herself.

"Good afternoon, Chuck," she said.

He jumped guiltily, his furtive hand catching, grasping the oak as if it had been there all along. "Hi." He managed a few halting steps into the clearing, being amateurishly nonchalant. "How'd you know it was me?"

"How do I know the secrets to all things?" She turned to him without rising, swiveling her entire lean body on the chair. With immense grace, she arose. "How do you like our forest?"

He thought. "It's just big enough to roam without gettin' lost. It's nice." He felt like a small boy as he approached the woman, though she was smaller, reaching just above his shoulder. He realized with chagrin that, in his guilt, he'd left his shotgun by the oak. He made a mental note to retrieve it. "So you really are an artist?" he asked.

She shrugged lightly. He saw the curve of her breast, the press of a nipple, saw that she wore nothing beneath the lightweight dress. "I try to be an artist in many undertakings." She gestured. "Over there, Chuck, is a valley. Come, let us sit upon the hill to see it."

Her hand was in his and Chuck followed obediently, sliding down beside her and staring out over a virtual ocean of trees. From this angle it seemed impenetrable, infinite; immortal. It was like being uprooted from his home and sitting on a hill in a distant country. The trees, he thought, had always been just as they were now and they would remain in stately, unspoken isolation even after men—perhaps time itself—were gone.

He gasped. Her mouth was on his neck. It nipped, playfully. Astonished, Chuck turned his head to speak words as yet unformed and found her wide, hungry mouth upon his, her agile tongue quickly probing between his teeth. Awkward, rough, he tugged her into his strong arms and met her tongue with his. Momentarily her tight, high breast was in the cupped palm of his hand and his fingers found the nipple beneath his thumb grow erect, urgent against the fabric.

When he felt her own fingers snatching at his groin Chuck pulled free, abashed and ashamed. He bounced on his buttocks a foot from the beautiful woman and stared in misery at the ground.

"It's my age, isn't it?" Her eyes were bright.

They sought data.

"Well, yeah," he said without pause, unfettered by maturity's manners. "And mine." He frowned fiercely and seemed about to cry. "Shit, I'm a *k-kid!*"

Computerlike, her fathomless eyes ran the length of his muscular body. "You do not appear a child, my Chuck. Your present form is that of a strong man."

Suddenly he craved her more, achingly. Staring, his mouth worked but nothing came out. He knew two things just then, only two: He wanted her desperately, and if she touched him once more, he would have her. She would be his first.

But Lamia Zacharius stayed put, immobile except for the timeless ebon eyes. "It is all a question of perspective, lad," she said in a soft, expressionless tone. Behind her the towering trees rose like the phallic symbols of a world that would always be. "To you, you are young, I am old. Yet your body finds me desirable, does it not? No, don't answer. But to others, you see, *I* am the child—the young woman who has all knowledge yet has much to learn. To those you have known I might well be older than the trees in this valley, aged and ageless, unchanged yet *all* change. It is . . . perspective."

He stared at her, his heart beating furiously. What was she getting at?

"Everything is change, Chuck, everything. Nothing—abides. Nothing. All is changed and changeable, always for the good."

He shook his head fiercely. "No, I don't believe

that, ma'am." His father's face had swum before his mind's eye, a youthful face now six feet beneath the surface of the earth. "I don't think there's anything good about—about getting older, for example."

"I want you to think of what I'm about to say, boy," Lamia said carefully, unbuttoning the top two buttons of her bodice. "To dream of it, in fact. It is all a question of *who* is in *charge* of *change*. You, or what we term nature." She parted the lips of her bodice and the curving apex of her small, plump breasts appeared. He felt his mouth going dry. "There are those who change things when they please, *because* they please. Who change anything—or *everything*."

"I didn't know that," he answered honestly, thinking that if he had to rise now from the ground it would be impossible. "I thought things . . . just happened."

"Not to us, in Thessaly." Lamia pulled from between her breasts a small silver amulet. It seemed almost masculine in design when she handed it to him, her fingers resting briefly, hotly on his wrist. "Wear that, Chuck, when you want to dream—*useful, changing* dreams. You have much to learn."

"Yeah, well, that's right." What was she talking about? He put it round his neck obligingly.

"You were thinking about your father, whose change was not his choice, whose change was death. Weren't you?"

"Yes, ma'am."

"When he did not choose, that was his mistake.

Where does he lie?"

"Washington Park Cemetery."

She arose then, walked quietly to Chuck and stood over the boy. He could see the dusky nest of her femaleness outlined by the breeze blowing her skirt against her legs. "He would not wish that you concern yourself with age or with dying. He would wish that you learn to be in control of *your* life's changes, and I think that you shall be. Trust Lamia, Chuck. Soon, I shall prove all this to you. You will learn it all—and more."

She pulled Chuck's willing, tortured face against her. His lips formed a kiss but he could not move. He was not surprised when he began to cry.

Above them, atop the hill, the wind gusted sharply and took from the easel Lamia Zacharius's life-picture. The one which, sketching it, had excited her. Now it fluttered to rest in the weeds, a drawing—in excellent detail—of a large, shining snake gorging itself on a nest of helpless, baby field mice.

In the cottage of Attica Avenue, Ellen fought the good fight against setting the table. As usual, her fourteen-year-old nose was deep in one of her beloved botany books. Ellen had every intention of teaching it to kids her age, one day, having been scholastically galvanized by a handsome young teacher. These days she took every book on botany, vegetable chemistry and phytology available from the library, again and again, making voluminous notes to impress youthful Mr. Schneider.

Soon, she knew, she would get out into the forest and begin collecting specimen leaves for her thriving collection. Ellen was putting it off, because she knew that once she fell under the enchantment of the Thessaly woods, she would be lost forever.

While the girl was sighing over her routine task, putting out paper plates and bringing the ham, bean salad, and potato salad from the refrigerator, there was a knock at the door.

Mary, in the kitchen putting bread on a plate, looked up in surprise, then dusted crumbs off her hands and hurried through the living room to the front door.

"Good evening, Mary," said Milo Traphonius, giving her a courtly bow.

"I hope we're not interrupting dinner," Velda Traphonius offered from his side, fluffing her handsome hair.

"Not at *all*," Mary replied, stepping back from the door and smiling. "Do come in." After all, she had prepared a buffet for any of the Thessaly people who came by.

She was startled when a third visitor, a tiny, completely hairless man with a myopic squint followed them into the house. "I'm George Aristides, Mrs. Graham," he said in a cultivated voice with the precise English of those who learn it in foreign lands. "I've heard so much about you and your charming family that I thought I should add my own welcome."

"How lovely!" Mary gushed, seating her guests.

"Please accept this token of our friendship, my

dear," Milo offered before he took his chair. His extended hands held a gift-wrapped package.

Mary took it, found it rather heavy. "You really *shouldn't* have done this."

"I quite disagree, my child," Milo replied with a note of regret. "Perhaps because of the full moon, or Lamia's peculiar temperament, or my own declining intellect, I fear that we have not adequately assured you of how *glad* all your neighbors are—*all* of us—that you are here. You and your family."

"Thank you." Mary removed the silver ribbon and paper with care as Chuck came in, greeting the Traphonius couple by name. She noticed how respectful was his tone, something he rarely displayed to older people.

The gift came into view as Ellen joined them and perched on the arm of her mother's chair.

It was a large, handsomely decorated earthen pot crammed nearly to overflowing with cooked fruits of all kinds.

"It's called a *thargela*," Milo explained with a slight cough.

"It's only offered by Greeks to those we like and respect," said George Aristides from the sofa.

Milo's eyebrows raised above his intelligent eyes. "I hope your little one, Joey, likes fruit? We were so sorry to miss him yesterday morning."

Mary laughed gaily. "Well, he didn't miss *you*, Milo! He was the little lightning bolt who streaked into the house as you were leaving."

"Does he like fruit?" Aristides inquired anxiously.

"He loves fruit," Ellen said approvingly, warmly. "We all do."

"So good, so *good!*" Velda Traphonius exuded with a little clap of her manicured hands.

"Now we shall all be the best of close friends!" Milo exclaimed, arising from his chair.

He wandered out to the dining room, to Mary's surprise, and pivoted after a glance with his palms up. "What have we here? Dinner! And you told us we did not intrude."

"We'd be delighted if you stayed to eat with us, folks," Mary urged them, hurrying to his side and resting the pot of *thargela* beside the potato salad. "I fixed plenty."

Aristides looked hungry but Milo answered for them all. "Regretfully, I am on a diet," he said in great sadness, his large fingers ruffling his gray beard. "But come! *Saboi!* What have we here?"

Mary stared where he seemed to be looking. "What's wrong?"

"Beans! Why, Mary my dear, you should not eat *beans!*"

The old man was peering at her bowl of bean salad as if he had seen something obscene crawling inside.

"Why not?" Mary asked in helplessness.

"Well-l-l, a harmless superstition of my people." Milo's pose was that of a courtly lecturer. "It could be viewed on that level alone."

"What's the superstition, Mr. Traphonius?" Chuck asked with sober curiosity.

Milo's eyes widened mysteriously. "Once it was believed that beans contain souls on their

69

first step to—to what we may call rebirth. *Human* souls. And one would not wish to be a spiritual cannibal, eh?" He chuckled suddenly. "It would anger the goddess Hecate, I fear."

"You sound like there's more to it than that, sir." Ellen was amazingly attentive, captivated, Mary felt, by the old charmer.

"To a thinking man, a man of science, such a superstition is sheer nonsense. Of *course!* However," he raised a warning index finger, "the way it was originally conceived in ancient Greece, Pythagoras claimed that beans tend to inflate. As a consequence, they prevent predictive dreams from being wholly truthful and accurate." He tossed back his head to laugh harshly, jovially. "You can see the logic in that, I believe."

Mary's nod was tentative. "Yes, but—"

"*But,*" the old man interrupted, "Cicero laughed at Pythagoras about that. He reminded us that it was the *mind* which dreams—not the stomach!"

Ellen and Chuck howled with glee. Joey, entering the dining room after a nap, stopped at the door to gape at the older people.

And Mary thought that the laughter of the children was excessive, even startling to see.

"You don't mind humoring an old man, do you?" Milo asked at last.

He's serious, Mary thought with shock. "And not eat the bean salad? Well, if it will make you happy, no." She cleared it from the table, brushing past the watchful Joey. Then, returning, she sobered. "Just this once, Milo, that's all. I want to be fair with you folks from the beginning. We do not plan to alter our entire way of life merely to please Thessaly's residents. Cooperate, be neighborly, seek friendship—but *not* alter our whole way of life."

"Yet ours is a way of life of quite long standing," George Aristides protested mildly. He was so small, so silent, Mary had lost sight of him. "A *proved* way of life, Mrs. Graham."

"And that's fine for you." She sought to change the subject as the three older people ambulated toward the front room, preparing their departure. "How does it happen that Thessaly is entirely Greek except for us?"

"An attempt at gathering those with a common background, common national interests," Milo shrugged, slipping into his fur-edged topcoat. "I founded it twelve years ago for that purpose."

"Are you actively involved in the politics of Greece?"

Milo turned back to her with a gentle, ironic smile. "Not *modern* Greece, child, that contemporary failure, no—but the Greece that was once preeminent in the world of scholars, scientists, poets and philosophers. In our small way, we restore the grand traditions. Greece today does not interest or involve us. Does it, my dear?"

Velda shook her sculptured white head. "Not in the least, Milo."

When they had gone, Mary attempted to draw the children out on the reasons behind their excessive amusement over Milo's comments. They seemed puzzled that she would ask. Noticing that Joey wasn't eating, she asked him why.

"Because Mr. Fratonitus didn't even speak t'me," he said with angry tears in his eyes. "He ig*nored* me, like I was a baby or somethin'."

Soon the topic changed and Mary learned that Ellen was full of news. She had met a boy, that day, whom she thought was "terribly cute." She warned her mother that she would bring him by the cottage soon.

"You aren't possibly thinking of asking me again if you can date?" Mary demanded. "Because the answer is still No, El. You're too young."

Ellen gave her one short reply, her eyes averted: "We'll see."

Alone in her room that night, Mary felt out of sorts, entirely discomfited by life. No, she corrected herself—out of place. In a foreign land, suddenly, even if it was only eleven miles from Indianapolis. A foreign land where she could not fit in.

But the children certainly seemed to be having no trouble fitting in. None at all.

Was she really that set in her own ways, was she getting old? Was she so opposed to changes in their little family that she imagined Thessaly was, somehow, taking her kids over? Because it was certainly beginning to seem like that to Mary Graham.

It was probably indigestion, probably that strange fruit concoction Milo had brought them. God knows what all was in the *thargela*. It reeked of wine and honey. Chuck must have eaten a quart of the rich, miserable stuff and neglected his regular meal.

Mary held her picture of Barry, tears in her eyes. His affable face with the soft gray eyes behind thick glasses and the full, on-verge-of-laughing lips reassured her a little. Oh, Barry, why can't I seem to re*late* to people who were going out of their way to be *nice?*

Why did you have to go and die . . . ?

Sometime around midnight, when all the lights in the Graham house were off, Mary awakened with a shudder. She felt simultaneously chilled and suffocated.

Again tonight she thought she was hearing the sound of hoofbeats.

She padded barefoot across the floor to the window and peered behind a lace curtain at the dark midnight world of Thessaly.

She arrived just in time to see an ancient drawn coach, pulled by four gigantic horses, plunge precariously down Attica Avenue, turning on Alexandria, presumably headed in the general direction of the great woods. She hadn't been able to see the coachman or to make out any passengers. Even the immense horses seemed virtually eaten by engulfing shadows, partial creatures whose beating hooves clattered eerily in the silence of the small community. There was a distant whinny and they were gone.

The entire episode, occuring as it had just as she awoke from sleep, had a distinctly nightmare quality to it. Mary found her heart throbbing, pounding anxiously. She tried to conclude that she had only imagined it, but her practical mind told her that that simply wasn't true.

What was going on here? What kind of people rode around in crazy carriages in the middle of the night? Did they do this kind of thing *every* night — and for what reason? Just who *were* these seemingly friendly Greeks, and what were their secrets?

She remembered the old saying about beware of Greeks bearing gifts, just in time to keep herself awake yet another hour.

When at last she tumbled into sleep again it was pregnant with ominously meaningful dreams, slices of insight, thumb-flipped images of truth — all of which she forgot completely in the early glare of morning.

IV

The world-wide warfare of the eternal Two
Well in the mass of human limbs is shown:
Whiles into one do they through Love unite. . . .
                                        —Empedocles

Four-twenty-six A.M. Indianapolis, Indiana, the
eastern outskirts of a sleeping city. A cemetery,
several graves expunged, left naked, by swift,
furtive digging and the illicit opening of long-
sealed caskets. Discarded now as unworthy,
inappropriate, their solemn contents left to rot
and disintegrate in the piercing morning air.

One gravesite selected with grim mutual
delight, coffin lid thrown back to reveal the
recently buried much-mourned body of a sixteen-
year-old girl. Nameless to the nocturnal preda-

tors, she had been uncommonly pretty until a slippery dusk when she was catapulted from her boyfriend's motorcycle and snapped her young neck against a storefront.

Now, greater experts than any mortician labored with proven methods of *grimmarye*—with mathematical formulae mumbled as incantation, with ensweetened, precious wine rubbed just-so beneath the skull, with a blending of herbs forgotten by most sane men—to restore her loveliness.

It was not a belated act of agonized compassion. Indeed, they had begun their grisly work by slicing forthrightly into the chest cavity to remove the heart, making as little mess as possible, setting the stilled organ aside for its unmentionable final part in the bizarre operation.

"The Patriarch must know nothing of this," the female one insisted in a hoarse whisper. She worked the limbs, found them supple again. "He would not approve."

"He gave you permission to try, to make the change. Did he not?" The male leered at her, his sharp teeth flashing against the darkness of the grave. He applied treated kykeon wine beneath the leg joints, a crazed masseur until he looked up again with purpose. "Besides, while *he* is the Patriarch, *I* balance his authority—as I always have. Do not forget this. I do exactly what I please, and I want *this* to happen."

Behind them, a horse whinnied, pawed spilled earth. It did not like this place of the human dead. It wanted to go home to Thessaly. Soon, burdened by an additional passenger, it did.

Thessaly seemed nearly deserted at six-thirty in the morning, Mary observed as she won the grudging cooperation of her old Granada and the motor chugged to life. Anxiously, she glanced at her wristwatch, refraining from tooting the horn out of respect for her neighbors. Each landowner had at least a half-acre, so that, while she could say she had "next door" neighbors, they were by no means on top of one another. Lamia lived on the next street over. Down this block, as she waited, Mary could identify the rather impressive, stone-fronted two-story where Milo and Veldo Traphonius lived. A single light burned on their second floor, as if it had been forgotten when the old people retired for the night. Didn't Greeks used to be farmers, accustomed to early rising—or was she confusing nationalities and periods of time?

Joey raced to the car, throwing the door open for trailing Ellen with a grand, sweeping gesture. It fooled no one. Mother and daughter knew this was his highhanded way of claiming the privileged front seat, not an exercise in manners.

Ellen got in the back seat without argument, scattering her books everywhere on the seat. Joey, Mary saw, was empty-handed. She bit her lip and said nothing.

No one in the Graham household arose early with ease or grace. Part of it was undoubtedly the wide array of jobs Barry had had, going to work at seven with one position, at one in the afternoon with another. Routine was lacking from their lives and Mary knew it. She felt an obligation to bring a measure of regularity to them.

The first part of the ride down Attica Avenue and through the tiny heart of Thessaly, past the small commercial aorta, was utterly silent. Mary saw that Nick Melas's general store was already lit up, although there was no evident customer and the expressionless middle-aged man could not be seen. He was probably in back, preparing stock for the new day. She wondered idly how he could survive on the small income provided by a town of two hundred.

She turned left on Alexandria, noticing how the look of the community quickly gave way to vacant fields and untenanted land, then to a neglected rural realm at the eastern edge of Indianapolis. Thessaly, she mused, was almost more a state of mind than a real place—belonging to a couple of hundred time-bypassed Greek-Americans who wouldn't let the past go.

Out here, East Washington Street was also U.S. 40 and she turned west, heading for Mitthoefer Road. She wound north gradually, past the sprawling Washington Square shopping world, heading for Marshall High School at 38th Street. There, Ellen would get out. Then she would drop Joey with his friend from their apartment days, Teddy Higgert, so that the two of them could walk the necessary two blocks to their grade school by eight. She hated giving him that much free time, away from home; but it was more risky leaving him in front of an unopened school.

78

"Try to pay a little more attention in English, Joey," she said to the rear-view mirror. Always restless, he had climbed into the back seat a few blocks back. Now his small frame was crouched in a corner, as if ready to spring. "You can pass it, if you try, Mrs. Hopping says. Also, in math, do the long-division the way I suggested to you and you *could* get a C."

For a moment she thought Joey wasn't going to answer at all. Then, in a small voice, "Wish Thessaly had a school."

"It's too small for one." Mary smiled. "You're really taking to our new home, aren't you?"

"I guess so," he answered deliberately. "Yeah, I am," with more assurance. Abruptly, his alert, pugnacious blond face was at her shoulder, emphasizing his question with enthusiasm. "D'you think Mr. Safronitus would pay more attention to me if I told him I'd shovel snow for him this winter?"

"His name is Tra-pho-ni-us," Mary enunciated carefully. "Why do you ask, son?" Was Joey in need of a new father already? "You don't usually care much for older people."

"But he's cool." The boy's breath was warm on the side of her neck. "He don't even seem old t'me. That new dude who likes Ellen told her Mr. Fratonius knows magic tricks. Really far-out shit. I want the old guy to teach me some."

Mary sighed. Bad grammar mingled with childish slang left her with a helpless feeling and an incipient headache. There was just too much about this boy that required improvement, but

79

she hated to be a nag.

"I see nothing wrong with offering to shovel his snow," she said at last, pulling up in front of Teddy's dark house. "Although it might be two months before we get any." *I hope*, she added, to herself.

"Or it might be tonight," Joey corrected her as he slammed the door after him and peered elflike through the window. "Don't forget crazy-ole Indiana weather! I hope your horsie comes today," he added, laughing and turning to spin away.

He appeared so self-sufficient, *wanted* to be *so* badly, and he was so completely helpless. She ached to help him, to better him for his own sake, at least to reach the soft, liquid heart of the child where she knew kindness and decency surely dwelt.

Joey would be all right, she told herself as she headed the Granada toward East 16th Street and the Dutch-Touch Cleaners. He would do just fine in Thessaly, and so would Ellen and Chuck. Soon Chuck would get a job, and unlike his father, *keep* it—work his way up, save some money, amount to something.

But for the life of her, where Mary Graham fitted in anymore—with the children, in Thessaly, or in Indianapolis—was more than she could see.

It was good to be back at work. Greta Bailess, the German-American owner of the establishment, had twice regaled Mary and the other employees with recollections of her innocent membership in Hitler's youth movement. It amazed Mary how naive Greta sounded, how quickly she had concluded that it was safe to speak of such terrible things in the United States. True; Greta had been obliged to be a member, at the tender age of ten, and had never hurt a fly.

But Mary remembered that her own father had inadvertently joined the Ku Klux Klan, thinking it only a civic-minded social organization, some thirty-five years ago. He had refused to discuss his youthful foolishness to his dying day, and that had seemed right to Mary.

As usual, fiftyish Martha Cummins was full of cheerful wisecracks that made the minutes speed away. Young "Huck" Ford was equally full of sexy innuendoes as the day's variety of attractive women coming into the store drew his keen attention. Work itself seemed nearly a luxury, an ameliorating influence on Mary's nerves. The bustling city with its diverse life styles, its modern interests, first contrasted with Thessaly's traditions and then simply overwhelmed them.

At noon, Mary washed up in the employee washroom and drove to the newly opened Wild Boar for lunch. She had planned to meet Jeanne Lange there and, sure enough, as she peered down the cafeteria line, there was hungry Jeanne with two plates the size of platters, piling the food high.

They sat by a window, opposite one another, Mary munching on a huge tenderloin sandwich and fat french fries. She had hoped to allow Jeanne to do most of the talking but, as was customary, Jeanne wanted to hear all about her.

She wasn't sure just what she should say, confronted with a point-blank question from Jeanne: "How d'you like that burg by now?"

Mary paused to consider.

"Well, Mare, if you can't answer the question, you hate it." Jeanne finished a rib and daubed at her mouth with a cloth napkin. "And I don't blame you."

"I didn't say I hated it, Jeanne," Mary protested. "The people are trying hard to be nice."

"They're trying, all right. And maybe too hard." The pile of blond hair atop the teacher's head seemed slightly askew, but her eyes were sharp and attentive. "Why are they paying so much attention to you?"

"Perhaps it's just their way, their custom, to drop in like they do."

"I doubt it." Jeanne sipped her beer, stifling a burp. "I know a little bit about Greeks—at least, the ones from way back—and they tended to be clannish. There were severe disputes among the Greek isles, places you couldn't safely go even within the same country. *I* think they're *after* something."

"Well, they did seem clannish, at first. Then that changed."

"So what d'you think changed it?" Jeanne asked sharply.

Mary forced a laugh. "Maybe they crave my bod for a human sacrifice."

"I doubt that too." Jeanne shook her head, glancing out the window. "Most of them weren't into that, the way some of the Roman, Hebrew, and early Christian sects were. Mare, look at that animal.''

Mary turned her head. Beyond the window, sitting on the sidewalk, a lean, hungry-looking yellow dog was watching them closely, his head tilted, his expression peculiarly intent. ''Poor thing looks half-starved.''

''Maybe *he* craves your bod,'' Jeanne muttered. ''Be careful of that mutt when you leave, okay?'' She finished her salad and reached for a slice of peach pie. ''I can't understand how you can eat a meal without dessert,'' she complained. ''Makes a person anemic.''

''I have to watch my girlish figure. If I don't, no one else will.''

''Mary, let's not leave the subject of your new home for a moment.'' The teacher swallowed an enormous bite of pie. ''That dame, Lamia, seemed downright weird to me.''

''She's really quite lovely. How d'you mean, weird?''

''It's hard to put.'' Jeanne searched for words. ''I think it's something to do with her eyes. Mare, everything else may change about a person—complexion gets muddy and wrinkled, you lose hair or teeth, all that—but the basic expression in a pair of eyes stays the same.''

''I thought Lamia had striking, beautiful eyes.''

''Oh, she does. Eyes that lie. Eyes that—well, it has to do with the ages of the people in Thessaly.'' Jeanne wiped with a pinkie at a dab of peach adhering to the left lens of her spectacles. ''I stopped by a couple of their little stores, after I left your place. The people are all the same."

"No, they're *not*," Mary insisted, frowning. She felt vaguely torn in loyalty. "The people of Thessaly are *all* ages, Jeanne, the same as anywhere."

Jeanne leaned closer. Her expression was intense and direct. "Aside from the fact that you're probably wrong, since I didn't see a single child Joey's age, that's not what I meant. Honey, age doesn't seem to—have an *effect* on them. Or—more than that—I think maybe age isn't *part* of them, somehow. It isn't . . . legitimate, what we think we're seeing."

"I've never heard anything so absurd, Jeanne. You've been reading too many books on the supernatural."

"Did I say they were spooks, or aliens from another planet?" the teacher demanded. "No, ma'am, I didn't. But you watch what I'm saying. You look into an old lady's eyes, and then the eyes of somebody around twenty, and you'll find that—there isn't any difference."

Mary twisted her napkin without realizing it. "Let me tell you, then, about my midnight visitor."

"You mean Lamia and the champagne or a mystery gentleman?"

"Neither. Something else."

Jeanne lit a cigarette, inhaling deeply. "They stay up late in Thessaly, don't they?" she said pointedly. "Odd for a small town, isn't it?"

"Jeanne, there was a—a coach-and-four that

84

went by my house last night." Mary had steeled herself for this. She guessed now that she'd intended to mention it since they made the luncheon date, even longed to. "I know it sounds crazy, but an old-fashioned, horse-drawn coach went careening down my street around midnight."

"It may be a death-coach."

Mary looked at her friend, stunned both by her acceptance of it and her term. "Wh-What's that?"

"Something that may never have existed, or may have," Jeanne replied with a shrug of her bulky shoulders. She seemed grim. "Usually it's English, or Welsh, I think; doesn't have to be. Probably got started after the wagons went around Europe picking up the dead, during the time of the plague. According to legend, it always comes late at night and it's difficult to see the driver's face. And you certainly don't want to."

"Why not?" Mary asked softly.

"Because," her friend answered, just as softly, "when you can see his face, it means he's stopping for you. And although no one knows precisely what the *purpose* of the death-coach is, everybody knows . . . you don't want it stopping in front of *your* house."

"I was hoping you'd tell me it was all my imagination," Mary said nervously, finishing her coke and squeezing the ice-soggy cup.

"It may be—or something just as good as that." Jeanne plumped her golden-haired wig into shape. Her pride and joy, it had deceived people for two years now. "There may be a sort of psychic memory-image clinging to Thessaly, just a mass of vibrations left there from some murder or drowning of the past. You know, psychic energy or matter rearranged and given life by the power of belief your nutty townsfolk seem to have."

"Is that what a ghost really is? Psychic energy—memory vibrations?"

Jeanne chuckled and patted her friend's hand. "That's one of the newer theories for the science-minded, honey. But don't let 'em kid ya: we still don't know a thing about it, not for sure."

Outside the Wild Boar, the lean and intent dog continued to stare at their faces, their eyes, their telling lips. Customers passing by were completely ignored. One, who affably paused to pat the animal's yellow head, received a cold, haughty stare and hastened on his way. But the dog went on watching Mary and Jeanne, its head unturning, appearing ornamental.

At dusk, this Friday, Chuck returned through the woods toward his home, and just as he drew abreast of the fringes of the forest and within earshot of the ragged line of homes nearest the trees, he heard a rustle of cloth. Shotgun dangling carelessly, his hands empty of rabbit, he turned to the noise.

Lamia Zacharius, beckoning him from the side of a moss-covered elm. Her eyes were as vivid and challenging as ever but there was something new there, too, he thought. Something of—fervent promise.

"Hi. Out drawin' again?" he asked, ambling toward the woman.

She watched him come, the six-footer with the football-player build. She noted the wide, deep shoulders. The crinkling of his almost turquoise eyes was a charming evidence that he was glad to see her. She longed to run her fingers through his yellowish hair, to feel his forceful weight on her; but she sensed that he found it impossible to hurdle their difference in years.

"Do you recall our conversation of yesterday?" she asked directly as he approached.

"Sure." He laughed a little as he stopped, his legs spread, balancing on one bouncy hip. "But I didn't understand a lot of it, actually."

"No, No, of course not," she said pityingly, patting his cheek. "But you shall, and sooner than you think. Let me start you on the road now, Chuck."

"Yes, ma'am?" He was so polite. He was like a loving puppy.

"It is not the age or the body alone that will please you, boy. Not in the long run." Her dark eyes were hot on him. "It is the fervent mind, the demanding spirit in the woman, that *directs* the body—and the age is then rendered meaningless. I promise you that, after tonight, you will begin to understand this."

"How?"

"Do you know where the general store is located?"

"Yes, ma'am."

"Continue wearing what I gave you. Behind the

store is a place thin with trees. Go there, after eleven o'clock." Lamia kept her hands from him with difficulty. Her tongue flicked out, lapped at her full lower lip. "You shall not see me, boy, but another. Her name is Lythia. She—lives with me, Chuck. And she will teach you everything you have longed to know and much more. She will be yours, boy. To do with as you please."

Ponderously, Chuck nodded. His eyes gleamed. "I'll be there."

"You must not speak of this to your mother, your sister, or the boy Joey." Her hands were suddenly on either side of his heavy neck, her body shoving against him, fitting. "Promise me that they shall not know. Especially the boy."

Her hips ground, twisted, and she seemed nearly naked against him—but not naked enough. "I promise," the teenager moaned, agonized.

"And Chuck?"

"Yes'm?"

"Remember this promise of *mine* as you have remembered much in your recent dreams. You have a great deal to learn." She touched the amulet on the string around his neck, the one she had given him. "You and I can be any age we please—any age *at all*. As you become one with Thessaly, *of* Thessaly, you will share its secrets. You will not have need of the dying, as your father did. Can you remember? Will you learn?"

He nodded.

"Good. Then you will be able to help us teach . . . the others."

Then she was gone, melting back into the forest

88

as if she belonged there.

At home, dinner was a quiet proposition. Mary still felt disturbed by the peculiar remarks Jeanne had made and found that she was inclined now to see, even in this old cottage, traces of nameless, wordless terror. That way, she told herself firmly as they ate, lay paranoia.

But her limping efforts at conversation with the kids fell short. It was always a mixed matter at best, given Joey's presence and his animated, hyperkinetic performance, which left one waiting to catch the next falling object. Tonight he had excitedly announced that "the old guy with the beard" would allow him to shovel snow that winter and then, seemingly dissatisfied with his family's cool response to the news, fell into one of his impenetrable sulks.

Chuck, often uncommunicative and moody for no reason clear to others, had to choose tonight for such an occasion. He limited his participation in the meal to eating double portions of everything on the table. And Ellen, after informing Mary that "my new Thessaly friend" would shortly drop by, hid behind silence as if it might shield her from Mary's probing queries.

They were clearing the table when a solid ratatat of knocking sounded at the front door. Mary sighed with something akin to relief, as Ellen went to answer it. At least this attraction of El's was normal; this was a human mother's task of consultation awaiting her: appraising Ellen's first candidate for boyfriendhood and attempting to establish some sensible boundaries.

The boy proved to be above average height, olive-skinned, with a thatch of tight, dark curls that gave him, with the customary darkly remote Thessaly eyes and a duo ringing of thick lashes, the demeanor of a young Olympic god. His name was Andruss—Ellen offered nothing more and Mary was unclear whether Andruss was the boy's first or last name—and he was the soul of courtesy and solicitude.

Beaming on Mary as if nothing would make his life more ideal than her sweet smile of approval, Andruss insisted on "helping out with the dishes."

"I've been one of nine children," he boasted boyishly as the soapsuds flew. "You learn to do your part in a situation like that."

His industry and proficiency in bringing cleanliness to the plates and silverware were undisputable even if he seemed to waste half a bottle of detergent in his zeal. Mary noticed that Andruss had given Ellen little more than a perfunctory nod before setting out to charm the family. Even Joey, beating on his strong young back as he washed the dishes and then calling him a chicken, warmed to Andruss.

It proved to be an easy matter to converse with the boy, too. Mary, sitting afterward in the front room as Andruss perched on the sofa beside Ellen and Joey, found herself liking the youthful Greek even while she felt that she understood his private motives. Few American boys these days cared a whit about the impact they had on their girl's mother. She found herself suddenly discussing the bizarre and frightening midnight coach as she studied Andruss's handsome face. To her pleasure, the boy didn't exactly deny its existence.

"People have been talking about that thing for years," he said with cheery forthrightness. "It's some kind of ancient Greek legend or something."

Mary framed her words carefully as she watched him. "Are you saying that the coach exists or doesn't exist?"

He smiled. "I could just say 'yes,' since that seems to fit in with the legends of your Santa Claus and Easter Bunny. Perhaps some of your minor deities, indeed." He scratched his black crown of hair thoughtfully before answering. "A lot of unusual things do happen here, in Thessaly, probably because the older folks expect them to," he said finally. "I'm only a boy. No one tells me what's actually going on. But I know that *I* sure wouldn't want that death-coach to stop in front of *my* house at night."

"Don't talk about th' Easter Bunny," Joey said with great solemnity, pursing his faintly scarred lips as he recalled his old dread. "I do not dig rabbits; I do not groove on them."

They all chuckled at his almost adult expression of open antipathy.

When Andruss had departed and Mary had gone up to bed, she undressed with a sense of mixed achievement. Ellen had accepted her premise that she might date one weekend night weekly, so long as it was afoot, held to the town, and some member of Ellen's or Andruss's family was present at all times.

But she realized now, with a sick feeling of having let Ellen down, that she knew next to nothing about the young man, including his age. She pegged him at near Chuck's age and recalled that he had spoken of having eight brothers and sisters. But his father's identity, what he did for a living, the family background, where they resided in Thessaly, were all still unanswered questions.

Was it her fault, or had Andruss skillfully guided the discussion with a verbal dexterity beyond his tender years?

She read parts of Peter Ustinov's amusing, surprisingly perceptive autobiography, *Dear Me*, as she sought sleep. Jeanne's words kept slipping through her concentration as if it were made of cheesecloth. At length, she reached above her head to switch off the bed lamp and try to sleep.

Bold diagonal shadows marched somberly on the bedroom floor, animated now and then as the lace curtains at the window shifted with a faint draught from beneath the window. Mary dozed.

When she heard it coming, she pulled the blankets instinctively higher, close around her neck. The death-coach rattled nearer, and nearer, as she prayed for the damned thing to come level with the house and quickly move on. *There is nothing to be afraid of*, she told herself, mouthing the words in the dark. *It's only some silly custom of the elders here, that's all.*

But when the horse-drawn carriage pulled clatteringly by, and she heard a sallying whinny echo on the midnight air, Mary found that she shivered uncontrollably for a moment and hugged the blankets to her naked sides. Perhaps the weekend would be better, she thought gamely. Maybe the death-coach had the weekend off, didn't follow its lunatic route on Saturday or Sunday.

She smiled quite feebly at her small joke and reached out in the dark to touch Barry's picture on the nearby dresser. Then she lay back, achingly awake, awaiting morning and daylight.

The overhead lightbulb dangling in Nick's General Store's backroom had been left on. Now yellow light splayed out for many yards in the clear December night, dispersing slowly in the stillness.

She was where Lamia had said she would be, behind the store and just back into the woods. She was approximately Chuck's own age and dressed even as Lamia had been dressed—in the light-weight knee-length gown with bare shoulders and a scooping, plunging neckline. Unlike Lamia, the young golden-blonde named Lythia was gifted with great globular breasts which pressed against the material, threatening to tear it.

In his haste, Chuck did. She had said not a word to him, meeting him with a low, moaning sound from deep in her throat and hurling herself against him with the ferocity of a beautiful young animal. The boy was not brilliant, but he could not conceivably have misinterpreted the motives of the wanton, utterly delectable stranger.

There was a small fire going which removed

some of the chill, and there were two immense blankets awaiting their use, Chuck saw over the girl's shoulder as her breasts filled and overflowed his hands. The amulet hanging from his neck felt tinglingly hot, a part of his mind managed to notice, almost as if charged by some lambent electricity. But he forgot it at once because of the heat suffusing his cheeks and forehead, pounding like fire between his legs.

He was neither gentle, his first time, nor patient. He ploughed ruttingly into the sixteen-year-old body, feeling an instant response as she arched and ground beneath him, her little sharp teeth nipping at his neck and shoulders.

Chuck was amazed by the girl's fury, the way her hunger at least matched his own, with the way she wrapped her supple legs round his waist to urge him on, and at his moment of soaring climax, tracked deep scratches along his broad back and shoulder blades with her nails.

When it was done he tried, when his interest swiftly began to return, to get her to remove the remainder of her clothing. She'd left on a pale-yellow, quite fashionable slip that rode above her lean, thrusting hips during their mating but still covered her stomach and a portion of her breasts. Happily, Lythia permitted him to feel her full bosom from the top of the chemise but not to grope beneath the open hem of the garment. When Chuck began to protest, playfully, she shoved him onto his back. To his amazement and pleasure she rose above him, then impaled herself upon his new erectness. Their backs arched and, in a moment, all words were not only unnecessary but quite impossible.

Afterward, lying side by side, Lythia told him that she lived with Lamia, who was her aunt, but had been away from town of late. The two of them were roommates and took turns caring for the house willed to them by Lamia's father. Now, Lamia herself had gone out of town, attempting to sell her sketches and paintings. And if she could arrange a showing, she might be gone for a long while.

"Did you like Lamia?" asked Lythia, her palm resting on his flaccid penis.

"She was gonna teach me more about Thessaly," he said, a mild complaint. His big hand stroked the contour of her sloping hip. "And show me how I'd never get old or die, because there were—some kinds of *changes* I could make."

"I am glad you liked her, but don't fret." Suddenly she sat up, leaning over the teenager. She kissed the length of his shaft and again found it rising to her lips. His eyes were huge. "I know every secret Lamia knew," she said huskily, her voice even sounding, just then, like the older woman. "And I promise you, lad, I'll teach you everything you want to know. *Everything.*"

She lowered her head, and the lessons continued.

In front of Nick's General Store, the deathcoach pulled to a silent halt. The coachman leapt down from his high perch with remarkable agility and padded almost noiselessly to the side of the building. There, he found a square, covered box. Within it was a brown dropcloth and it covered what he sought.

Grinning horribly in the grip of rigor, her arms and legs frozen at strange angles, the body of Lamia Zacharius was picked up as rudely and informally as another man might pick up a sack of old potatoes. The coachman toted the stiff, nude body to the opened door of the death-coach, then paused to get a grisly fresh grip. Having purchase, he tossed the body unceremoniously inside and slammed the door. Part of Lamia's dark hair was pinned beneath the door but he ignored it. Quickly he mounted to his high perch, reaching for the reins and whistling an aimless little tune as he headed the horses toward the stone-shielded gravesite known to old residents as the Vale of Aphaca.

"What was that?" Chuck whispered, lifting his head and blinking past a corner of the blanket.

"Nothing," Lythia replied, resuming her labors. "Just—night sounds."

V

Fools! for their thoughts are briefly brooded o'er.
Who trust that what is not can e'er become,
Or aught that is can wholly die away.
                                        —Empedocles

It had been another largely sleepless night, and
when sleep did mercifully numb her awareness, it
brought Mary torporous nightmares heavy with a
portent she tried to grasp but could not. At one
point they accelerated, the images charging,
racing through her mind—pictures of each of the
children in dreadful peril at which they laughed
inanely, like infants being tickled. She awakened
after a dream of her own body heightened,
widened, stretched like a great shielding door
between the giggling children on one side and—

something—on the other side. She was turning her head, to look at it, when she reached consciousness.

She sat for a long while on the edge of the bed, her shoulders heaving. Perspiration trickled like ominous fingers between her shoulder blades. With a shudder, she heaved herself erect and went to the bathroom where she gargled a mouthwash for a full minute, knowing that she was symbolically washing away the alarming dreams.

When she was only half-dressed, Joey burst through the bathroom door with a delighted expression on his face. "The old dude's here!" he announced explosively. "And he wants to see you."

Mary smiled, partly with amusement, partly with annoyance. For Joey, it was like a royal command performance that old Milo Traphonius had asked for her. But it was only eleven o'clock on a Saturday and, in Indianapolis, only children who sought other children visited that early.

She finished buttoning a comfortable flannel shirt, one of her favorite garments, and let the tail hang over an old pair of blue jeans. Then she ran a brush through her thick dark brown hair, and unknowingly looked grand. That'll have to do, she told her mirror image.

The "old dude" sat in her own chair, almost primly, spine straight and his knees together. Even on Saturday he wore a dark business suit which somehow accentuated his encircling mane of gray hair and beard. He arose when she entered, even gave her a slight bow.

"How nice to have visitors early on a Saturday morning," she murmured, taking his extended hand.

"Early?" He seemed surprised and glanced at a watch on his hairy wrist. "Why, it's less than an hour till noon." His eyes became roundly solicitous. "I do hope I've not awakened you. Were you ill?"

"Not at all," she laughed with a merriment she didn't feel. "I have tons of things to do today, anyway." She perched on the uncomfortable edge of the sofa and waited.

"I'm afraid that I come with unpleasant news," the old man said with a sigh. "I was aware that you, and the children, were becoming fast friends with Lamia Zacharius. For that reason, I felt it best if I were the one to come today. To—break the news."

"Break the news?" Mary repeated. "Is there something—?"

"Something wrong?" Milo nodded his head. "Indeed, there is. I'm afraid that Lamia has—perished. Yesterday, just before her niece Lythia arrived home. The poor young girl discovered the body, I fear."

"How dreadful." Mary had always been more kindhearted than she tended to appear. Her words were genuine. "I am sorry to hear it, Milo. Lamia . . . tried . . . to welcome us to Thessaly. Chuck, in particular, was quite attached to her." Mary's mind swept upstairs, to the boy's bedroom. She had caught a glimpse of his large, bare feet through his partly opened door before coming downstairs. "Was it her heart?"

"Apparently. Her own doctor came and went so I don't have it direct from the horse's mouth." Milo's solemn expression became moreso, more earnest. "We are honoring Lamia, in our own little way—a way she would have approved—tomorrow." He paused. "Sunday."

Mary nodded, waited.

"It will be at the church, over on Kadia. Will you come?"

She paused, feeling uncomfortable. "I—don't know that I should, Milo."

"Why not?" he asked, beaming paternally upon her. "You'll be more than welcome, I assure you. You'll meet more of the residents of our little community, all those neighbors who wish so much to be your friends."

"I'm Catholic." She looked at her hands, hoping God would forgive her. She hadn't been to mass in years.

"Well, just as the Catholic mass was once spoken in Latin, some of what you'll hear is in Greek." He explained carefully, as if addressing a child. There was a great deal of the professor in Milo Traphonius. "And what you hear may even prove to be interesting, thought-provoking."

"Is it Greek Orthodox?" she inquired, sliding now.

Milo gave an explosive miniature laugh. "My, no! More, perhaps, Greek *un*orthodox if the truth be known." He stood, briskly. "But you shall see for yourself." He turned to Joey who, throughout the adult discussion, had quietly listened with an attentiveness rare to him. "Please bring the child. And all your family, of course."

"Can we, Mom?" Joey pleaded, suddenly on his feet. *"Can we?"*

She peered down at him in astonishment. Joey Graham, pleading to go to a *funeral?* She shrugged helplessly. "Of course, Milo. We'll be honored."

Shortly after Milo had driven away in his Oldsmobile, Mary was fixing two cold meat sandwiches with the intention of awakening Chuck when Ellen opened the french doors at the back to step in and hurry to the kitchen.

"G'morning," Mary murmured. "Want a sandwich?"

Ellen shook her head. "Any of that *thargela* left?"

"No," Mary replied, "your brother cleaned that up yesterday. Where've you been so early?"

"Over at Andruss's place."

"I should have guessed." She put extra mustard on Chuck's meatloaf and the bread adhered like glue. "We're going to a funeral tomorrow. I'm sorry to say that—"

"I know all about it," Ellen interrupted, lounging against the door between the kitchen and dining room. Her eyes seemed brighter than usual and yet introspective, as if thinking of something exciting at a distance. "Andruss told me about Lamia. After the services we're all going to a sort of indoor picnic."

"A picnic!" Mary turned to her daughter, incredulous. "After a *funeral?*"

"Andruss says it's natural here, almost a tradition." Ellen's fingers toyed with a pendant unfamiliar to her mother. "Lots of people'll be there. You see, Mom, it's not like Lamia really died. She only—changed."

Mary laughed. "Well, death certainly is a change—I can't deny that."

"I don't know why folks laugh at things they don't understand." Chuck appeared in the other doorway wearing old slacks and a heavy high school sweatshirt. He seemed sleepy, almost exhausted, rubbing his eyes with thick knuckles and trying to focus them as he yawned. "El's right. Lamia just faced up to the need for change. No big deal, actually."

"How do *you* know about it?' Mary asked, startled.

"Her niece told me. Lythia." He lifted the top piece of bread on his sandwich and thoughtfully applied still more mustard. "We got t'talking last night, when I was out, and she's goin' with me to the services and the picnic."

Mary's eyes narrowed. "That's pretty fast work for you, Charles. Meeting a girl and making an immediate date."

He gave her his boyish grin. "Speedy Gonzales Graham, that's me. Your little boy's growing up, Mom. Might as well get used to it."

He took his sandwich and a huge glass of milk and went out to sit in front of the television set and stare at cartoons, oblivious to the paradox. Mary looked at him for a moment before half-smiling, turning back to address Ellen.

102

But Ellen had slipped back out the french doors and was striding purposefully toward the woods, fifty yards from the back door. Mary watched her go with a mixture of pride and regret. There was a lot of herself in that girl, even though they didn't really look alike. Their coloring was similarly fairly dark with brown hair, but Ellen's was lighter and more naturally curly. Both were relatively tall but where Mary's weight was proportionate to her height, Ellen seemed an adult mixture of willowy slenderness and jutting young breasts.

More than direct resemblance, Mary thought, it was something in the businesslike walk with the head up, eyes straight ahead, determinedly fearless of anything that the world might throw at her.

The way Mary had felt before coming to Thessaly.

The thought had come with a pang. Why did *that* enter her head?

She turned away from the doors. She noticed Chuck was absently playing with a necklace of some sort dangling from his throat. It looked surprisingly like the pendant, or whatever, that Ellen had been wearing.

A mutual friend? She thought of asking who gave it to him but reconsidered, afraid to sound like she was meddling.

Instead, she went to the front door to see if the mail had come. It hadn't but she watched Joey playing in the front yard, shooting invisible bad men—she *hoped* they were bad—and getting shot in return. She was glad to see his sudden burst of zeal, to see the old Joey. He had been subdued recently and Mary was inclined to see, in any kind of alteration, a vaguely alarming threat. She'd prefer that Joey settled down as the direct outcome of a well-reasoned argument she had presented to him rather than for reasons she could not perceive.

And wasn't that what her concern was about, really, the odd way that she persisted in feeling a foreigner in Thessaly despite every effort on Thessaly's part to welcome her, to make her one of them? Wasn't it that she resented not being in control of her destiny—and didn't *that* stem from Barry's untimely, unexpected, change-bringing death?

Perhaps she was fundamentally wrong, despite the things Jeanne had said, to be so concerned because the kids were adapting so well to this new home. When in Rome, and all that, after all.

She turned back into her house from the front door in time to see Chuck replace his pendant or amulet beneath his heavy sweatshirt. But why didn't anything else make sense these days? How did it happen that Chuck and Ellen suddenly had identical necklaces? Why didn't Joey mention his Christmas birthday anymore, plague her for gifts the way he usually did? And what of the minor, seemingly unimportant changes in the children— the way that Joey's entire day appeared to have been made exciting by the appearance of a bearded old man he barely knew?

Mary went out to the kitchen to wash the dishes

as it dawned on her that, if failure to change meant she must forever be isolated in her own family, a tacit outcast, she'd give anything to be swallowed up by this or any other community.

The Synod's special council, the Syndic, met in midafternoon on Saturday. The four remarkable men—the Patriarch and the countering Vrukalakos, George Aristides and Nicholas Melas—briefly grasped hands round the table bearing the *Logos*.

The book of miracles and truth lay beneath a glass that protected it from the ravages of time as the Syndic prayed to Apollo for guidance.

Only the tall, saturnine Vrukalakos would have seemed truly unusual in other company, company beyond Thessaly. His perpetually angry black eyes were set closely together above an aggressive, pointed nose, which, in turn, shielded an ebon mustache that drooped on either side over a cruel slash of a mouth. There was something quicksilver to his lean, hungry body, a hint of constant, threatening motion, as if he might choose to fly away at any moment and was held there only by some uncommunicable mutual need.

Of late, his long-standing animosity for the Patriarch was beginning to surface from time to time, to make the others restless. The Patriarch hated Vrukalakos, they knew, at least as much as he was hated. Petty and self-satisfying acts were rare with the *pater familias*. Through the years he had always taken action for the good of the entire

105

Synod, always by first calculating the precise wishes of the *akousmatikoi*—his fellows in the Syndic. No one doubted this, not even Vrukalakos, who despised the old man for his character—and for the incredible involvement with each other that nature's secrets, the secrets of the *Logos*, had thrust upon them both.

Because they prevented Krukalakos from rending the Patriarch to ribbons.

Now the old man was staring at him with that weary, reproachful expression that bespoke his displeasure more than any words could do. "You should not have defiled that cemetery," the Patriarch said in his level baritone. "There was no need for that change, at that time."

"It doesn't matter," Vrukalakos replied with a shrug.

"It was not mathematically plotted for perfect safety and *Bauernpraktik* were not consulted," the old man insisted. "You might have been seen."

"If we had been, I would simply have slain the observers."

"Is killing all you know? Even for you, Vrukalakos, there are a number of adversaries which can restrain you. I know that number and it is not infinite."

"Threats, after all this time?" The swarthy creature smiled cruelly. "You know that you require me, even as I need you—curse Apollo for it! Let us speak of significant issues. I say that we take this boy now, without waiting."

"And what of the mother?"

"Why, kill her!" His eyes flashed hatred.

"Who *cares* what we do with her? Give the word and I'll take her to Aether!"

"You have always been a fool, Vrukalakos," the Patriarch observed with regret. "The boy's presence at Commemoration will be best utilized if he is happy to be with us, to lead us. I feel strongly that this would not be the case if we murdered his earth-mother."

"She may become one of us too, in time," Aristides said. The chandelier overhead made highlights on his bald skull. "She can still be purified, long before Commemoration."

"Besides," the blank-faced Melas added, "she is connected with the outside, in Indianapolis. Her unexcused absence would be remarked."

The Patriarch nodded decisively. "It is that which troubles me today, this more pressing problem. I speak of the mother's friend." He sighed and reflectively stroked his gray beard. "Her words are . . . countering . . . what we say, *all* our efforts. Vrukalakos has watched her for us and is obliged to tell us the truth, by our contract. He says that this Jeanne Lange has considerable influence upon Mrs Graham."

Little Aristides slumped in his chair, shaking his bald head. "I hate this," he moaned, "I hate this. The *thallophoroi*—especially four of the most brilliant men to walk the globe—should be able to consider . . . better measures."

"I quite concur," the Patriarch said sadly.

"*Leave her to me.*" It was Vrukalakos, his voice a harsh, hideously eager echo of the violence they had endured so long. "*I will handle her.*"

"*Saboi,* I do not wish you to do so," the old man told him, avoiding the ugliness of the evil eyes.

"You must." Vrukalakos made a sound of crimped laughter. "You have no other choice. Only mine."

"Be quick, be merciful," the Patriarch urged, giving in.

"Yes—quick! Do it quickly!" Aristides urged him.

The practical Nicholas Melas changed the subject. "Is there any progress report where the mother herself is concerned?"

"I believe so," the Patriarch answered thoughtfully. "The *grimoire*"—he touched the glass case housing the *Logos*—"indicates numerous means. One, as you know, is attempting to ingratiate ourselves with her even while isolating her from her children. Psychologically, it is quite effective. Then, at the proper moment, when she is receptive, we tell her the full truth."

"What is another way in the event that this fails?" asked Aristides.

"Terror, of course." The old man sighed once more. "The application of terror added to our other, earlier efforts must do the trick." He hesitated. "So long as it is achieved before the Commemoration and preferably before Joey's birthday. Please approach the *grimoire.*"

Each man, including Vrukalakos, stepped forward. The Patriarch lifted the shielding glass to reveal, momentarily, the enormous and ancient manuscript contained there. Each man extended his index finger gently, laid it carefully on the top of the great manuscript. For them, it was like touching the hem of God's garment. An expression of ecstasy slowly spread across their swarthy faces.

"Man—enfolding Earth," intoned the Patriarch.

"The cloud-collecting," said Aristides.

"The blood-full liver," chanted Vrukalakos.

"Life-giving," continued Melas.

"Evening, the day's old age," recalled Vrukalakos.

"The belly," said Aristides.

"In seven times seven days," pledged the Patriarch.

Often, on Saturday evenings in Indianapolis, Mary had persuaded Chuck and Ellen to play three-handed pinochle. An inveterate card player from a family of card players, Mary was even trying to teach Joey. The boy showed promise but appeared physically incapable of sitting through an entire game.

This night, the older children were out, due home at midnight. Joey was already in bed, dramatically claiming exhaustion. Now it dawned on Mary, as she sat sewing and pretending to watch TV, that this was how it would be one day— one day soon—without Barry: long evenings of aloneness, of the kind of quiet they once had hungered for when they thought it would be shared, a time for being together.

Instead, it would merely be—aloneness. And loneliness.

True, it didn't really have to be that way. Pleasant, robust Mrs. Aristides, down the block, had come by during the afternoon to suggest that Mary drop down to take a look at the old-fashioned crazy quilt she was making. With only a phone call she could probably arrange, within minutes, to be in several sociable Thessaly homes, eating and drinking God-knew-what and being exposed to peculiar customs—but *not alone*. Being by herself, she realized in a flair of annoying honesty, was still her own choice.

Once she had had a keen interest in the workings of the human mind. Her own friendship with Jeanne had begun during classes at college, developing over shared, gabby study sessions. She used to read a mixture of psychology and philosophy that tended to bore Barry, and because of that, she had laid the interest aside.

Now, on the spur of the moment, she went to the bookshelf against the dining room wall and browsed. Her fingers closed on a small volume entitled *The Presence of Other Worlds*, by Wilson Van Dusen, a discussion of the brilliant and misunderstood visionary, Emanuel Swedenborg. She remembered having promised herself, one afternoon, that she would read everything written by the amazing scientist-philosopher—until she discovered that Swedenborg had written eight lengthy volumes alone of biblical exegisis.

Now, opening at random, she found her eyes dropping to a remembered passage: ". . . Swedenborg said that ideas of time and space could impede our understanding of heaven. What corresponds to time," it read, "is change of state."

Change of state. Wasn't that what was occurring in her little world? Was that what Milo meant when he said Lamia hadn't died, but changed? Was it possible that these Greeks, with their ancient traditions, were closer to the truth than she was, with her free-spirited modern openness of mind?

The death-coach—from nowhere, it seemed—jattered along Attica Avenue, sounds from another age, from another place, no lights to illumine its way, nonetheless unerring as first it approached, then cannonaded past her house. Mary hadn't budged, sitting in a chair with the Swedenborg book limp in her fingers, simply holding her breath until it had gone. The dreaded coachman with his huge horses certainly impeded her understanding of heaven. She hoped that they would never make accessible a clearer understanding of hell.

For the first time in years, she crossed herself, eyes pressed together in an agony of need for intercession.

VI

And thou shalt From Hades beckon the night
Of perished men.

—Empedocles

She received the telephone call at ten-thirty,
just as she was pinning on her hat and double-
checking on her best Sunday appearance. She felt
better when she discovered the caller's identity. It
was Jeanne Lange and it warmed Mary to realize
theirs was a friendship undisturbed by distance or
time, that they were almost like sisters.

"I'm worried about you, Mare," said the
slightly nasal voice at the other end. Mary could
imagine her blond wig askew, a pencil probably
jabbed aimlessly in the yellow mass, chewed to
ribbons by her nervous teeth. "Have those

weirdos sacrificed anybody yet?"

Mary forced a laugh. "Not really. It's mostly the midnight coach that scares me. As a matter of fact, I'm giving in a little to get them off my back. I'm about to attend a funeral. That Lamia, whom you met—she died suddenly of a heart attack."

"You're kidding. Well, if they die and everything, just like normal people, maybe I wasn't entirely right about them."

"They call it change," Mary explained. "Not dying, but changing."

Jeanne sighed. "Back to weird. Look, babe, I want you to come by my place for lunch tomorrow. Okay?"

"Instead of eating out?"

"I've been taking some notes, doing some research on your friends, and I have more to do." Jeanne didn't wait for a commitment. "Get your butt over here anytime that you can tomorrow."

"That's very kind of you," Mary said slowly, "but I'm sure we're both exaggerating my danger—"

"Sure, sure. But it doesn't hurt to have a little background, does it?"

Joey was tugging on her sleeve and continued until she eventually hung up. For once, the little guy seemed to be keeping his shirttail in his waistband and the snap-on tie somehow gave him a nearly cherubic appearance. He appeared something of an armed and dangerous choirboy. She followed him out to the Granada where Ellen and Andruss were waiting.

"Where's Chuck?" she asked, getting into the

driver's seat.

"He left early to pick up Lythia," Ellen replied from the back seat.

"You look lovely, Mrs. Graham," Andruss said politely.

She glanced around at him with a flashing smile. "I could get using to having you around, buddy," she said, starting the engine.

It was only a few blocks to the small church. It sat atop a slightly sloped hill, and was composed of white stone that seemed pebbled and enduring in the Sunday sunlight. There was no Christian cross ascending from the roof, somewhat to Mary's surprise. Instead, she saw what seemed to be an immense lower-case "e" with the right-hand side broken. It took her an instant to realize she was seeing the Greek E, epsilon.

Before she could ask Andruss why the fifth letter of the alphabet was emphasized by his people, the boy was addressing her: "There's a parking place just to the right," he said, adding, "You'll find the church is a large single room. And it's called a *megaron*."

Mary guided the old car into the available space. "Is there anything Ellen and I should know so we can seem like true—ah, true—"

"True *orgeones*," Andruss helped her. He chuckled as he slipped out the passenger side and assisted both the ladies. "Worshipers are *orgeones*. Actually, Mrs. Graham, Ellen is pretty well briefed on what's going on. I've been working on her."

"I see," Mary said as they walked, not sure that

114

she did see or wanted to. "And I? What am I supposed to do?"

"Just behave as you would in any church, with respect and silence while the minister is speaking. Play it by ear."

Although the church or *megaron* wasn't huge, it would still seat close to a hundred, and Mary was surprised to see only fourteen or fifteen people in the congregation. Andruss guided them near the front. She found herself sitting beside Joey with Chuck on the other side of the boy. To Chuck's right, she saw, was the beautiful sixteen-year-old girl called Lythia.

Chuck introduced them in low tones. Lythia's response was not the shy, half-giggling nervousness Mary expected of teenage girls. Instead, she reached across Chuck to take Mary's hand and murmured how happy she was to meet Chuck's mother.

"I can see why he would be taken with you," Mary said easily.

The girl's enormous dark eyes appraised her steadily. "It is too bad that you don't realize why a girl would be taken by him."

Mary stared ahead, wondering if that was a compliment to Chuck or an insult to her.

Ellen, seated to her left, indicated the altar. "You'll notice it isn't ornate and showy, like our churches back home," she whispered in a tone not so much of scorn but of the convert-to-better-things. "Simple laurel leaves everywhere, as an appreciation of God's nature. Used this way, they're called *korythale*."

115

"Isn't she great?" Andruss asked, impressed.

"What's the stick with the pine cone on top?" Mary asked softly.

Ellen looked blank. She nudged Andruss and he whispered with good humor in her ear. She turned back to Mary. "It's a *thyrsus*. A focal point for worship and prayer."

"A crucifix or statue of the Virgin works pretty well too," Mary murmured.

"Mother!"

"I was only teasing." *Was I?* Mary wondered.

In front of the altar the coffin lay on a stand, intricately carved from some dark burnished wood. It was closed, undecorated by cloth or holy ornamentation. As Mary watched, a man in his late fifties approached the altar, shuffling his feet slightly, his gaze averted.

Then he turned to them and she was startled by his prominent, piercing blue eyes set in a rather pale, hairless face beneath a mop of curly golden-brown hair. He smiled directly, unmistakably, at her.

"I am Reverend Bandrocles, Mrs. Graham, and welcome. Our services, in the Church of Mycone, are a mixture of formality and informality. This affords me the opportunity to thank you for coming."

"Thank you," Mary said, with her lips only.

The minister nodded, then inclined his head. Little George Aristides, dressed in an ancient Greek tunic, his head bowed humbly, stepped from an anteroom adjacent to the altar pushing a serving cart. His appearance startled Mary for an instant but she had no need to resist a smile. The bald man appeared quite natural, somehow fully at home, as he moved down the aisle and paused beside Andruss to pour from a large metallic container into a small, lovely silver cup.

"The wine is kykeon wine," Reverend Bandrocles said from the altar, "and the cup into which it is poured is a *kernos*—a special wine cup of considerable antiquity. Each person in attendance is asked to sip it."

The *kernos* was passed from Andruss to her. She paused, then allowed Joey to have a sip. His eyes, she saw, were wide and fascinated by the procedure. He seemed almost reverent.

Then George Aristides was reaching into a hamper covered with cloth, revealing several loaves of bread.

"These are *hygieia*, essential to the faith," Reverend Bandrocles murmured in explanation. "It was sanctified by proximity to the *Logos* before I came to the *megaron* today."

"What," Mary whispered to Andruss, "is the *Logos*?"

The Greek boy stared at her with enormous solemnity. "All I can tell you is that it is the most important book in the history of civilization," he said simply.

She broke off a piece of *hygieia* as Andruss did and tasted it. It seemed a bit stale, presumably from lying for a period of time next to an old book. But it was edible, might even be good if fresh, she concluded.

Soon the Reverend Bandrocles was addressing

the *orgeones* and Mary found her attention wandering. What he was saying when he spoke in English, she thought, sounded not unlike the preachments of priests who had frightened her since early childhood. His message was a combination of disappointed criticism of the sins committed by his faithful and reassurance that their repentance "in time for Commemoration," could yet provide salvation.

She mused about Commemoration, wondered what it was. She started to ask Ellen but the girl was absorbed by the minister's sermon.

Distracted, stifling an urge to yawn, Mary let her eyes rove around the church. The attitude of the people there, while they were not warmed by sunlight streaming through a stained glass window, was polite and respectful, entirely familiar to her. Yet there was still something about the *orgeones*, about their ages, that was troubling to Mary. She finally realized what it was. Everyone appeared to be sixty or older or, at the other extreme, young people between the early teens and mid-twenties. Those in their thirties, forties, and fifties, as well as small children, were not present.

Odd, she thought, and remembered what Jeanne had said about these extraordinary people of Thessaly. "Age doesn't seem to have an effect on them," her friend had observed over lunch. And something else Jeanne had said: "I think maybe age isn't part of them, somehow." There was more but she couldn't quite recall just what.

Yet those now, in this church, who *were* old

certainly had the requisite gray hair and abundant wrinkles. The young people were among the most fresh-faced, healthy kids Mary could remember seeing. What was it Jeanne was suggesting—that these were androids or clones?

But she did get an inkling, now and then, of what her friend had seen. With Andruss, Ellen's boyfriend, it showed in his mature manners, his knowledge, in his personality itself. It seemed to her suddenly that if she could only stare into the eyes of someone here—Andruss, or Milo Traphonius, even the minister—if she could just *probe* behind the sheerly physical makeup of Thessaly's public mask, she might be able at last to grasp the meaning of the mystery Jeanne had intuited. Yet that was ridiculous, of course; if she could probe behind the public masks of many Indianapolis politicians and business executives she would doubtlessly find ample corruption, abundant secrets.

It was getting hard to stay awake. She tried to concentrate on what Reverend Bandrocles was saying in his persistently affable, even-toned, utterly boring sermon. She caught allusions to *Logos*, and to such well-known Greeks of the past as Empedocles and Pythagoras—but no reference to God or to Christ. The discernible emphasis on the Greek names was similar to that afforded her own deities by priests in Indianapolis, and it both offended Mary and annoyed her.

Empedocles, she recalled with some difficulty, was a poet from about the fifth Century before Christ, and maybe a philosopher, too—she wasn't

119

certain. All she could remember about Pythagoras just then was that he had been a learned, early mathematician who taught something weird, something about numbers being the underlying motivation of all. She had been sure, in school, that it was Pythagoras's way of impressing his students with the importance of math.

For what earthly reason were those names being invoked by Bandrocles?

Gradually, the minister focused on Lamia Zacharius, of whom he said certain obligatory complimentary things, then reiterated what appeared to be the prime concept of this Church of Mycone—that Lamia had not died, but changed.

And then he opened the casket in front of him and the mourners were asked to approach, to pay their last respects.

Well, Lamia certainly *looked* dead. The odd thing was that she really didn't seem terribly changed. Perhaps the mortician who'd been summoned had used marvelous new cosmetics. Whatever, Lamia's coloring was good, her features composed, only the absence of breathing and the shut eyes a certain indication of her state.

Her change of state, Mary thought, turning away. Impediment to heaven.

She felt dizzy, then found Andruss's and Chuck's hands beneath her elbows, supporting her.

Absurd! Mary Graham had never fainted in her life!

She shook them off and paused for Reverend Bandrocles's final words. "There will be a brief walk to the place of burial," he intoned, in his formal tones, "in the beautiful Vale of Aphaca."

The brisk, early-winter temperature quickly helped Mary to clear her head. But she felt oddly agreeable, compliant, and docilely followed the others as the mourners of Lamia Zacharius began their walk up the hill behind the church to the nearby woods. The line of trees caused Mary to feel that she was entering another room, making a deeper commitment, somehow. To her left, she saw Milo and Velda Traphonius trudging along, their aging heads lowered either in respect or in order to see. The ground became rocky and unsteady underfoot.

Among the stones, autumn leaves that had turned deep brown, crisp like overdone toast, snapped beneath Mary's feet. Andruss and Chuck remained on either side of her—like sentries, she mused, or guards? Her son occasionally glanced with boyish concern into her face, seeing if her illness had passed. Once she patted his cheek maternally, calling him a nice jerk; behind them, Ellen and Joey giggled faintly.

It was strange, this funeral procession. It seemed to Mary that she was somehow removed in time to something quite old, something once entirely proper that had occurred thousands of times with nothing altered now but the faces of the mourners—and the corpse. Her sigh turned to a tremor. It wouldn't be long now until the Indiana winter descended on them all with the usual mindless midwestern fury. God's natural vengeance, she sometimes thought: snow mass-

121

ing in its obdurate, insistent way, making the slightest travel unpleasant, and with frigid temperatures, locking one away until one felt literally restrained—trapped in a prison of grim, relentless nature.

She realized that a hint of *déjà vú* arose now because it had been such a short while since she approached another gravesite, similarly aided and sheltered. When Barry was dropped into the unforgiving ground forever. Change—they spoke cheerfully of *change?* When would change ever be for the good, she wondered with pain—a source of comfort, inspiration or solace, a means of getting through one single day unscathed?

They drew into a clearing in the woods, well-trod and barren of leaves, as if dozens of feet walked this out-of-the-way area often. It *was* lovely here, in the sense that a black-and-white sketch or engraving may have a stark, frosted beauty. She saw a great heaping of stones in front of a rising, rounded mound. Snow flurries were beginning to strew white polkadots before her eyes. She felt that she was peering through a veil as Reverend Bandrocles approached and sternly rapped on an overhanging rock.

It was quite still, very quiet, and Mary thought he had knocked symbolically for silence. But as the small congregation held its collective breath, an immense stone set doorlike in place shifted—mysteriously, frighteningly. It moved, apparently unaided, with a shudder and clatter. Then Mary saw that the trick was done from within, by the man who had waited for them in death's garden.

It was a tall, saturnine figure with smouldering eyes that seemed averted, as if the man disliked the afternoon light and spent hours in darkness. The casket, brought there by the minister, George Aristides, Nick Melas and two other men whom Mary did not recognize, was solemnly passed into the mouth of the enormous cave. To her astonishment, the wraithlike tall man waiting took it alone, in his two powerful arms, bearing it inside with incredible ease.

"That's Vrukalakos," Andruss whispered in her ear, "keeper of the Vale of Aphaca. Symbolically, he's taking Lamia to Hecate and she will be guarded always, in the underworld, by that goddess, as well as her great black dogs."

Mary nodded but scarcely heard the boy's words. Before the keeper shut the enormous stone in place again, Lamia's body claimed, Mary thought she had heard . . . peculiar sounds, from below: water gurgling, as if another door somewhere had been expectantly, breathlessly opened. There seemed a babble of many voices, some of which sounded fearful, entreating, and anguished—

—And something *else* was down there, too, she thought. At first, she could not even find words for it.

Only as she felt little Joey pressing against her for reassurance did the descriptive terms come to her mind. She thought she had heard hollow, resounding footsteps moving well below the entrance, not with stealth but with measured cadence, as if at the end of impossibly massive legs that took time to climb upward through the shadowed tunnel. . . .

She shuddered, suddenly freezing, and desired very much to be elsewhere. Then Andruss was picking Joey up from the ground, slinging him to his sturdy young shoulders. Everyone moved off and she followed them, reluctantly, quite perplexed, as they altered direction toward the west, and jovially chatting among themselves, hurried through the chill afternoon with a destination well in their foreign minds.

Unable to know her own thoughts just then, Mary centered her eyes on little Joe, buoyed by Andruss, his old self now as he was being shown attention.

Too much attention, the mother thought abruptly—Joey was getting far too much notice. Each of the dozen or so strangers seemed to be approaching the pale lad, calling out to him in unreal warmth, touching his small leg or foot as if seeking some gesture of attention from *him*.

Kinglike, miniature royalty on the throne of a young Greek prince, Joey ignored all the supplicants and dug his sharp heels into Andruss's ribs, urging him onward.

The Olympi-Inn was on a sidestreet running at a ninety-degree angle to the block of other commercial enterprises in Thessaly. Since Mary had driven in the opposite direction on Alexandria to reach U.S. 40, she hadn't seen this place before.

Its appearance was outwardly that of a neighborhood bar and grill one might encounter in any city or town. But no beer or whiskey were served and the food appeared to be strictly Grecian in character.

Mary Graham, not at all hungry and still vaguely upset, accepted a chunk of goat's milk cheese forced upon her by Andruss and Ellen, plus a glass of wine. The cheese tasted sharp, strong, and the odor was overwhelming; yet it did taste good.

An utterly unfamiliar array of strange foods was brought before the others at the table. She noticed with dismay and ongoing surprise the way that Ellen and Chuck happily reached out to snatch the foreign dishes: a variety of olives, like so many nasty prying eyes; musty yet meaty figs; barley and corn in a variety of alien forms. Mary asked Chuck's girl Lythia why there was no meat here but he answered for her, explaining that meat had always been scarce in Greece and simply wasn't part of the regular diet. The center dish on their table seemed to be a giant helping of cooked fruit not unlike the *thargela* that Milo had brought to their home.

"No, that isn't *thargela*," Andruss said when she mentioned it.

"I'm sorry. It looked the same."

"This is only *pankarpia*," Andruss commented, bold eyes gleaming.

"When it is taken to people as an offering," Chuck put in, anxious to display his new knowledge, "it's called *thargela*. This isn't quite as rich or hard to prepare."

"An offering?" Mary repeated. Confused, she

drummed her fingers on the table for a moment. "Milo Traphonius brought us—an *offering?*"

"And why not?" demanded the old man, overhearing her question as he was passing. Smiling broadly, he drew up a chair and sat beside her. There were four tables in the Olympi-Inn and she saw, with dismay, that Chuck and his girl were moving to another as Milo's entrance provided the chance. "We truly enjoy welcoming such an interesting family."

"I guess I always think of an offering as something one presents to God," Mary responded, her tone a trifle sharp.

"And so it is." The old man scratched his beard and gave Andruss a wry, humorous frown. "Your Greek is abominable, young Andruss. I see that I shall have to spend a little more time with you. And with George, our language specialist."

"I'm sorry, sir," the boy said with sincerity. He lowered his gaze.

"Perhaps I shall give you another chance, boy," Milo said with a conspiratorial wink at Mary. "Suppose I recite an ancient toast to our guests, and *you* explain it to them." He didn't wait for a reply but fixed a bright eye on the distant ceiling. "'The protection of Agathos Daimon upon you,'" he intoned. "There. What does that mean, Andruss?"

The youthful Greek brightened. "When you dine with us, Mrs. Graham, you earn our protection because of your presence as guest. During the time you spend with Greeks, in their places, you are fully accepted as a member of the family—as one of us. It is our ancient custom."

"Why, thank you, Andruss," Mary said, smiling. "But protection from what?"

"Excellent, my boy," Milo boomed with a little chortle. "And it is true, my dear Mary. We very much want you—*all* of you—to be with us in the full sense. Permanently." He paused and saw her indecision, then lifted the palm of his hand. "I would like you to meet some of the other citizens of Thessaly."

He turned slightly in his chair, and with a hand cupped round his mouth, called in Greek across the Olympi-Inn. Chairs scraped away from tables and a number of people began to move slowly across the room to stand before Mary, Joey, and Ellen. Some smiled, some bowed their heads in something akin to respect. Their common denominator was that they were uniformly into their sixties, some pushing eighty.

Milo was on his feet, playing host. "Here are Leo and Elis Krakides," he announced, gesturing to two quite thin, almost emaciated souls. Together they could not have weighed two hundred and twenty-five pounds. Elis put out a timid, blue-veined hand with crimson nails. "And here's Sam Poppagoras, one of the wittiest men on earth." Sam alone weighed well in excess of two-twenty-five, a jolly-faced fellow with marble eyes and a fringe of dyed black hair. He beamed upon the Grahams with humor and twiddled sausage fingers.

"And these lovelies," Milo continued, drawing the newcomers nearer, "are four sweet sisters.

127

Mormo, who is a capable registered nurse and knows more medicine than most physicians; Gello and Karko, who are retired now; and Sybaris, who acts as a sort of unofficial historian for the people of Thessaly."

Mary resisted a laugh with difficulty. The quartet was in its middle sixties, ultimately ill-wigged, awesomely obese. Sam Poppagoras had been fat, but any of these "sweet sisters" nearly doubled his bulk. It was like looking at a quartet of unemployed circus fat ladies.

Then Mary's hilarity faded. She had glanced accidentally into their eight businesslike eyes. And the thought came to her at once.

Without exception, the eyes do not belong.

She couldn't see how she could be wrong about it. They were the eyes of other people, of persons who were more slender, youthful, perhaps quite bright. There was nothing foolish, aging, or gluttonous about the serious, level eyes which regarded her above inane smiles that simpered on cue.

Suddenly, with a panicky feeling, Mary didn't want to be there anymore. She ached with the need to let down, to stop worrying about these bizarre acquaintances. For a moment she felt she would suffer a relapse and again be afflicted with the sudden nausea and faintness that had troubled her in the church. It was loathsome to think of the nurse, Mormo, tending to her well-being.

—What was Milo saying now? she wondered distractedly.

". . . Important thing to remember is that Thessaly folks are better educated than those of other communities. Since I helped found the town, Mary, I sought out Greeks whose backgrounds were similar: strong in scholastic endeavors, students as well of human nature, who go *on* studying in adulthood. Change as improvement, you see."

She nodded absently, her gaze beginning to wander. Lythia, Chuck's date, sat with him at another table. She had appeared to be a silent, uncommunicative child except for her single observation in church. Now she was animated and happily voluble, laughing as she leaned her head against Chuck's shoulder in a manner that seemed mature and proprietary. Mary felt a surge of bilious distaste, even dislike. She had prided herself on being youthful still, able to be quickly accepted by friends of the children. Lythia hadn't really given her any chance at all to become friendly.

She started, then. *Something* about the girl, the way she held her head, half-covering her lips as she smiled—she was familiar somehow.

"I'd like to clear away any little mysteries you might have about our services today, my dear," Milo was cueing her.

She forced her attention back to the old man. "As a matter of fact, Milo," she said, "I was quite curious about a great number of things. For example, why do you bury your people underground?"

"Well, don't *you?*" he replied, seemingly

mystified. "I mean, don't you bury *your* people underground?"

"Not in a—a tunnel leading straight down into the earth. And the *sounds,* like someone or something *lurked* down there!"

He shrugged good-humoredly. "How to explain customs, eh? Perhaps there is an underground stream—I shall get a dowser to come inspect it sometime." He untangled his beard with a hard, quick tug. "I believe that the tradition of the Vale of Aphaca goes back two thousand years or more. We re-enact it here, you see. It's quite lovely in the spring."

"I'm sure it is. But Milo, there was no reference to Christ at all. I can only assume that the Church of Mycone isn't a Christian faith. Are you all praying to the gods of Mount Olympus?"

The old man beamed amusement. His beard danced as he chuckled. "Dear me, no. We refer at times to those fellows but our concept of divinity is actually a bit older than Olympus."

"Older? Really?"

He bobbed his head affirmatively. "So I'm told. Our faith is something more than a belief, you see—it is a theogony rooted in the past, in nature, in gods or goddesses that predate or cohabit with those of Olympus. They are more symbols of what we seek than creatures in whom we believe. I'm not sure you could easily grasp it, my dear, without a firm grounding in our little history. And there'll be plenty of time for that as the days and weeks pass."

"You pray to gods yet you don't *believe* in

130

them?" she smiled.

"Let us say that, not unlike you, we pay lip service generously to many cherished customs which time has rendered . . . unworkable. Not unlike you, child, we worship a Giver of all life, the Giver—when one knows the way—of eternal life. We believe, in a word, in that which is functional."

"Functional?"

"Yes." He gave a brief, almost curt nod. "In that which demonstrably *works.*"

"For you, you mean."

"Oh, yes," he agreed with a sly smile. "For us, by *all* means! We are not overly interested in faith, *per se,* in putting credence in remote possibilities, vague hopes." He paused and his eyes shone brightly. "It seems to me, as a matter of fact, that stupidity has done more harm in this world than evil has ever achieved."

"It sounds—cold, somehow." Upset by what she was hearing, Mary twisted in her chair and poked at the rind of her cheese. "Are you equating faith with stupidity, then, Milo?"

He laughed. It was no less amiable—or booming—than before. "Not at all, my dear. We all grope muddlingly in the dark for that which is perfectly workable, until we can establish and prove the facts. It's forgivable for the seeker to make a few little errors when his beliefs go astray."

Mary studied the old man's face intently. "You believe in what is proved, subscribe to what's logical. But what about your outlook on change as

131

opposed to death? Isn't it illogical to hide the ugliness and sadness of death with a bland word like change?"

"Not at all, my dear, not at all! Consider: Isn't everything, really, a change instead of a finality—does *anything* truly end? The seasons change but spring always returns after a long winter, does it not? Spring has not died for good—and nothing else has, either. Ever! Death is only the disguise that change wears until it is sure it is wanted."

Barry—a fleeting glimpse of his face—filled her memory. "I—I'm not sure that I can accept that concept."

He was hearty. "You will, child, you will. In time. By the way, 'Christ' is from the Greek—*'Christos.'"* He paused. "We all want you and your charming family to feel welcome in Thessaly, to become one of our own—under our protection forever, against whatever comes. But we can be patient if you will only promise to *think* about it, merely consider the offer. Will you do that much for an old man?"

The Olympi-Inn was starting to spin, novalike, sucking in and out on itself; Mary felt somewhat faint and distinctly nauseous. The wine, maybe; the cheese. To end the conversation, she murmured an agreement as sweetly as possible—it was unthinkable to be rude to this dear old man—and shoved herself rockily to her feet.

As she staggered, young Andruss was there at once with a helping hand. Solicitous, the boy began guiding her toward the door. The place rang with hollow voices, glasses and cups tinkling. Joey joined them, taking her hand manfully.

Trailing after, Milo caught up, and at her side, said with polite forcefulness: "We must know your answer soon, my dear. It is important."

Then he swooped down upon Joey, tossing the delighted boy into the air, and as he came down, giving him a smacking kiss on the forehead. "Beautiful, adorable child!"

On the way home, Andruss driving the Granada for her, Mary saw wanly that Joey was now afloat in a seventh heaven all his own. He had been catered to, noticed, adored; he was happy.

The balance of Sunday was to be one of those weekend days one can only recall in slivers and slices. Mary remembered resting in her front room chair for some time, doing nothing except soothing her nerves and stomach; later, there was a brief, dreamless nap from which she neverthe-less emerged in a queer panic; she saw an NBC "Big Event" and wondered about its estimate of dimensions; there was a speedy gin game with Chuck, who seemed distracted and was easily vanquished; and cold cuts for a rather silent supper. Afterward, Mary tumbled into her bed and a deep sleep that lasted until she awoke to Joey screaming horribly in the throes of his worst nightmare. . . .

The meeting of the Syndic was brief. After all, only three of the four officials were present: the Patriarch, Aristides, and Melas.

Besides, they had seen one another—and much of the larger Synod—just that afternoon.

Some things, naturally, had to be said which were clearly unfitting at the services for Lamia.

"Is the one who would interfere being properly handled, Patriarch?" It was the direct Nicholas Melas.

"Yes, although it is a certain pity. Tonight it will be done." He sighed. *"Saboi!* I despised releasing that vulturous Vrukalakos!"

"It was the one way," George Aristides sympathized, and changed the subject. "I liked the Graham woman."

"As did I," commented Melas. "She has fire; a real woman, and beautiful. A suitable mother for the child."

"Oh, yes," said bald Aristides, nodding with large eyes. "Oh, yes."

"And what of her?" continued Melas. "She can be convinced?"

"You saw that the persuasion has begun in earnest," the Patriarch said with faint asperity. "Soon we shall ask her."

"When?" pressed the practical Melas.

"Soon. This week, in fact."

"And if she then declines?" asked Aristides fearfully.

The Patriarch frowned. "She will still be persuaded, *akousmatikoi*—or driven quite mad."

VII

Each slits the throat and in his halls prepares
A horrible repast. Thus too the son
Seizes the father, children the mother seize,
And reave of life and eat their own dear flesh.
— Empedocles

A house may be a home but a town may not be a city. It is constructed of different needs and emotions, takes a different type of pride—an often perverse pride—in untrammeled individuality. There are towns that exist for the sole reason of being unlike any others, earning their bread from curiosity seekers—tourists for whom the townsman willingly does his quaint trick, again and again, jumping for the stick, rolling over, playing dead.

Thessaly, while it was unlike any other town, enjoyed more subtle distinctions.

It caused *intruders* to jump, roll over, and play dead.

The town had had few immigrants, and fewer visitors, over the twelve years of its existence. There was no commerce worthy of the name to draw a man eager to seek a union-controlled income for his family. There was no garish, natural, or performing attraction. Unlike most Indiana towns, Thessaly had never boasted an outstanding high school basketball player, and its population never turned out en masse at Market Square Arena or at the Indianapolis Motor Speedway. It believed in carriages and chariots, not race cars.

Yet old-fashioned Thessaly had reasons to take pride.

Each person living there was an undisputed genius in his or her field of educational endeavor, a true Olympian of intellect, a walking computer of specialized data. He, or she, could be counted on absolutely to perform tasks necessary for the good of all. At once, and better than anyone else. One call from the Patriarch and the task was done, perfectly.

Within its three parallel streets and bisecting pair of avenues there was very little crime, none of the kind that really outrages a citizenry. Such theft and murder as occurred was more or less universally acceptable to town members. Consequently, it wasn't illegal. It had no racial problems since, with the exception of the newly arrived

Grahams, there was only one race present.

Because Thessaly was united by a bond stronger than blood, than family ties: the bond of a shared secret that guaranteed each man, woman, and child a very long life. Its citizens, each having done almost every kind of labor known to humankind, had no trouble getting work in neighboring big-city Indianapolis whenever it wished—and all worked from choice, not need. A prudent, old-fashioned people, they had saved their money over long years and owned income-producing property, in a variety of Greek names, all over the world.

Now the Thessaly townsfolk shared something else: a terrible fear of something much worse than exposure, or crime. Collectively, they understood that their abiding godhead, the *Logos*—unseen by all except members of the Syndic—suggested a way out only through the symbolic instrumentation of a small boy named Joseph Hadley Graham. There was, as well, a time factor: The escape must be engineered by the time a frightening anniversary rolled round: that of Commemoration.

They talked, that wintry Sunday night, of Joey and the other Grahams. Those who had put in an appearance honoring Lamia Zacharius's change quite naturally visited others who had not been able to attend—the handful of young children, and the larger group of people between the ages of twenty-five and sixty-five—those who could not venture out in the daylight. The questions were asked repeatedly: What is he like? Is it *true* about the boy?

There was nothing ominous about the people or their heated interest. They had no desire to injure Joey Graham; quite the contrary. They wished to purify and venerate him.

When they were told that it was true about how he had been born, how he looked, that he had indeed arrived on the schedule indicated in the *Logos,* there was great excitement. Cries resounded in house after house, all over little Thessaly: "The child is ours—he belongs to us!" "He is truly one of our number—our Leader!" "We must seize the boy now, to protect him, to be ready for Commemoration!"

All the people were nice enough, really, where their attitude toward the boy was concerned. In truth, they were devoted, industrious, brilliant, talented, religious, caring people—

—And their viewpoint was summed up by one gentle woman in her forties, a person who knew more about the ancient trade routes, hermetic magic, and the actual geography of the ancient world than anyone else alive. She peered mildly over her pince nez at the obese sister, Mormo, who had brought her the information; she gave her thoughtful comment: "We must do whatever is necessary to obtain the full cooperation of the Grahams—*anything at all."*

Mormo, stuffing her fat mouth with chocolates, nodded a large head in agreement. When she was able to speak once more she merely burbled, "Don't worry, Professor. It's all being done now."

*　　*　　*

The long, lean, yellow dog prowled restlessly outside the apartment building on the north side of Indianapolis, its knowledgeable nose trickling along the pavement as it sought the wafted scent. An ugly beast, people who saw it tended to walk quickly past, shying away, with their own more ignorant noses wrinkled in disgust.

It was Sunday night, the temperature dropping steadily, and most residents of the brick building were already home. The dog knew that its target was inside, somewhere, but the exact apartment temporarily eluded it.

Utilizing all its keen senses and astute natural intelligence, and more, the yellow hound honed in and finally found what it sought so diligently: a fresh trace of Jeanne Lange. It issued from a closed window four stories above its nondescript and angular head, as unmistakable to the animal as a fingerprint.

For a long while it sat on its haunches, considering, peering up as if it had treed a cat. Its throat vibrated as it keened. It experienced an excitement, triumph and hunger only partly canine in nature.

If Jeanne had seen it on the street below, recognized it as the same plain mutt who had stared at her from outside a restaurant window, she might very well have remembered beasts who were the familiars of witches—combined loyal companions and capable aides, who sought out the prey for odd, old women with bizarre notions.

She would have been entirely wrong in such an assumption.

This creature was a familiar of no one.

In any case, Jeanne was otherwise occupied that Sunday night, even though her attention was gradually riveted upon the supernatural. Jeanne had eaten a meager supper, for her, at eight o'clock. She had thought of cleaning up the apartment in readiness for Mary's luncheon call tomorrow, but Mary was no more preoccupied with the niceties of tidiness than she was.

Instead, Jeanne cleared off the table and spread on it a stack of note paper and several unusual books, a few quite rare. After reading awhile, and taking notes, she had gone into her bedroom, put on her glasses, and brought more books back from her shelves. This wasn't going to be easy.

As a matter of fact, doing this sort of research was always hard. Any of her students would have balked, understandably. She wasn't really sure just what she was looking for, to begin with. There was such an abundance of material, much repetitive and contradictory from volume to volume, so much that was patently a case of self-perpetuating trash getting in the way of real facts.

She had begun simply enough, by looking up allusions to Greece as well as any references to names that Mary had mentioned.

Those things alone proved to be more than enough to whet her appetite.

The name of the old man, for example—Traphonius. Under a slightly different spelling he became a famous Greek oracle, a man capable of foretelling the future, whose name was given to a region with numerous caverns, a place where those seeking information about the future slept for days and experienced terrifying visions.

That lent credence to Jeanne's supposition that this peculiar community was somehow intentionally linked to ancient Greece, to customs and beliefs practiced and accepted before the birth of Jesus Christ. Squinting through her rather thick glasses and a cloud of heavy cigarette smoke, she read on, occasionally making notes for information to give her friend Mary.

Then she whistled.

In a seventy-year-old book entitled *The Fragments of Empedocles,* by William Ellery Leonard, the teacher learned more about the poet who Mary said was important to Thessaly's citizenry. He was said to have been a brilliant but moody, egotistical philosopher, politician, healer and heuristician. Pausing, she recalled that a heuristician was one who aided others in making discoveries—who was so knowledgeable that he laid out a course of study enabling others both to learn what he knew and to extend that knowledge.

It was a strange combination of gifts this man Empedocles possessed—and an impressive one. A practical man, he had sought the very sources of the universe, she read, adding the element earth "to the water of Thales, the air of Maximenes, and the fire of Heraclitus," declaring them "the promise and the potency" of the entire universe. The writer had declared, "These are the celebrated 'four elements' of later philosophy and magic."

The very *source* of all philosophy and magic!

141

Jeanne was impressed. She hesitated to try to grasp the idea of a civilization so old that the concept of earth enabled one to erect a foundation suggestive of universal truths.

It was when she went on reading, learning of Empedocles's greatest and most controversial discovery—his insistence upon the existence of the Vortex—that Jeanne became certain that she was onto something. "The eddying center of the Mass," the old poet wrote; here was a clue to Thessaly's strange origins.

Jeanne froze.

The sound of wings batting frantically at the window in the tiny kitchenette made her jump. It was some latent, inherent terror she felt of that which rustled, slithered, and threshed about—an evolutionary memory, perhaps, of existence as a bird who awaited helplessly the creeping serpent. She paused, a pudgy hand over her heart, then heard the sound again—and dealt sternly with herself.

It was probably a poor little birdie who had flown too high and got himself trapped, she decided, striding quickly for her bulk. She had instantly and even more firmly dismissed the idea that it could be a bat—that was just unthinkable.

Peering out the window, she was trapped by the fierce red eyes glowing like embers. They seemed to hover, disembodied, floating free like voracious insects with an inhuman ability to *command*. Her body swayed; then she opened the window wide, and stepped obediently backward.

There was a terrible and shattering cacophony

142

of undulating wings as the creature penetrated her apartment, found its feet and enlarged, extending to its full, semihuman form. Some still-independent chamber of Jeanne's brain worked its warning, flinched away from proximity to this un-man, urged her body to run or at least cover. Perspiration speckled her forehead; small, anxious noises seeped through her lips.

Vrukalakos ignored everything in his horrid commitment to living, to his obsessive ritual. The nails of his hands were like talons of the finest forged steel, the muscles of his arms and shoulders dynamically structured for tearing. He reached slowly behind Jeanne's taut neck, beneath the blond wig, groping—locating—seeking purchase—and *rending*.

She didn't feel a thing as the spine ripped through flesh and muscle, and her round body folded in upon itself like a deflated concertina.

The creature sniffed the air cautiously to be sure that he was alone with his kill. Then, with enormous sang-froid that amounted to a hideous caricature of dignity, he sank deliberately upon his lean haunches and reached out for her. . . .

Sometime later, Vrukalakos climbed heavily to his feet in order to transmigrate once more. When he no longer resembled a man in any way, his claws reached for and found what was left of his meal, gathered it all beneath the massive ebon wings that folded back like a ghastly cloak, and half-vaulted, half-flew out the window into the winter evening.

The wings beat the air steadily, smoothly.

Halfway back to Thessaly, the creature began to release the terrible fragmented burdens a little at a time over the sleeping, modern city of Indianapolis. The flight was uneventful; the task was completed.

An hour later, past midnight now, Mary sat beside Joey in his bedroom, occasionally feeling his forehead to detect any early signs of fever. He wasn't so much hot to the touch as clammy, moist, his eyes moving like twin small beasts beneath the fragile lids in the third level of sleep, continuing his nightmare.

Outside, other nightmares proceeded as Mary watched them, shrinking in fear behind the boy's muslin curtains. The great steeds seemed to be trotting tonight, not speeding by, almost—she thought—as if urged to mark and learn the area, the area of her home. The death-coach flashed into view and moonlight frosted the face of the coachman, enabling her to see it for the first time.

Something in the mad, dark eyes was somehow familiar but she couldn't place the driver at first. When she did, she was startled and wondered if she could possibly be right. It had appeared to be the terrible, dark, wraithlike man who had been at the Vale of Aphaca, standing inside the yawning graveyard to accept, and welcome, the dead.

She held Joey's damp head in her lap protectively, against her warm body, and stared for a long, miserable time at the window looking out upon her adopted town.

Part Two

*

The Dying

VIII

... This feeding's monstrous crime!
                                    —Empedocles

Mary awakened on Monday just ahead of the alarm clock, tapping in the switch quickly before it could jangle. For awhile she stared into the dimness of her bedroom with an unpleasantly vague sensation of unfamiliarity with her surroundings. Lying back, a rounded arm thrown out on the other pillow, she wondered when she would ever begin to adjust to the new surroundings. It was a revelation, a painful one, she thought, to learn what a creature of habit she was.

Even this room, the one part of the old house which the children ignored, obliviously leaving their individualistic smudges everywhere else, seemed all wrong.

She remembered the completely casual atmosphere of the room she had shared so long with Barry. He had never taught himself to hang up his trousers overnight. His dresser had always been littered with bottles of after shave given him for Christmas, birthdays and Father's Day by the kids, each just enough depleted to keep them happy—plus endless paraphenalia from his pockets. She had piled clothes requiring mending atop her own dresser in those days, often obliged to lift the stack just to find a clean pair of hose or panties.

She giggled; her lovely green eyes shone. What a couple of dreadful mess-makers they had been, two overgrown children playing at house and marriage, living each day as it came with a child's simple confidence that nothing serious would ever change things.

This room, she felt, was austere and uninteresting by comparison—*half* a room, at best, without Barry—clean, tidy, everything in its place, everything oddly unemotional, almost dead. No: It had simply never lived. Possibly she could buy a couple of inexpensive paintings to brighten the off-white walls; perhaps bright, gay new drapes would help.

And perhaps nothing would, but Barry.

Or another husband, came the unbidden thought.

Perhaps. Just—barely—perhaps. But even that might turn out to be next to impossible if this day developed as it seemed that it might.

Determined not to make Monday any worse than it had to be, she arose and got ready for work as swiftly as possible.

Joey still felt clammy, with a suggestion of some faint temperature, as well. With regret, she asked Ellen, who was dressing, to stay home from school and look after the boy. Ellen's grades would stand it.

"Sure," she replied brightly at once. "I can use the time to study my botany."

"By now you must be just about ready to write a dissertation for your Ph.D.," Mary joked.

"It's for me, not school," Ellen replied in that solemn, unblinking way she had. "Nothing much will happen today, anyway."

"Why not?"

"Tomorrow is the start of Christmas vacation."

Christmas! Mary shook her head, marveling at the way she had forgotten all about it. None of the children had mentioned it even once that she could recall. Evidently they were growing up.

Which was both good and bad. The bad part, right now, was that it meant they would be leaving her someday soon, alone in this foreign place.

She shook off the depressing visions and went after her purse. Before coming downstairs, she looked in on Joey and Chuck, both of whom were asleep. Then she kissed Ellen on the cheek and went out to the Granada to head for work.

As she drove along U.S. 40, battling with other traffic returning to the city, she began to mull over her lot—to try to sort out some decisions. Perhaps it was time to begin thinking about a career, for the first time since high school. Maybe her major problem these days was stagnation. Well, she still had a little singing voice left. It was just possible to conceive of getting club dates, once she worked herself back into shape.

Silly! Who wanted a pop singer in her thirties—a pop singer who sang genuine songs instead of rock nonsense? Popular music was as dead as the dodo bird, as Thessaly's ancient Greek gods.

But Dutch-Touch Cleaners was merely a job. That was all it could ever be. There was nothing in it to fulfill a need Mary always felt—to be fundamentally *necessary* to others, preferably vital. Besides, the job was devoid of intellectual challenge; she could do her tasks in her sleep. While she had never really welcomed change, even before Thessaly, she knew that the fully unchanging nature of her Dutch-Touch duties would eventually represent a truly staggering boredom.

What else was there? Well, only the entire *world,* she scolded herself.

It would be fun, in a way, to be a sort of professional student—to attend a variety of courses each semester, every year, into ripe old age, mastering subject after subject and collecting impressive degrees by the bushel.

But as she pulled into the parking lot she smiled sadly and knew, without doubt, that whatever turn of personality it took to attend college forever, she didn't have it.

During the morning hours Mary went on

feeling slightly dejected and preoccupied, incapable quite of communicating with Greta Bailess, her employer, or Martha Cummins, her wisecracking pal. Knowing her occasional quiet moods and taking this for one of them, they left her alone. Not young Huck Ford, however. His sexual double entendres about female customers sounded more and more pointless to Mary, tasteless, and worse, unfunny. She began looking forward eagerly to lunching with Jeanne at the teacher's apartment.

Finally she was free for the entire afternoon, the little German boss grumpily and grudgingly giving her permission because of an appointment Mary mentioned. The fact was that the appointment, which she had discussed with no one, was much later. Mary planned on going to Jeanne's place first.

The skies appeared clogged with snow, choked almost to the point of bursting, as Mary headed across to Keystone and north toward Broad Ripple. Other motorists obviously felt as she did, that they were about to be inundated with snow, and reacted with erratic nervousness. Twice she was almost involved in accidents. She wondered every winter how so many people could conceivably forget, in less than a year, how to drive in winter weather.

The elevator was waiting on the ground floor and whisked her quickly up to the fourth floor, Jeanne's level. Mary padded down the carpeted hall and stopped at 401 to knock.

There was no answer. She rapped again, harder.

Once more, no reply, no cheerful "Get your ass in here!" from her waiting crony.

Instead, a draft fluttered chillily down the hall, and shivering, Mary put out her hand to try the door.

It was unlocked.

There was something of the happy, cluttered look of her own former living quarters about Jeanne's apartment, but no Jeanne. Calling her name now and then, Mary moved slowly and a trifle fearfully through the apartment.

Jeanne simply wasn't there.

She stood in the dining room, purse dangling at the end of her arm, feeling a bit helpless, annoyed, and concerned. Not that Jeanne hadn't done things like this in the past. If a student had a serious problem, Jeanne was quite capable of forgetting anything else going on until the child's mind was at ease. Once they had planned to take a week's vacation together in Chicago but Jeanne showed up two days late, full of warm pleasure over the way she had put a student's parents back together again.

Generally, however, Jeanne took the problems of others one at a time. And she had seemed genuinely concerned about Mary's well-being.

The dining room table was littered with notes, Mary noticed, lying loose as if Jeanne had intended to leave them only for a moment. Several books were beside them on the table and more were stacked on the floor.

Idly, she stooped to pick up a volume and read the title: *Encyclopedia of Occultism*, by Lewis

Spence. Typical Jeanne Lange reading. She glanced at a few others and discovered similar titles, similar interests.

Bless her heart, Mary thought, she was actually researching this stuff in order to help me.

She saw her name on a scrap of paper, and pulling out the chair, sat down at the dining room table.

"Tell Mary that Greece was more than intellectual capital of old world—their genius is 'essentially magical in conception and meaning, in their literature, sculpture and history. The natural features of the country appealed powerfully to the quality of their imagination. Mountains and valleys, mysterious caves and fissures, vapours and springs . . . dedicated to the gods.' Spence goes on about 'subterranean waters' of Trephonius's Oracle."

Mary, eyebrows lifted, fingered the note. She didn't know quite what to make of it.

Another paper with Jeanne's writing drew her attention. She read: "Mary mentions importance of Pythagoras in Thessaly. He must be studied further to learn why. Not only great mathematician but magician who sought knowledge at all costs. Had tremendous influence throughout his society. Pyth. had miraculous powers, some said, passed along to him through a secret book of magic called a grimoire."

She turned it over and made out further crabbed scrawls: "Pythagoras could tame a bear or lion just by whispering in its ear, they wrote. This is spooky crap."

Beneath the cover of a notebook Mary discovered a cache of Jeanne's notes and glanced at the top one: "Thessaly—according to Apuleuis—was the ancient Greek city 'where, by common report of the world, sorcery and enchantments were most frequent. I viewed the situation of the place in which I was, nor was there anything I saw that I believed to be the same thing which it appeared to be.' He goes on, an *eyewitness observer*, 'I persuaded myself that the statues and buildings could move; that the oxen and other brute beasts could speak and tell strange tidings; that I should hear and see oracles from heaven conveyed in the beams of the Sun.' *I think Mary must be warned. Two Thessalys?*"

This last was underscored twice. Mary stared at the note, worried and perplexed. Did Jeanne actually believe that Thessaly—sleepy, companionable, polite Thessaly, Indiana—was a literal rebirth, a namesake, for the ancient city of sorcerers? That was a little much, even for Jeanne.

Yes—where *was* Jeanne?

Mary shuddered and bit her lip.

Get a firm grip, old girl, she told herself. It was not unusual, when you considered it rationally, not at all. Jeanne is doing research for me and gets a telephone call. One of her students in trouble. She takes off, and being unafraid of anything in this world, leaves the door unlocked.

Poor Jeanne, fearless about thieves and muggers and rapists, terrified of things that did not exist.

There was a sharp breeze somewhere.

She arose from the table and wandered back into Jeanne's kitchenette, where she saw the window, wide open.

When her eyes dropped to the floor and saw Jeanne's blond hair spreading wildly from beneath the sink, she made a little screaming sound and her fingers crammed fearfully against her front teeth.

Mary laughed then. One of Jeanne's damn wigs.

She bent to retrieve it, a trifle shakily, half expecting her friend to pop out from under the curly hair. There was a surprising brightness, a stickiness along the edge of the binding. Gingerly, Mary touched it. Nothing came off. It could be blood, but of course it probably wasn't.

Well, she mused with a sigh, there's nothing to do but wait for Jeanne to phone her again at home. It would certainly be tempting to give her a piece of her mind, dragging her way out here for nothing.

It occurred to Mary abruptly that these notes were meant for her. She paused, honest to the core, then scooped them up, and as an afterthought, stuck them beneath the cover of the occult encyclopedia. It might make interesting reading, and there could be some information about the silly tradition of Thessaly's mysterious death-coach.

She scribbled a hasty note to Jeanne, saying that she had taken the notes and borrowed the book, then hurried to the door. At the last instant she decided to switch off the light and lock the door behind her. Surely Jeanne had a key, and if she wasn't worried about burglars hiding behind chairs in a dark apartment, Mary was worried for her.

The elevator took her downstairs quickly and she strode out of the building toward the parking lot without glancing to left or right.

She failed to observe the large, unpleasant-looking gray cat perched on the apartment portico. It followed her progress step by step, inch by inch, its gaze coldly unblinking. Once Mary had backed out into the street, the gray cat also left the area of the apartment.

Only it wasn't a cat anymore.

Mary drove to the Wild Boar alone, settled for the salad bar and a Diet Pepsi, trying to decide whether she should be concerned enough about Jeanne to chase her down. Since Christmas vacation began tomorrow and Jeanne was a teacher, she would have two weeks off and might well have driven to see her mother in Kokomo. It wouldn't hurt to call there—except that it would seem critical, as if she were upset over Jeanne forgetting their luncheon date. Mary hated "making a production of everything," as she felt most people tended to do. At last, as she was leaving the restaurant, she made the decision to wait until Jeanne contacted her.

Then she drove with anxiety to the doctor's office.

The old man, who had brought her into the world as well as all of her offspring, confirmed what she had suspected for nearly a month: She was nearly three months pregnant.

As usual, she took the news with equanimity and was halfway across U.S. 40 to Thessaly before everything built up within her to an intolerable peak. She pulled the Granada off on a dirt road, a cloud of shimmering white dust filling the air, and began to cry.

Face buried in her hands, shoulders trembling, she wondered how much more she could possibly take. First the irreplaceable loss of Barry, then this crazy town with its strange customs, prying callers, and frightening midnight coach, now the prospect of raising an infant alone. How could she possibly manage? How would they all *live—that* was the crucial question—when she was unable to work at Dutch-Touch any longer?

The one cheerful thought that enabled her to start the engine again and drive on was the realization that a new baby, while it might not be much company, meant another twenty years before she would be entirely alone in the world.

As she began backing out onto the road, her elbow caught the occult book she had borrowed and flipped the cover open. One of Jeanne's notes fluttered to the floor of the car. Mary picked it up. "Important!" it read. "Persuade Mary to put up branches of whitethorn and rope if possible at her windows and doors. Could save her life someday. Don't let her talk you out of doing it. May be *essential!*"

Well, she thought forlornly, if it would ease Jeanne's mind she might do it. Besides, there was the baby to think of now. She maneuvered the remaining miles with the news growing both in significance and pleasure in her mind.

Home at last, she parked the Granada in the drive and hurried to the front door, anxious to tell the kids, and entered with a glad smile, full of her news.

In the living room, sitting at the card table under a full flood of ceiling lights, were Ellen, Chuck, Andruss and Lythia, concentrating on some kind of peculiar wooden board with such serious intent in their faces that they didn't hear her enter.

All four of them were stark naked.

IX

As far as mortals change by day, so far
By night their thinking changes. . . .
                                        —Empedocles

Mary stood in the doorway to the house, her *own* house, stunned and dazzled, staring in total disbelief. There was an aroma in the air of perfume and perspiration.

Ellen, her high-positioned breasts conspicuous above the card table, looked up to smile. "Hi, Mom. How was work?"

Andruss had the decency to keep his eyes lowered to his lap for the moment. The hair on his chest was curly, matted, oddly shocking.

Lythia, looking like a *Playboy* centerfold, stared at Mary with such intensity it appeared actually to be the heat of indignation.

Chuck jumped to his feet, his male organs swaying beneath golden fleece, his face crimson with embarrassment. He did not appear to know what to do with his hands. "Aw now, Mom," he moaned finally, "you weren't supposed to be home from work for another hour."

"Obviously," Mary said, tight-lipped, and unable to gauge whether her predominant emotion was outrage or astonishment. She swept across the room to the card table, her eyes working; she stared down at the wooden board and the triangular object set on the table. "What the hell *is* this thing?" she demanded. "Some hippy version of strip poker?"

"It's a kind of Ouija board, Mom," Ellen replied mildly, scratching in the region of her bare navel. Only her mother could have detected, in the carefully unmocking gaze, the glint of challenge, of dare. "The great-granddaddy of the Ouija board. The Greeks invented the original, of course."

"The Greeks, the goddamn Greeks!" Mary exploded. "What happened—did it tell you to take your clothes off? Come *on*, I want *answers—explanations!* What makes you kids think you can have an orgy in my living room?"

Andruss sighed, stood, and arose with absolutely no evidence of embarrassment. "No one has so much as touched anyone else, Mrs. Graham," he offered evenly in his surprisingly mature manner. "It is not a sexual game. Truly." The boy was built, in one way, on an enormous

160

scale, Mary saw to her dismay, finding it almost impossible to avoid looking at him. A part of her mind sensed that the youth realized her plight, but he went on calmly discoursing. "We merely wished to communicate with the spirit world and this was the most convenient and certain way. Paradise does not have Hart, Schaffner, and Marx."

Red-faced, Mary spun on her heel, searching. She soon discovered unfamiliar male garments over the back of a chair and tossed them at Andruss. "And *my* house does not have your kind of games! *Ever!*"

"You're really so frivolous and unevolved, so earthbound." It was Lythia. She tossed her long blond hair back from her face and stood, graceful and poised. For the first time Mary saw that she wore a half-chemise beginning just below globular breasts with nearly orange nipples and a faint ring of passionate toothmarks around each. "If I wished to make love to my Chuck—or anyone, including Andruss, or even Ellen—I would not require your stupid little house in which to skulk. I go where nature leads me."

Mary started, rendered speechless. Andruss, now restored to his pants, was resting a hand on her shoulder—quite gently, almost paternally. "To reach spirits without impediment, man must be without impediments. It's as simple as that." He paused, and even then, she could not twist away from the gently resting palm. Did she imagine that his eyes swept her own body from head to toe? "Why don't you join us, Mrs.

161

Graham? Then there would be five—an adventurous number that might enable us to reach new levels of contact with the beyond."

Ellen, yawning, arose and sat on the edge of the card table. It was the first time Mary had seen her as a young woman and it was difficult, noticing how relaxed she could be in a bizarre situation, to realize she was not quite fifteen. "You can still change, Mom," she urged, swinging one leg lightly. "C'mon, take off your clothes and join us. If we learned, you can learn."

"Get out." It wasn't a shout nor was it especially intense. It was a plain command which might, given the passing of awkward minutes, become a plea. "I want you two to get out."

"Of course." Andruss withdrew his hand from her shoulder, smiling.

"We have gone about as far with you as we can," Lythia hissed, snatching up her lightweight dress. Her breasts rose, tightened, her covered abdomen flat as she slithered the dress over her blond head. "We have tried to be accommodating, to understand your backward, hesitant ways. But you are forcing us to—"

"Lythia!" Andruss exclaimed warningly, taking her arm.

For a moment it seemed she might strike him.

Then she was hurrying out the front door. The Greek youth paused as he slipped into his shirt and found his jacket. He shrugged. "Look, I am sorry about this, Mrs. Graham. Will you please try to understand and to forgive? We meant no harm, really. Will you try?"

"We'll see," Mary said, breathing hard.

"See y'tomorrow, Andruss," Ellen called from her careless perch on the table, waggling her fingers.

He nodded amiably at her and Chuck clapped his shoulder, then closed the door.

"You two have done it now," Mary declared dangerously, turning. "You *won't* see that boy tomorrow, young lady. And if you *ever* want to see him again, you'd better go right back to being *yourself!*"

Ellen, for the first time, appeared slightly hurt, involved. "Mom, I'm still *me*. I haven't changed— that much."

"Heck, no," Chuck mumbled, "there's been no need. Look, Mom, we weren't bullshitting you. That game was invented by Pythagoras, and it really works. If you'd only try it with us, you'd see there's no harm to it. We just—talk to spooks, and they sort of . . . talk back."

"Ellen," Mary began tightly, "get dressed and start preparing dinner at once. Chuck, get your clothes on and set the table, help your sister. When I come back downstairs I want this to look like our *home*, not a brothel!"

Trying to hold back a sudden surge of tears, she fled upstairs, nibbling frantically on her full lower lip.

Joey! God, Ellen was supposed to have been looking after Joey!

In discovering Jeanne's odd disappearance, and learning that she was pregnant, Mary had temporarily forgotten her youngest child's nightmares, and more importantly, his temperature.

She opened his bedroom door quietly, started to turn on the light and realized that he was still asleep. Her eyes adjusted quickly to the evening gloom and she hurried across the room where she looked tenderly down on him.

He seemed to be serenely, peacefully asleep. When she laid her palm on his forehead, he appeared much cooler than he had been that morning. His thumb was firmly stuck in his pathetic little mouth. She could see, in the dim light, the scar from his harelip, and she wondered both how long it would be until it faded, and how long it would be until he stopped sucking his thumb.

Gently, she pulled it from his mouth—

—And took two steps back in horror.

The tiny thumb was covered with blood from tip to root!

My Lord, in his sleep Joey had not only sucked the thumb but chewed it almost to the bone!

She held his hand at the wrist, frightened and sick at heart. How could he *do* such an awful thing in his sleep and not even awaken?

When she replaced his little hand on his narrow chest and turned to go in search of disinfectant and bandages, Joey's eyes shot open, red-rimmed and fever-bright.

Instantly awake, he smiled up at his mother, his lips edged with gore and bits of human flesh between his small teeth.

"I was sound asleep, Mom," he said lazily, yawning, "havin' a nice dream."

But dreaming of *what*, in the name of God, Mary wondered grimly as she hurried to the bathroom.

Perhaps *only* God—or one other—should ever have to know the content of Joey's dreams and nightmares.

Dinner was an insufferable procedure for all concerned. The children did not ask to leave the house, to Mary's relief, although Joey seemed rested and much improved, other than his wounded thumb—enough to chatter about Christmas vacation and all the fascinating things he would be doing around Thessaly.

Chuck and Ellen averted their gazes, not so much in shame, it appeared, but in a wish to avoid further discussion. They did their best to ignore the frigid tone in their mother's voice, and after eating, Ellen retired to her botany books and Chuck parked himself silently in front of the television set.

Once she was sure that Joey was occupied with his coloring and connect-the-number puzzle books, Mary went to her own room wearily and tried to read portions of Jeanne Lange's occult encyclopedia. The words and terms seemed absurd to her, made irrelevant by the passage of time and the advent of demanding science, almost impossible for her to consider.

It was here and now, right in Thessaly, Indiana, that caused Mary anxiety, not mystical experiences and outre commitments of a world centuries old. She didn't want to read about alchemy, witchcraft, demonic possession or the enigmatic mysteries of Stonehenge or Easter Island—she wanted to know why all her children seemed to be altering their personalities before her eyes.

What difference did the Aztecs or Atlanteans or even Unidentified Flying Objects make to her when her family was being absorbed by a townful of affable Greeks who dwelt in a past that may never have existed?

Mary sat at her writing desk remembering a book by a leading psychologist who had claimed that American children, born in Dayton or Brooklyn or San Diego, could be persuaded—by virtue of continually living with them—to assume all the mores and beliefs of people in Borneo, Thailand, Singapore, or the Australian outback. There were only a few requisites, the psychologist had averred: that the ex-American child was young enough and impressionable enough, and that the adopted society that was urged on him was tradition-oriented and mystically tacit about offering explanations.

It had sounded unbelievable to Mary when she read those claims. Bronx stickball players, miniature cowboys, or pretend race drivers from Indy deciding to wear bones in their noses or to hunt kangaroo for game was palpably absurd.

Or so she had thought then.

For the first time she confessed that it could be true.

Clattering hoofbeats; a whinny.

Mary Graham stayed where she sat, at her desk, eyes going blank even as muscles became taut, stressful. She would not move, she told herself. She would not look out the window because there really was no such thing as a death-coach. Either it was a ridiculous custom for which they hired a weirdo cemetery caretaker on a part-time basis or it was a peculiar power of suggestion. At worst, it was nothing more than a collection of psychic memories somehow impressed, like ectoplasm, on nighttime in Thessaly.

What it *wasn't*, she informed herself firmly, was a genuine coach of death wending its way through Thessaly on hideous, unguessable business.

Soon, to her immense relief, the hoofbeats faded into the distance, and the ride was done for the night.

She went to her bed and turned the covers back, wearily. It had been a terrible day, but it was over. She undressed, and then, finding it chilly in the room, put on a pair of pajamas Barry had given her for their final Christmas together. Sighing, she slipped between the covers and fell into a dreamless sleep that was much more like unconsciousness.

Someone was staring at her.

Her eyes snapped open and she saw, in the open bedroom doorway, a shadowed form standing silently like a watchful nocturnal spectre. Her heart throbbed wildly until she realized that it was neither a ghost nor a prowler, but Ellen.

"What is it, honey?" she called out, squinting in the semidarkness.

No reply. The apparition in the flannel

nightgown went on standing, and staring; then it turned, in utter silence, and slowly walked away.

It came to Mary with a shock that Ellen was sleepwalking.

She threw her legs over the side of the bed, trying to remember how sleepwalkers were supposed to be handled. Not awakened suddenly, she recalled; eased out of it or, better yet, she thought, prevented from hurting themselves but allowed to awaken on their own.

She padded barefoot across the bedroom and out into the hall, peering.

As quiet as death, Ellen walked slowly down the corridor ahead of her and turned into her own bedroom.

Mary followed, gathering her senses, moving cautiously.

Ellen had returned to bed, lying on one side. Apparently, it was over.

Then Ellen was rolling over, and with a start that jolted her whole body and caused Mary to switch on the light in panic, sitting upright with a piercing scream.

Mary ran to her, her maternal hands out to help. Ellen's face was contorted with the scream and then she shrieked again, louder, eyes wide and gaping, her young bosom heaving in absolute terror.

"Ellen! What is it?" Mary cried.

The girl could not reply. Her hands were caught like birds in her brown hair and were pulling at it. While her eyes were opened wide they did not seem to see. Or, perhaps, saw *elsewhere*.

Chuck bounded through the bedroom door, looking sleepy and frightened, staring at his sister. "What's wrong with her?"

Mary leaned toward the teenager anxiously and peered closely into her young face. "Honey, *tell* Mother—what's *wrong?*"

Suddenly the fourteen-year-old seemed to be drunk, an intoxicated young madwoman. She whipped her hands free of her hair, leaving it in a crazy tangle, the arms shooting to the ceiling, grasping handfuls of air. Her mouth dropped open dully, the lips flecked with foam as it drooled on her pert chin.

"I know, I *know!*" she exclaimed, half-shrieking, staring past her mother and brother as if they didn't exist, seeing that which they could not see. "It's true—he *told* me!" She tossed her head from side to side frantically, making raspy moaning sounds deep in her throat. *"Doomed!"*

Chuck looked with fright into his mother's face. "Maybe I should get Milo Traphonius from down the street," he suggested, looking terrified. "He knows about—about things like this. He can help."

Mary hesitated, considering. Then her own head whirled from left to right in an enormously defiant answer of No. Maybe she *did* need the old man's help, maybe he *could* help. But *asking* for it, *seeking* the help of people in this damnable town, was like—like *conceding* her helplessness to Thessaly. She refused to do it, to give in.

She looked back at Ellen, saw the words starting to rise up inside her, beginning to pour out.

"*Aesculapius has told me!*" the girl screamed abruptly, "he *told* me, he *told* me!"

With that, a torrent of words spewed wildly from her spittle-streaked lips—meaningless, maniacal sounds that cascaded into the bedroom heedlessly, as if the girl were floating, forever damned, in the lost eternity of infinite space.

Wordless, Chuck fled the bedroom. Mary raised a hand in helpless protest, then returned her attention to her daughter. She pulled Ellen to her, tried to hold, caress, and calm the girl. But Ellen's slender arms began to flail the air frantically like the wings of a great bird, and to Mary's further consternation, her legs kicked aside the blankets and sought to thrust her body free of the mother's desperate, clutching hands.

As Mary's grip weakened, Chuck was back, his muscular arms full of laurel branches. He hesitated only a moment, then tipped his sister's spit-damp chin to make her see them. Nodding pacifyingly, the boy began draping the branches around her shoulders and strewing them in the lap of her flannel gown.

Ellen let go. To Mary's astonishment, and relief, Ellen relaxed almost at once with a tiny, childlike moan of exhaustion.

Behind Mary, Chuck was placing incense on Ellen's dresser and lighting it with hands that still trembled from his honest concern. The powerful odor rose at once, quickly choking the room and permeating their senses.

Mary glanced back again as Ellen sank slowly, languidly among the laurel leaves like a cartoon animal revelling in nature. They framed her frightened, tear-streaked face, but at last it was starting to become calm, to become rational once more.

She whispered something and Mary inclined her ear to the girl to hear.

"*Antipodes,*" she whispered as if it was important to hear the word. Her terrified eyes stared with awful certainty and she gave her mother a decided, definite little nod. "*We're all headed for Antipodes. It's written.*"

Her eyes closed in sleep.

While Mary did not understand the meaning of her daughter's message she felt suddenly quite cold, as if all the heat in the house had gone out and they were exposed to winter's cruel mercies. She looked at her own shaking hand and found another emotion tearing at the corners of her worried mind: stark terror.

X

Far from the Blessed, and be born through time
In various shapes of mortal kind, which change
Ever and ever troublous paths of life. . . .
                                    —Empedocles

Sometime during an endless night that was largely sleepless, occasionally clouded by the scattered storms of ghastly dreams, Mary reached the conclusion that she would make an effort to sell the house in Thessaly. It had to be done. It was unthinkable that her Barry would expect them to remain, under the circumstances. Whatever, precisely, they might actually be.

There seemed to be every reason for telling no one about the decision, even as she had—so far—told no one that she was pregnant. Her Thessaly neighbors with their mystifying hold upon her kids would just have to learn of both developments as they were all going out the front door! The problem would be winning the children back, so that they would willingly return with her to Indianapolis. Timed well, the information about a new baby brother or sister might help turn the trick. Surely Chuck and Ellen wouldn't desert her at such a time.

In the meanwhile, she would play down the nude game of yesterday, try to seem both understanding and affectionate. She'd quietly seek prospective buyers of the property after she was in Indianapolis, and keep her eyes open for another place there. It was conceivable that Jeanne might be helpful, when she returned.

That Tuesday morning they were all up very early. Mary found that Ellen was astonishingly well, despite her nocturnal terrors. When they met in the bathroom, Ellen said that she had no recollection whatever of sleepwalking, of unseen voices in her mind, or of fits of shouted prophecy.

"Aesculapius?" Ellen repeated, as they went downstairs together. She appeared genuinely puzzled, even embarrassed. "Who's he? One of the men in town?"

"Look, that's what I'm asking you," Mary said lightly as she poured coffee for the two of them. Chuck looked up from his eggs with open interest. "You said that he was somehow telling you things. Terrible things."

"I don't know what you're talking about," Ellen persisted with a shake of her pretty head.

She took the coffee cup from her mother and sipped. "Really I don't. Does it have to do with all those laurel leaves strewn on my bed?"

"They were necessary, El," Chuck remarked soberly. "You were really out of it. They saved your ass."

"Oh, come on," the girl said lightly. She looked embarrassed, perhaps a trifle frightened, as she arose. "Gotta go to the john. 'Scuse."

Taking her coffee, she went upstairs. Chuck glanced seriously to his mother before speaking. "It could have been communication with her own astral body. Maybe she projected it somewhere and it returned to inform her."

Mary stared at him, seeing the grin but able to tell, from the gaze she knew so well, that he was serious. "Where'd you learn terms like those?"

"Lythia and Andruss, mostly. Mr. Traphonius likes my interest in Thessaly and pitches in, too, sometimes. T'teach me their ways." He appeared almost his old self this morning, dressed in blue bib overalls with his yellow hair needing a trim and his affable grin easily in place. "Or it could just be spontaneous on El's part. Pythagoras once said that prophecy was simply a—a heightened form of a normally unused imagination."

Mary sipped her morning Diet Pepsi, studying Chuck with good humor. She knew these brief intellectual periods. "Since when do you care about math, Charles Martin Graham? I seem to recall that geometry was one of the reasons you dropped out of Marshall."

The boy nodded his admission, sopping up the

rest of his egg yolk with a brown scrap of toast. "Oh, Pythagoras was a lot more than a mathematician. A helluva lot more. If the teachers taught neat stuff about the way people *are*, or were, back in history, maybe kids would care a little more about *what* they did."

"You might very well be right. Why not educate me about Pythagoras?" She was pressing again now, and knew it. She badly wanted to get closer to the kids while there was time, to know what they knew without letting them realize she planned to quit Thessaly. "I remember his theorem, of course. And reading that arithmetic, to his people, was studying the concept of numbers as they applied to nature. Didn't he even have a regular school of students?"

"Very good, Mom!" Chuck praised her with a nod. "Yes, he did—on Croton, a Greek colony in southern Italy. But he was actually born on the island of Samoa around 569 B.C., and he travelled all over Egypt and India learning fantastic crap that was *already* ancient, then. He didn't exactly teach math, I understand—he taught special doctrines and principles for living, and for learning the, *um*, source of things. Math was his means of doing that."

"What kind of 'doctrines'?" Mary inquired, curious, unwilling to break this fresh flow of communication. It occurred to her an important clue might develop.

He paused. "Well, we've lost a lot of that by now, of course. But he and his followers were inspired by religious beliefs of the time. In terms of purifying men's souls or redeeming their minds."

Mary frowned, uncertain she'd followed. "Redeeming their minds *or* their souls?"

"I don't think Pythagoras felt there was much difference. He sought to teach people how to save their minds from the prisons of their bodies." Chuck had finished breakfast and stood, fetching his rifle from the wall. "I'm still tryin' to shoot me a rabbit or two. It'll save us money."

"Chuck." Mary sensed a strange correlation. "These students of Pythagoras," she pressed. "What was *their* role? What did they *do* for him?"

He paused, again, looking impressed. His gaze held hers. "Anything at all, I understand. He was the absolute leader. Once they joined Pythagoras, they were pledged to secrecy. More'n that, they were required to join for life." He worked the bolt of the rifle with two plunging snaps and appeared satisfied with its operation. "I don't think anybody ever left his school. *Ever.*"

"Well, it sounds more like a cult than a teaching fraternity."

Suddenly Chuck was anxious to leave. "Look, if you're truly interested in Pythagoras, I've got a fact-sheet about him." He fumbled in the pocket of his coat. "Lythia gave it to me. Be sure y'give it back to me tonight, okay?" He turned to leave.

"Chuck?"

"—Yeah?"

She hesitated, feeling foolish. He was such an enormous boy, yet a boy. "Be careful. With that rifle."

"Yeah; sure, Mom."

When he opened the door the obvious beginning of a blizzard blew with hasty terror through the front room, striking the dining room in a wild torrent of biting wind and a handful of coldly searing snowflakes. Only teenage boys went out willingly on a day like that, Mary thought with a laugh, if they didn't have to.

But she would have to go get ready soon for work herself. Sighing, a little afraid of the weather, she went to the telephone table to dial Jeanne's number. Today was the official beginning of Christmas vacation and the teacher might already be home.

But there was no reply, at Jeanne's, only an incessant, changeless drone.

With a sigh Mary moved upstairs, stopping in the bathroom to run a hairbrush through her dark brown tousle of hair, startled to see a few new worry lines beginning at the corners of her eyes. Cobweb traces of inner anxiety. She turned from the mirror. Ellen was apparently holed up in her room with her botany books. Mary thought briefly of dropping by, to chat again.

But it was difficult, after the furor of last night and Ellen's claims of ignorance today. Independent, rigid, the girl was simply not easy-going Chuck. Suddenly the living room display appeared to her nothing but a silly kids' game, essentially harmless—though Andruss's great organ made it hard to think of them as children. Still, Mary felt an honest twinge of regret at having lost her temper and ordering both the boy and Lythia to leave. Even the girl's outspoken reaction now seemed suddenly nothing more than an expression of nervousness.

Mary took a chair at the vanity table in her own room after checking the clock and learning that she had some thirty minutes before she must depart. Joey was still asleep, Ellen incommunicado, Chuck gone; she felt totally washed up, just then, worthless and unnecessary.

Alone, where no one could see her display of understandable human emotion, proud Mary felt tears well up and flood her light green eyes. They spilled over. She let them go, permitted them to run untouched down her cheeks as she stared fondly over at Barry's photograph. If only he was there, now, to help with the kids. That wild imagination of his might come in handy; he might know, instinctively, what to do. What her practical ways could not fathom.

She touched the familiar face in his picture; she felt paper, only paper. No way to reach him now, to know him ever again. Not ever. She replaced the picture on her dresser, inhaled, dried her eyes on a Puff tissue from the ornate container on the vanity table. At last she picked up the fact-sheet Chuck had left for her to read.

The tiny, brownish-gray sparrow that had perched stoically outside Mary's window took a final, inquisitive, appraising look in at her, its little head cocked reflectively to one side. Then it moved its wings rapidly and lifted gracefully from the sill, quickly disappearing into the gray December morning.

Mary unfolded the crumpled sheet. Why would they have a fact-sheet on Pythagoras, a man dead thousands of years? Was he a sort of patron saint here in town? There was no clue in the document itself. At the top it read, simply: PYTHAGORAS, PERSONAL DATA.

Okay, then, she'd explore. Mary shifted her body in a way that allowed maximum light from the bedlamp and scanned the wrinkled page with building curiosity.

Chuck was right, she saw that at once. The ancient Greek was a great deal more than the mathematician teachers limitedly indicated in high school. But exactly what, it was difficult to tell. . . .

The Pythagoreans were called the *akousmatikoi* and dedicated themselves not only to arithmetic but to the study of philosophy, science, magic, and early astrology manuals called *Bauernpraktik* —all half-a-thousand years before the Galilean Christ trod the earth. Going so far back in time that they had no symbols for numbers, the *akousmatikoi* represented whole numbers with pebbles on the ground, and with dots of sand, becoming the first people to identify square numbers and perfect squares. But to Pythagoras and his group, numbers were not only symbols for quantities. They were at the heart of special, secret concepts and relationships of unsuspected but vast meaning—much of it darkly mysterious.

Chuck's fact-sheet claimed that all the aspects of the true nature of numbers had been established, even though time had eradicated their

179

methods of discovery. It was as if time was yet so new, then, that a sense of wonder was attached to everything—what today's youngsters found stultifying had seemed, to the ancient Greeks, warmed by the sweet smile of God. As the essence of universal matter, *odd* numbers (to the Pythagoreans) represented *male* traits, creative and active ones, while *even* numbers represented *female* traits, receptive and passive ones. The information page specified the qualities for which each number stood:

1—purpose, action, ambition
2—balance, passivity, receptivity
3—versatility, gaiety, brilliance
4—steadiness, endurance, dullness
5—adventure, instability, sexuality
6—dependability, harmony, domesticity
7—mystery, knowledge, solitariness
8—material success, worldly involvement
9—great achievements, inspiration, spirituality

These numbers formed a basis for other great developments of the *akousmatikoi* rather than being of intense significance by themselves alone. Mary blinked. Unlike other Greeks, Pythagoras's people believed that the earth was in motion, astoundingly anticipating Copernicus by two thousand years! From each of the other planets there issued a different musical note dependent upon its distance from the earth. The combination of all the sounds formed a perfect cosmic octave. From this had evolved the enduring, poetically lovely concept of the "music of the spheres."

The brilliant mathematician and scholar concluded that although they could account for nine heavenly bodies, there had to be a *tenth*, an invisible body which he named "counter-earth." With the natural earth and the other planets, it was said to revolve around a central, fixed fire. Pythagoras, with his dedication to Empedocles, the poet, believed that its location was actually ascertainable. He set out somehow to find counter-earth.

The fact-sheet stated that since there had to be an ideal ten bodies in the solar system, the universe must be describable in terms of categorized opposites, or *pairs:* polarities such as old and young, right/left, odd/even, male/female, good/evil. She nodded. That made sense. It—

She jumped at the sudden noise. Then she realized it was merely Ellen, leaving her room to go downstairs.

She continued reading the strange data sheet, mystified as to its very existence in Thessaly. It concluded with a biographical sketch of Pythagoras, stating that the Greek genius definitely knew he had lived many other lives. Mary paused. Even though her Catholicism did not encourage it, she had, for some while, wondered about reincarnation. She felt drawn to its special logic, its rationale. Pythagoras claimed he'd been a warrior named Euphorbus, slain during the

Trojan war, a prophet named Hermatimas, burned to death by his fierce rivals, a Phoenician prostitute, and the wife of a storekeeper in Lydia. As Pythagoras, he'd been devoted to higher instruction, in a complex philosophy that presented perfect order through a calculated pattern. He developed something called musical medicine, and offered a variety of mystical teachings, including his doctrine of the transmigration of souls. About most of these there was little surviving information.

Mary stopped to think, puzzled. Wasn't transmigration just about the same thing as reincarnation? She wasn't sure and tried to make a mental note to look it up in Jeanne's occult encyclopedia.

Concluding, the fact-sheet said that rumor had it that Greece's profound Pythagoras was driven by jealousy from Croton, fleeing to Metapontum in southern Italy, where it was said that he—like his hero, Empedocles—might have been brutally murdered or forced to suicide. Certainly he'd disappeared, forever.

She folded the paper and slipped it thoughtfully into her purse. For the first time, she thought, she might possess a few clues to what was happening around her in Thessaly. If the society of the town was patterned on the principles and beliefs of such a brilliant and strange ancient personage as Pythagoras, a lot might soon be explained.

Ruminative, she went back downstairs, and on the spur of the moment, rushed up to her daughter. Ellen was dressed in tan slacks and a heavy sweater, her feet propped up on a hassock.

She was reading.

"Botany so early in the morning?" Mary asked gently.

"Hm-m?" Ellen looked up, vaguely startled. "No, some poetry."

"Greek poetry?"

"Yep." The girl made a pouting face. "I suppose you're going to object."

"Not at all. I came over to ask you a favor."

"Sure. What?" Ellen asked with a measure of suspicion.

"Is there any whitethorn in the forest?"

Ellen blinked. "Why, sure. I guess it's here and there. Why?"

"Well," Mary told the lie, "I think it's pretty. It's time I made use of nature's beauty since we're so close to that wild woods. Hold on a sec." She left the room momentarily and returned with two bright vases from the kitchen cabinet. "Would you gather some whitethorn while I'm at work, Ellen? Just put it in these vases. Put one on the table by the front door, and one in my room. Okay?"

Ellen nodded somberly. Her expression said what she dared not put in words: Mothers were all, obviously, quite mad, present company not excluded.

Feeling she had made use of all Jeanne's efforts in her behalf, and that she'd learned something about Thessaly by studying the fact-sheet Lythia had given Chuck, Mary bustled around to finish getting ready. She was tugging her topcoat down from the closet when she heard the knock at the door.

It was Milo Traphonius, a Grecian Santa Claus with freshly clustered snowflakes glittering in his massive, enwreathing beard. "Mary, my dear! I'm so happy to catch you before you leave for work!"

She looked out at the smiling old man, trapped. "Well, I *am* running a little late, Milo," she answered tentatively, hoping he'd take the hint.

"Won't keep you, child," he beamed. "I just wanted to ask if you would care to participate in a little gathering. A sort of, ah, town meeting."

Mary paused. She truly wanted to like, to trust, this old fellow. He was so warm, so pleasant. "When is it?" she asked.

"Day after tomorrow—Thursday evening at eight. We plan to meet at the church and discuss various relevant matters. Matters of importance to those of our little town." He gave her his most stunningly paternal smile. "Witnessing the progress of your children, we're still anxious to make all of you a part of us. Indeed, we're looking forward to little Joseph's birthday next week."

Something about his proprietary air and the way Milo recognized Joey's birthday while quite ignoring the fact that it was Christmas as well annoyed Mary anew. Her lips tightened faintly. "Frankly, sir, I'm not really pleased with what *is* happening to my kids. One of them has had—hysterics—and another has very nearly chewed his thumb off. To be truthful, I rather wish that we could all be . . . left alone. For awhile, you see."

For a long, contemplative moment the old man

stood quietly in the doorway, looking ever more like an aged snowman, studying her pretty face and severe stare. She saw again suddenly how huge, how powerful, he was despite his age. For the first time, when he replied, Mary sensed a distinctly ominous inflection. "I'm sorry you feel that way, Mary. Truly sorry. But I am afraid that you cannot possibly be left alone, my child. Not— *ever again.*"

"Just what does that mean, Mr. Traphonius?" she demanded. So it was coming out in the open, was it? "That sounded very much like a threat."

"You are a resident, a member of the community, quite uninvited," he murmured, choosing his words and speaking in measured tones. "We have preferred to welcome you. Whether you like it or not, in a small town such as Thessaly, you can't remain an island. It is— unnatural."

"Well, we shall see." She began easing the door shut. "I really must go to work now," she said, managing a slight smile, shutting the door the rest of the way.

Quickly she made Ellen promise to keep an eye on Joey off and on during the day and to make him go to bed if he seemed to be running a temperature or indicated that he remained ill.

Then she went out in her coat to the Granada, scraped off the accumulation of rather mushy snow from the windshield, and got it running. The sound was muffled, sputtering. Allowing the motor to warm up, she stared out at the still dark morning streets, wondering. It was pitch dark here. Someone could break into the car, rape and kill her, and unless "Mayor" Traphonius decided to care, he could wander into the dark night, forever safe.

Milo's newly adamant, almost hostile stance had frightened her. What could he have meant when he said that they would never be left alone? Just how much commitment did he, and the others, feel her family must make to the town of Thessaly?

Deeply troubled, but eager to be on the road to Indianapolis, she drove to the end of the block and turned left, obliged to ram the Granada through drifting snowbanks. She passed the first vacant, white-sheeted field with her mind trying to sort out the enigmas of this strange place. She—

The deer vaulted suddenly in front of her car, a flash of light, soft brown and dazzling fur-white, inordinately huge in the headlights. Involuntarily, Mary hit the brakes—hard. The car lurched in protest, writhing on the thin coat of icy snow, veering toward the unprotected edge of the road and very nearly careening into a yawning ditch. It shuddered; held.

It was over then.

On the brink of tears, Mary sat root-still, statuelike, gathering her dwindling nerves together like a frayed security blanket. At last she began backing up, out onto the road. She began again, nervously, her eleven-mile drive to Indianapolis.

Her hands trembled in gloves tightly squeezing

the steering wheel. It looked like a long day ahead.

Vrukalakos reported to the Patriarch with a note of uncharacteristic optimism in his slightly nasal, sharply accented tones. "She still adores her husband," he said plainly. "I have seen her weep for him and that shall be beneficial to us."

"Aye, and I have seen that the lady will not listen to reason," commented the Patriarch, his inflection sad. "It certainly cannot be said that we haven't tried."

"You have behaved wisely, as always," Aristides praised the old man.

"No one could conceivably have done more," Melas noted supportively.

Once more the Patriarch turned with reluctance to the wraithlike Vrukalakos. "Mrs. Graham must be brought to reason. There is no alternative. I want that entire family to accompany us when Commemoration comes—and the boy must be purified before that. Do I make myself clear?"

"Perfectly!" Vrukalakos smiled, scarcely able to conceal his exultation. The smile was not nice to see.

"No, my old comrade and adversary, I do not think you see at all." The old man pointed a gnarled finger. "Under *no* circumstances is she to lose her life. Is that clear? That shall *not* be part of our present contract, yours and mine."

Vrukalakos scowled. "It is clear," he growled, "if unfortunate. However, I know what to do."

Melas changed the subject. "What is the progress with the boy Joey?"

The Patriarch brightened. "The progress is excellent. On his birthday—his tenth, the number of perfection, the number which symbolizes counter-earth—he will become one of us." He beamed. "That much is certain."

"And the other young Americans?" inquired Aristides. "What of them?"

"The boy Chuck is almost ours now. The female, Ellen Graham, has been stubborn. But she shall be dealt with this afternoon. And that matter will surely be concluded."

Shortly after one in the afternoon Ellen Graham bundled up warmly and strode purposefully into the deep woods beyond her home. With a surprising expertise for one so young, she sought, located, and gathered the whitethorn branches in short order, then headed back to the house. Swirling light snow blew in her face and prettily speckled her dark hair.

It was odd, but carrying the whitethorn seemed unpleasant. She squirmed just to retain her hold on the branches. For some reason they made her feel . . . *creepy,* peculiar. The young botanist decided, as she shoved upon the french doors, that whitethorn was not among her favorite plants.

Avoiding becoming pricked by the devilishly sharp thorns, Ellen made two floral arrangements in the vases Mary had brought her, reluctantly carrying one to a place beside the front door and the other to her mother's room. She couldn't imagine what Mary wanted with them; but Ellen tried always to be obedient and planned to continue—unless Thessaly's demands made that impossible.

When she was leaving the house again to visit Lythia, Ellen found Andruss at the door, blithe and darkly handsome. She was vaguely flustered as she always was when her steadfast plans were interrupted. But he was so good-looking that she decided she was glad he'd come. Immediately Andruss proposed that they continue trying to reach the spirit world.

"Well, come in," she offered, stepping lightly away from the door, "but I won't be able to strip anymore. Mother's orders." She accepted his nearly fraternal kiss on the cheek without acknowledgment, her eyes flustered. "Honestly, Andruss, she's been so jumpy and changeable lately I don't dare disobey her. Not after she caught us all yesterday." She thought of how masculine he'd been, reddened, and turned away.

"Have I asked you to disrobe?" he inquired, following her into the front room.

"No, but I thought you might. Besides, Joey's upstairs, just getting up. And he's got the biggest yap in the world."

Andruss's eyes glittered. "I'm not alone hungering for your body, Ellen," he remarked. "I crave it, I know that we will be wonderful together. But you're more to me than that and so are Thessaly's traditions."

"Well, thank you." She perched on a chair arm.

"At least you say your mother is changing," he

189

said with a sigh, his gaze crossing her bosom with a flicker of desire. "That's a beginning." He found the card table in the corner and began putting it up, his brown hands strong on the snap-legs. "Come, we shall play the game clothed. Sometimes the spirits overlook our mortal weaknesses."

"Just the t-two of us?"

He laughed easily. "Just us, Ellen. Afraid?"

She shivered. "Andruss, you don't really believe in ghosts, do you? I mean, this *is* just a game—right?"

"Like everything," he replied, staring levelly at her and touching her cheek with two fingers, "it is what one makes of it. Bring candles, please. They may assist our communication."

Not fully willing now, but trapped, Ellen went to the hutch in the dining room and rummaged around, finally locating two lengthy yellow candles. Deep shadows fell across the french doors; the small house seemed abruptly, to Ellen, struck off from the early winter sunlight, cut off from other, safer places. Already it looked like dusk. She trembled.

His gaze followed her as she brought the candles to the card table and bent, a book of matches in her fingers, her young face intent.

"You are very beautiful," Andruss said. Her young breasts swung forward as she bent, pressing against the material of her blouse. "The most beautiful girl your age whom I have seen in many years."

She noticed where he looked so hotly and

straightened. "You haven't lived that many years, idiot," she joshed, laughing. "And you aren't Irish, so quit being so charming."

"For you, m'lady," he said, "I would be anything you desired."

They sat opposite each other to play the ancient game, and it began to feel to Ellen that they were the last two people in the world. The rules called for the touching of hands from time to time, and hand-clenching. She experienced a sudden rush of appreciation that this handsome, self-assured young man cared for her.

"Ask the spirits," the boy prompted, "whom you will one day love."

She blushed faintly but complied.

For the first time the trivet began working smoothly, quickly. It darted to the letters, spelling out: A BROUCOLACK GOD.

"How strange." Ellen gaped at the answer. Then she asked the board's spirits, softly, "What's his name going to be?"

The trivet flowed, spelling: HAS HAD MORE THAN ONE NAME. YOU CALL ANDRUSS.

"You *moved* it!" she protested with a trilling, half-fearful laugh. A shadow passed over the table and she withdrew her hands.

His deep, dark eyes peered seriously into hers. "No. But it *was* . . . moved." His face was the only thing in the world for Ellen, then, hollowed by shadows and licked by golden light from the candle. Outside, the winter wind picked up, slipping chilly fingers between the french doors and trailing eerily across the floor. Then he was leaning across the board to her, his breath hot on her cheek. "Ellen, the truth is always spoken in this ancient game. I am a god." He kissed her, first on the lips, then, thrillingly, on the side of the neck.

She half-shuddered. A thrill of mingled flame and ice spun the knotted route of her spine. It was hard to resist this boy. He was different from the few others she'd known at school in Indianapolis, different indeed from anyone at all whom she had met.

"I think I could be happy here, in Thessaly," Ellen said obliquely. "Andruss, why does the board say you've had other names?"

He raised his eyebrows in mild mimicry. "Because I am a man of infinite mystery," he murmured grandly. "But I shall always be a Broucolack. Whatever else I become, wherever I go . . . *a Broucolack.*"

"But what is that?" she asked softly, whispering, drawn by him.

He arose and came round the table to her, kneeling. His hands moved up to cup her breasts, the fingers lightly squeezing her nipples; then they moved caressingly to the sides of her youthful face and she stared at him, helpless. Gently, Andruss leaned forward to kiss her throat.

"I shall show you what a Broucolack is, my girl," he said huskily, with a trace of emotion, of heat. "You must be purified, and this is—*one* way."

Andruss's teeth fastened, biting. Yet they did

not exactly hurt, nor did they meet any protest from mesmerized Ellen Graham.

The snow was intent on jumping upon the ground in great, stomping wads as Mary drove back to Thessaly that Tuesday evening. It was becoming hard to see; the wipers kept clogging. But she drove with determination, longing for a long, hot bath. The day had been exhausting, excruciatingly endless. It seemed that everybody in Indianapolis had brought his clothes to Dutch-Touch cleaners for a holiday fresh-up. For some time there'd been a comforting sense of teamwork, with Greta, Martha, and Huck working cooperatively with Mary. But by afternoon it had become only individual hard labor and she'd yearned for home.

Parking in the driveway, Mary locked the car and then tromped through the clustering, protesting snow to the front door. Once inside the house she found Ellen seated quietly on the couch, leaning against Andruss. El had a notepad open on her round knee, a pen poised studiously in her hand.

Fleetingly, Mary recalled that she'd ordered the girl not to see Andruss until further notice. But she felt so tired, it had been too long a day to start a scene. "Is Joey all right?" she asked, and caught a brief, answering nod. Ignoring Andruss, she removed her coat, and hanging it in the closet, called, "Please set the table, Ellen. It's going to be a light meal tonight. I'm just beat."

Grudgingly, her movements slow and turgid,

Ellen put her notepad aside and rose. Andruss's dark eyes moved between the two females like wary rabbits. Apparently he decided to avoid risking a quarrel since he stood as well, languidly, then moved silently toward the door.

But Chuck arrived then, flushed with achievement, slamming the door behind him. "Look what the mighty hunter brought home!" he exclaimed jubilantly, raising his arm.

A pair of quite dead, very stiff rabbits dangled by their ears from his meaty hand.

Before Mary could reply, thinking of Joey's horror for rabbits, the boy Andruss was taking a step away from Chuck, his face working. *"My Zeus!"* he muttered. "Where did you get—*those?*"

"Why, the woods," said Chuck blandly. "Shot 'em myself. Mom'll clean 'em for supper t'morrow, won't you, Mom? And save me a foot for luck—okay?"

Andruss issued a sound of serpentine hissing that startled the Grahams. A sinuous, quick arm sought to snatch the dead rabbits from his friend. The taller Chuck pushed Andruss slightly, in reaction, making him back up. Chuck held grimly to his kill. Andruss's face crimsoned. He leaned close to Chuck, blurting: "Damn you, they must be dismembered and buried! They *must* be!"

"Don't be a shit," Chuck snapped. An injured expression moved on his face before the seriousness of his new friend. "Why should I, Andruss? Huh?"

For an instant the Greek was too flustered to reply. His eventual answer was bold. "There's so much for you to learn, Chuck. Magicians and sorcerers often use the hare's body, for—for quick transit. *Saboi!* You could be eating—"

He halted. "Eating what?" Mary asked, approaching. "Eating what, Andruss, other than two old rabbits who were too slow to escape the mighty hunter?"

Andruss ignored her totally. His lithe body moved like a streak toward his companion. To Chuck's astonishment he found himself nimbly thrown to one side by the lighter, agile boy. The floor came up fast and he collided with it, half-stunned, amazed and angry. Above him Mary gasped and took a maternally protective step toward any further attack from Andruss.

But he didn't even see her. Still red-faced, he raised the palm of one hand toward Chuck, fending cautioningly, taking the rabbits from Chuck with his other hand. "Listen to me, Chuck," he whispered hoarsely. "Chuck, this is the *will* of the Patriarch. Do you *hear me?* It is *his will.*"

The anger fled Chuck's face at once. He got to his feet, subdued, momentarily silent; Mary stared at his changed expression. He touched the Greek's arm lightly. "I—I just didn't know all that, Andy."

"Sure," Andruss smiled. To Mary's further astonishment, he gave Chuck a swift, comradely hug. At last he turned to her, solemn. "I apologize for the latest difficulty, Mrs. Graham, truly. There will be no more of this."

With that, coatless, he opened the door and vanished into the whistling winter evening. He took the dead rabbits with him.

Mary looked at the door, then held her son's biceps firmly. "Chuck, who is the Patriarch? Answer me!"

"I—can't explain, not now. But I will later, Mom, I really will." Furtive, embarrassed, Chuck snatched his coat from the easy chair by the front window and slipped quickly into it. Snow still gleamed wetly on it. "I'm goin' to Lythia's for awhile. Go ahead and eat, if you want. I'll fix something when I get back."

Deeply confused and equally concerned, Mary turned to Ellen after Chuck slammed the door behind him. The girl had observed the entire confrontation without uttering a word. "Young lady, what's going on here? I want to know, now! What hold do these people have over you kids?"

"*Survival.*" The girl spoke quickly, too quickly. Immediately she regretted the answer.

"*Survival?* What the hell does that mean?" Mary demanded, fierce and fearful.

"Mom, I—I think I love Andruss."

Her head whirled. Frantic, Mary shook her head and the room spun slightly. "El, you've never even been with any other boy alone. You're a child; you can't know what that word means." She saw Ellen about to protest. "No, Ellen, not another word—not now. I simply cannot—deal with it."

Seeing the notepad Ellen had grasped when she arrived, Mary picked it up with idly nervous curiosity, absently glancing at it. There were several childish legends, symbols of girlish affection: ANDRUSS AND ELLEN. ELLEN & ANDRUSS. ANDRUSS, BROUCOLACK. ELLEN, BROUCOLACK.

"What is all this business?" she asked, whirling. "El, what kind of a—a title, or a role, is a 'Broucolack'?"

The girl's movement was sudden. Gasping, she retrieved the notepad from her mother's hand. As she did, Mary saw the angry scarlet toothmarks left on her daughter's throat. But before she could inquire, Ellen had burst into tears and fled the room. Racing footsteps going upstairs.

Silence. Shadows lying like fathomless pools on the cottage floor. Above her, the door slamming behind a daughter she no longer knew. Here, alone, in a strange house called home.

Dazed, Mary stood in the entrance to her dining room with a greater feeling of helplessness than she could recall having experienced before. She stared up the stairs her daughter had climbed; in the distance there was the sound of crying. Desperate now, Mary turned to her hutch, spur-of-the-moment energetic, ripping open a drawer, finding the occult encyclopedia where she had left it.

After some searching, some cross references, she found the word at last and the quite brief, utterly shocking definition: BROUCOLACK, *a young Greek vampire.*

Clutching the heavy volume tightly to her breast, Mary felt the world shift maniacally beneath her feet, twisting on its ancient axis. For a moment she felt she must surely faint.

Was the world going quite literally mad, at last? Did it all begin here, in Thessaly, a virus of insanity that destroyed solid reason and logic everywhere in its careening path? Had everything familiar lost its meaning, become twisted in the folds of lunacy?

She knew then that she could not go on like this much longer. Her friend Martha Cummins had known of a nice little double that was available for a song in Indianapolis. The other half would provide income. Tomorrow she would see about a loan, buy the place virtually sight unseen, and *get them out* of this mad place.

Greek vampire indeed! Idiocy! Resolute, if no less bewildered, she went sweeping up to look in on Joey. She found him sleeping again. Everything changing before her eyes; he slept so much these days and often, so often, awakened at all hours of the night. Could that mean he—?

She shook her head angrily at the ludicrous concept and backed out of his room into the hallway. Then, on second thought, she went in reluctantly to inspect his poor, wounded thumb. Thank God, he was still leaving it alone. The bandage was boyishly filthy, but intact.

It was time again now to prepare dinner. Number 39,461, or was it 39,462, she wondered wearily. Then, with a feeling of terrible exhaustion, she wondered also how many more depressing, silent meals she could tolerate—how many more days she would be filled with maddening questions no one would answer.

Outside the house, the wind screamed like

celebrating fiends, the catcalls of a disco dance in hell. Branches thudded applaudingly against the house, bizarre, rooted creatures trying, she felt, to get in.

"At midnight, then. Is that when it occurs, Vrukalakos?"

"Of course." The lean being nodded, its eyes burning with its only intense involvement in life. "All is readiness, Patriarch. It shall be done."

The old man fixed Vrukalakos with his steely gaze and spoke so that Aristides and Melas heard every word, confirmed what he said. "She is not to be murdered or, *ah*, occupied. Remember? She is to live—if her heart survives the shock."

"Our contract is clear." Vrukalakos nodded, solemnly, an upstanding citizen.

"I regret this matter deeply, but you must be certain that *It* gets into the house. That *It* approaches the woman directly, clearly. She must under no circumstances be allowed to think it is only imagination." He paused. "Do your best to control It. Disposition, tonight."

Vrukalakos's sinister lips drew back in something not quite a smile. "I am always in control, Patriarch." With the others of the Syndic he drew nearer to the *grimoire*, the *Logos*, and all of them extended their index fingers with respect. "Anything that the woman imagines, after this night, will surely rise confusingly from the terrors of Antipodes. Or it will be whatever *we* have chosen for her to believe. For the good of Thessaly."

"Which is precisely why it is regrettable," said the Patriarch, heavily, convinced reluctantly of their wisdom, "but simultaneously an act of good. Of purity."

Respectfully, he lifted the glass container, exposing them, as he almost never did, to the *Logos*. They bowed.

XI

The mortals round me, doomed to many deaths!
—Empedocles

The evening wore on and yet proved, at
dinnertime at least, to become an astonishing
improvement over what Mary had anticipated.
When she went downstairs to prepare the meal,
she had been suffused with gloom. It had
appeared likely that Chuck would be gone and
Ellen evasive or sullen. There was apt to be little
clowning, little warmth, at this meal. She dragged
her way from the refrigerator to the stove, getting
bowls and plates from the cabinet with leaden
hands and spirit.

But to Mary's amazement, the next hour
proved to be Magic Time—something bordering

on a miracle, it seemed just then. Ellen set the dining room table quickly and quietly, without being asked, her attitude accommodating if uncommunicative. And as Mary was lifting the meal from the stove, Chuck entered the front door and quietly slipped up behind her. He put his strong arms around her waist to play "Guess Who?"

"Well, I don't know who *you* are," she responded airily, with courage; "but *I* am a person. *You* are only a people."

"Won't I get to be a person someday, Mummy?"

"Ordinarily, people never ever become persons," Mary replied teasingly, giving the teenager a light kiss on the cheek. "But since both your father and I were *born* persons, well, you have a chance. Someday. If you're very, very good."

It was another old game Mary had played with Barry and the kids during their best times together, another nonsense contest at which she excelled, never losing her sober expression, never allowing a giggle to surface. The children all adored the game—or had, at any rate, before moving to Thessaly.

Now they were playing once more.

It seemed a blessing that Chuck, the big, lovable oaf, was again giving her his goofy grin, even flashing his ghastly partial plate at her as she handed him a platter for the table.

Her good fortune held true even when she sent Chuck to awaken Joey for the meal. Not only was the little boy downstairs promptly, but *dry*—free

202

of the accident that so often plagued him when he slept. He had even washed his hands voluntarily, if not perfectly, and now tugged good-humoredly on his big brother's belt as Chuck dragged him in to the table.

They ate in a cheerful mood, and quite cautiously, Mary began broaching to them her concern, her fear, that she was going to lose them to this town—and to ways which were not their own. "I've heard of future shock," she tried to joke, "but never before of *past* shock."

The message actually began to sound foolish, however, as she looked round the table at her attentive, fresh-faced youngsters. They seemed to be hiding nothing at all; they did not look at their hands in shame or otherwise avoid looking at her. In midsentence, then, Mary found her words faltering as she thought: Could there *ever* have been three more normal kids? Chuck, bolting enough food for two; Ellen, still daintily picking at the foods she chose and cleverly hiding her peas beneath a bread crust; Joey, all eyes, working his way around the plate from the things he preferred to the things he disliked—all three of them listening closely to her every word.

Suddenly she couldn't go on at all, feeling herself the victim of some monstrous practical joke or, at best, of neurotic suspicions brought on by Barry's death. Tears sprung to her light green eyes and her fingertips covered her lips briefly in shame.

"We still want you, Mom," Chuck said matter-of-factly, touching her arm. "We're just tryin' t'fit in here. But *you* figure in *all* our plans. Really."

Even that sounded ominous. What plans? "We'll never leave you for these folks," Ellen added reassuringly, with a glance at Chuck. The girl had cleaned up for supper, all the way to pancake makeup carefully applied to her face and throat. "We're a family, Momma. We only wish that you'd try to like our new friends and see them as yours, too."

"A Broucolack is a vampire!" Mary said suddenly, snapping it out almost in defense as she remembered what she'd read. Her eyes flashed at Ellen as if defying her to deny it. "I looked it up! That's precisely what it said!"

Ellen stared blankly at her mother for a moment. Then a slow, delighted smile spread across her pretty face. "That book of Aunt Jeanne's!" she exclaimed. "The funny, weird one! Is *that* what you think the people of Thessaly are into—*vampirism?*"

Mary paused, frightened by a feeling of unreality. Why were they talking such lunacy? "I—don't know what to th-think," she confessed. "Or what else to think," she went on. "The book says . . ."

"Broucolack was once a Greek god but he walked the earth among mortals and one of them, a genius with lying words, gave him a bad name from jealousy." Ellen's eyes were huge. She seemed pale. Her gaze was so intense, so direct, that it seemed to shine with truth. "Shit, Mom, it's half-myth anyway—and I'll tell you *one* thing:

204

Andruss is almost a one-of-a-kind. Don't think they're all what *he* is." She took a breath. "Andruss's family is so old they say it goes back *before* the vampire legend. It's one of the oldest traceable families in the world!"

"Your neck." Mary said it limply, pointing feebly. "I saw your neck, Ellen—and it's . . . bitten."

Just fleetingly, Ellen tugged the collar of her dress down and gave a clear giggle. "Oh, Mom, you've *caught* me!"

"What?"

"I'm afraid Andruss gave me a hicky," she confessed, reddening. This time she did avert her gaze. "I'd just balled him out when you came home." She looked briefly at Chuck. "I imagine that's why he got so picky with ole Chuckie."

"Andy is a nice guy," Chuck muttered, picking the thread up lightly and stuffing in a final mouthful of mashed potatoes. "He's pretty neat, actually. Smart."

Andy? Mary observed the word, its sound, blinking. How that humanized the boy, *normalized* him somehow. Not Andruss. Just plain, old-fashioned, American-sounding . . . Andy.

She felt numb, her mind awhirl again, out of focus. Was she right or wrong? Could she believe her kids, the way she yearned to? Suddenly *they* were no longer a threat to her; they might be in Thessaly's grip but they still loved her, they would do nothing to harm her. Yet, they were so *united*. Not against her, of course, as much as merely *with* their new town, their new friends—

the special, enigmatic appeal of an ancient heritage. And they were coming close to begging her simply to go along.

A part of Mary longed to make the commitment. She remembered what she'd thought—that anything was better than being isolated from her loved ones. Well, then, wasn't she basically being absurd about it all?

She shook her troubled head, incapable of following her line of logic. "I'm tired, gang, I'm an old dame," she admitted wearily. "I think I'll just skip TV and games tonight and go on up to my room. To relax. Can you do without me?"

Ellen glanced at Chuck. He glanced at Joey. "We'll manage," El said.

"Call me if you need me," Mary murmured, moving toward the stairs.

"Oh: Speaking of Aunt Jeanne," Chuck began, as his mother paused.

"Yes, honey?"

He paused, then said it: "She called when you were on your way home. Missed you at work, I imagine."

"Was she all right?" Mary inquired, anxious.

"Oh, yeah. Sure! She said she was sorry she didn't phone you about some lunch or other but they were transferring her to another school that same day." He sipped on an after-dinner can of chilled Diet Pepsi. "Said she'd call you when she got settled again."

"Thank you, son," Mary said as she reached the bottom of the stairs. "That relieves my mind considerably."

"I thought it might," came his voice from the dining room. It was sincere.

She ascended the steps slowly, feeling suddenly quite old. Well, that was just like Jeanne. You saw her every day for three weeks and then she disappeared for a year!

She took a long, leisurely bath, letting the hot water soothe her jangled nerves, even turning on the faucet again in mid-bath to warm it up. Then she dried herself off, slipped into a robe, and went in to lie on the bed for a few moments. She hadn't decided what to do with the rest of the evening, but there was plenty of time to figure that out after she relaxed a little more. . . .

Fast asleep, Mary dimly heard the hoofbeats, and, for long protective moments, they were a part of her dream. Then she was sitting bolt upright on the edge of her bed, staring in panic at the winter-frosted window across the room. It was a pale, censuring eye staring back.

The clock, she saw in a quick glance, must surely be wrong or she had slept over four hours. It was nearly one A.M.! She gave her head a slight shake, as if trying to be sure that she had actually awakened. God, the hoofbeats had never been so *loud* before, so *demanding*.

She took a deep breath, steadying herself. Have to do something about this imagination of mine, she thought, willing the thoughts, envisioning words. Maybe see Dr. Laird; he might give me a prescription.

Prescription, she thought firmly as the hooves clattered; *p-r-e-s-* . . .

The hoofbeats had stopped.

Not gone on. Not dwindled away, into the distance.

Stopped.

Outside.

Waiting . . .

Mary sat a moment, hugging her arms around herself tightly. She was so cold, so very cold. *That* was it: She was coming down with a cold, she was feverish, hallucinating even. Perhaps the carriage *had* moved on; sure, it probably *had!* It was gone, and she just didn't hear—

A horse whinnied; snuffled. *Waiting.*

My horsie's come at last, she thought inanely, spiritedly seeking the humor in it, replacing one unreal fantasy with yet another, a safer one.

Except it didn't work.

The knock came at the door downstairs. Twice—sharp retorts.

Numbly Mary evaluated them, found the raps solid, peremptory, very genuine. Real. Yet just *two* knocks, not a businesslike three or a friendly ratatatting half-dozen. A faintly and weirdly inexplicable, but real, *two.*

Nonsense, dammit, this was all nonsense. There was a midnight caller, yes, sure, one who had nothing to do with anything so ludicrous as Jeanne's "death-carriage." Now—she thought as she drifted across the room—it might very well have something to do with old Milo Traphonius or his wife. They were getting on, certainly subject to infirmities—nocturnal problems. Why, her *help* might very well be needed while she just

208

dawdled here like a neurotic old maid!

Mary started downstairs in an imitation of her old briskness, persuading herself that it was something to do with Milo, or with Velda. Or perhaps it was a man with a telegram. No, a cute little boy would be there, scarcely old enough to have a job, a zillion zits on his sweet face, and eager for a quarter tip. Or—

Two. Two, more, raps. Sharp; insistent.

She paused, taking a deep breath that shuddered and caught.

Nothing to do now but go down. Less hastily, she descended, holding her floor-length blue robe—an old Mother's Day gift from Ellen, an Ellen she used to know so well—closed at the neck and the waist.

The downstairs was empty, the children all presumably in bed, and it was chilly. A single lamp burned on a table just inside the living room entrance from the stairway. Three corners of the room were clogged with lurking darkness. Approaching the front door, eyes wide and staring, feet cold, she reached past the vase of whitethorn Ellen had placed there to switch on the porchlight.

Mary's heart sank. It had burned out. She saw a shadowy form on the other side of the door. She took a breath then, and slowly—with immense caution—she opened the door.

It seemed an eternity before the light from within filtered out to illuminate the midnight caller, before her green eyes could adjust to the dark. From behind the figure, however, Mary heard the indignant snort of an impatient steed, the alien animal-pawing of a massive hoof. She peered, searchingly, for another moment—

—Before she began to scream.

It was a rasping, choked kind of scream, the kind that would have to come from a woman who had never before lost her modern nerve, her brave iron control, her dignified grip on sure reality.

It lurked there, unmoving.

It reeked with the lambent memory of death, from its putrifying, pale face to its fetid feet. Its eyes were sightless, by normal means, dumb hollow things behind the incongruous spectacles it wore in life. Its mouth was agape with the democratic stupidity of the dead; from it issued the nauseating odor of garlic which someone had inserted tenderly between the cracked, gray lips. Its suit—especially purchased for the occasion of death and burial—seemed grotesquely, crisply fresh and businesslike, except for the snow and the gravesite mud clinging to the cuffs and caking the shoes. Its suit jacket hung nakedly open, revealing a ripped white shirt through which Mary could perceive, agonizingly, the rotted, mangled cavern of flesh where once a human heart had throbbed with life.

It was Barry, two months dead, an arm lifted to her in the mockery of a late-to-dinner, apologetic spouse, presenting, she saw, a solicitous . . . *gift*.

In a translucently white, department-store-dummy bloodless hand with inch-long fingernails grown dumbly in the peaceful fertility of death's grave, hanging by strands of light brown hair, was the slightly shrunken head of Mary's friend, Jeanne Lange.

The two dead heads—one attached, the other unattached—appeared frozen in polite attentiveness, *regarding* Mary Graham. Her eyes rolled back in her own head as the creature who had once been her mate took a sickening lurch across the threshold, *toward her*.

Her own body seemed peculiarly rooted, quite incapable of movement, as the decaying thing's free hand groped upward, fumbled—*caressingly*—for her paling face. . . .

Then, somehow, *It* sensed or reacted to the whitethorn in the vase just inside the door on the end table.

The arm was yanked away, its rotting flesh burnt to white bone from its sheer proximity to the whitethorn brambles. The Barry-thing opened its pallid mouth wide, drooling green garlic, in a noiseless, unheard shriek of infinite agony, its fingers loosening on their dreadful burden—

—As Mary slumped to the floor in merciful unconsciousness.

XII

From what-is-not what-*is* can ne'er become. . . .

But come! but hear my words! For knowledge
    gained
Makes strong thy soul.

—Empedocles

The planet Earth continued, unheeding. Its people started and ended battles (often bloodily), won with brilliance and joy and lost with despair and humiliation; small personal triumphs and abject failures occurred; people showed how much they cared, and conversely, showed that they did not care at all for their fellow beings. Fortunes were achieved, and expunged; talent was finally fulfilled, inventions were discovered or developed; contracts were drawn and broken. Marriage was legalized, consummated, children were conceived, were born, died.

Time passed.

And Mary began at last to sense again the presence of other beings on the spinning planet. It was a coming-back to Time, in a fashion, a resumption of her old internal acknowledgment that she was a part of the conscious world. She slowly returned to the great partitioned ballroom that Time was, readying herself once more to begin the stately old dance anew.

She opened her eyes, and . . . remembered.

Shock—enormous, engulfing—shone from her emerald eyes as she sought to file the details away in a memory less distorted, less unreal, less mad.

Milo Traphonius reached for her with infinite gentleness, took the pale hands raised in stabbing, defensive terror before her shrieking face, and brought them down enough for Mary to see that they were alone in her own bedroom. Her Thessaly bedroom.

Bright morning sunlight infiltrated the drawn curtains and crept on golden feet across the carpet, camouflaged in normality. Everything seemed in order in her room; she saw that she wore her blue robe over a nightgown; a wobbly hand, trembling, told her that her hair was brushed and in place. She put a name—the name of terror—on that old man sitting on the edge of her bed, smiling at her.

"Welcome back," he said cheerfully.

Her eyes, frantically wild and disoriented at

first, blinked several times. Inwardly she made a decision that she'd imagined it all. Blinking, her eyes assumed a calmer glint, and when she spoke, it was quietly, revealing the most passionate wish of her whole life:

"I had the most *terrible* dream," she said, almost conversationally.

"No, dear, you did not." The old man said it with the certainty of fact, forcefully, and shook his maned head regretfully.

"—*Not* a dream . . . ?" Small-child eyes widened in disbelief, and more: Terror.

"No, my child." Milo shook his head. "No dream. It was real."

"Real? That was reality?" She spoke the words as if she might hide from their meaning, as if they contained a trap. "Oh no, *that* cannot be," she assured the old fellow. Her tone was reasonable, sweetly reasoning. "No, Milo, it had to be a dream."

He gave her a reassuring smile but continued holding her gaze. "Barry was, indeed, at your front door. With that . . . thing . . . in his hand. You must know and accept this. You must. It was, all of it, quite real."

She blinked again. "S-such things are impossible. . . ."

"Not for us, Mary. Almost nothing is." He fumbled in his jacket pocket to produce two squares of heavy paper. He gave her one, gently forcing it into her fingers. "Here. *Look.*"

It was a photograph.

Barry, a hideous, otherworldly, dead Barry,

with Jeanne's head, was just turning away from the house—her house—lurching toward a waiting carriage. A death-carriage.

Her hand tremored. "Real?" It was a small voice, wincing as if from a severe toothache. "It happened. It happened then."

He nodded. "You had to see what we can do, Mary. You had to be persuaded to become one of us—for that remains our purpose. Our intent." Milo's chuckle was throaty, affable. "Happily, you did not lose the child you carry. Why did you not tell us you were expecting?"

"H-How did you find out?" she countered, her voice scarcely audible.

"Mormo, my friend the nurse. And we think it's just wonderful. All the good citizens of Thessaly are pleased for you. Truly."

Her mind felt drugged, she realized. Perhaps it was. There were thoughts trying to get through which were being impeded. That word—*impeded; impediment*—meant something to her also. She concentrated. "Why did you consider it so important to persuade me?" It was almost offhanded. "And why didn't you ask?"

"Oh, we asked, my dear. Quite often." He smiled. "Honestly, you are a tough customer—a goddess among modern women. You've earned my respect. I, personally, tried many times, many other ways at first, to get you to *want* to be with us."

"But you all tried to chase us away, first," she accused in the bright I'm-onto-your-tricks voice of a precocious child. "You did! Don't deny it."

He nodded sadly. "We thought you'd be in the way. But I never wished you harm, not any of you. But then we learned about—Joey. It was only natural that we should want to keep his family together. It's merciful to take *all* of you. When we go."

Was she supposed to comprehend that? "Go? Go, where?"

Milo patted her hand, paternally. "There's plenty of time for that, Mary." He paused, permitting a faintly threatening tone to enter his deep voice. "You *do* understand now, do you not, that we are very serious about this? That we can always take more drastic steps to make you all members of our big family?"

Mary nodded quickly. "I do, yes."

Too quickly. "Ah, now-w-w," the Patriarch sighed, "I can see that you are lying again. My goodness, that's a pity. You're thinking of stealing the children and going to the police in Indianapolis. My dear child, that just wouldn't be intelligent."

"It wouldn't be, no," she agreed, trying to nod and shake her hurting head at the same time. "No, wouldn't be smart."

"I will show you why." Milo handed her the *second* photograph.

It pictured the mobile dead body of Barry entering the underground burial site called the Vale of Aphaca, between the parted, great stones. He was trailing after the terrible tall, dark man whom she'd seen there before.

And on either side of the rocks, looking into the

camera and smiling affectionately, stood Chuck and Ellen.

Hi, Mom. We found Dad. Love, your kids.

She began to weep.

"They are prepared to commit you to a home for the insane should you take this preposterous, unprovable tale to the authorities." Milo Traphonius's tone of voice was lightly conversational, stating facts as if discussing yesterday's snowfall. "You have no evidence of what is happening here, Mary. Not one shred. Another, discarded body now fills Barry's grave so there is no sign of grave-robbing. Oh, there's the evidence of these photographs, isn't there?" He withdrew the photos nimbly, yet with a measure of politeness. Then he tore them into tiny pieces and slipped them into a side pocket.

"The children," Mary said, grasping at straws now. "They don't . . . understand you. I can—explain."

His eyes grew sharp, stone-hard. "They understand far better than you."

"I can persuade them to see the truth," she asserted in a tiny voice.

"Only your truth. That won't be sufficient. Not when they have—*seen*."

"How did you steal them from me? How did you do it so e-easily, so swiftly?" she wondered.

Milo looked proud. "We Greeks invented a form of brainwashing, child, some thirty centuries ago. We are genuine experts in a subtle variety of that old skill. And once sold, a person cannot easily change his or her mind." He patted her hand. "But please, don't look on us as *villains*, my girl. We mean no harm to anyone."

She wanted to protest, tearfully, but could not honestly cite an example of how they had been harmed. She felt she should be able to do so, but her mind continued to feel weighty, stodgy, only partly functioning. "How long was I out of it?" she asked at last.

"About a day and a half," he replied. "It is around noon on Thursday. This evening is the occasion of our little town meeting at the Church of the Mycone. D'you recall that I invited you? The Greeks originated the concept of the public forum," he went on, blithely and cheerfully, "as indeed we originated—*most* things. Those things of lasting importance, based upon lasting intelligence. Is it any wonder I take pride in who I am or that I defend it?"

"Milo, I'm so tired," she whispered, sagging back against her pillow wanly.

"Of course you are," he said, sympathetically. "You've been through a great deal, poor girl. You shall sleep until evening, with my friend Mormo's assistance. Then you shall come with us, *see* what is happening for yourself; hear your own children's honest words about what we are achieving here. I'm certain you'll find that reassuring, eh?" He grinned almost boyishly, scratching at his gray whiskered mane. "After that, just the four of us— you, Ellen, Chuck, and I—will get together. To answer *all* your questions. I do believe, pretty Mary Graham, that you will be *happy* to become a member of our family."

"Just the four of us?" It was feeble, accompanied by a frown.

"This is not for such babes as Joey. He shall stay here, with Mormo to care for his every need."

"I thought this all *involved* Joey. . . ."

"Oh, it does!" His eyes reflected passion. "But his time is coming on December twenty-fifth. *That* day—next week—will be our beloved Joey's time."

Methodical, they're so methodical, she thought. After a fatherly pat, he left the room and was replaced by the obese nurse, Mormo, the huge sister with the incongruously perceptive eyes. But even before Mormo reached the bed, the hypodermic flashing in her fat fingers, Mary was asleep.

And, when she awakened later, the sun going down behind the lace curtains, Mormo was yet waiting—eagle-eyed, prepared, polite yet oozing unyielding firmness of intent. Mary gauged her own chances quickly, the chances of escape. Although Mormo was in her sixties she appeared healthy and her great weight suggested a strength that she would not hesitate to use. Forcefully.

The nurse followed her to the bathroom door, waiting outside as she bathed, trying to wash away both the cobwebs that clung to her mind and the terrible state of terror which lurked just below the level of her consciousness, ready to clutch her in icy fear. The hot water streamed over her full breasts; she could not seem to get it hot, or clean, enough. Where could she go even if she left the kids here? To whom could she turn for help? Who in this world, with Jeanne dead, would believe a word she said?

It was all an incomprehensible, living nightmare, a town of madness that was contagious and infectious, spreading like a virus to subvert the loyalties of children, and eventually—surely—to destroy the sanity of adults.

No: That was unlikely, Mary thought as she climbed from the tub, toweling. Impossible, even, in psychological parlance. If she had ever understood anything in college psych classes, now was the time to use it. Mass hysteria was always possible, in any group, of course, given proper stimulus. But after a few days, it had to pass. An entire town could not go mad. Go *wrong*, go *bad*, yes—she thought of Hitler's Berlin—but not technically insane.

Then what were they doing, what *were* they all seeking to accomplish that was worth going to such lengths? How could they do such incredible, terrible things—in the name of *what* unguessable cause? Were they even who they pretended to be?

What prompted them, *what motivated a town*, to go to such mad lengths? And wasn't this just what Milo Traphonius had in mind: making her wonder—making her begin to look forward to his damnably quaint town-meeting where she might, at last, begin to get some answers?

Barry. His poor image came to mind. She blinked it away in incipient terror as it was replaced by another image of him, a later one. . . . No, she had to be strong now, prepared. As steely in her ways as they were in theirs.

She dressed in one of the gowns Barry had liked so much, a red cocktail dress that came to the neck and left her lovely arms bare, her full breasts pressing against the bodice. She felt, as she got ready, the incongruity of her actions: Here she was dressing up, a kidnap victim of sorts, to be led to the council of a town that sought to enlist her cooperation and the aid of her children in some unspecified, unvoiced, horrible crusade.

Mormo accompanied her downstairs. Milo was waiting for her, wearing a handsome black suit and dark patterned tie, smiling—an old suitor picking up his young courtesan for the evening.

She despised leaving the sleeping Joey in the clutches of the hulking caricature of a woman named Mormo but she appeared to have no choice. She got into Milo's Oldsmobile and rode through wintry, chilling Thessaly to the church.

Surprisingly, it wasn't candlelit like the somberly superstitious black mass of the Satanists that Mary had half-expected. The one-room church was well-illumined, almost aglare with modern electricity.

She was equally surprised to find that the entire town of two hundred seemed to have turned out for this meeting. The pews, largely empty for Lamia's services, were crammed with Thessaly's citizenry. Many of them turned to stare curiously at her as Milo led her, stiff-backed, down the center aisle. She ignored them entirely, concentrating on a newly aroused, passionate hope that Milo was telling the truth, that they meant no harm. She found herself clinging to his old arm, and she was startled by the firm, well-developed bicep beneath her fingers.

At the front of the church, once again, Mary was guided to her seat before the altar. Chuck and Ellen were on either side of her, giving her quick, affectionate kisses on either cheek. "So glad you're feeling better, Mom," Ellen asserted. "Me, too," Chuck added with a guilty-little-boy smile. She ignored them as well, staring straight ahead, outraged, unsure of what she should say or do, or, more importantly, what she should feel, other than deep-seated fear.

Then Ellen was whispering in her ear, urgently: "Mom, *listen* to them with an open mind. *Please!* It's for your own good and ours. Really!"

"I may as well listen," Mary said stiffly. "I have no choices anymore."

There were four seats arranged in twos around the altar itself. A banner bearing the Greek "E" hung behind them, and seated there, Mary saw Milo, George Aristides, Nicholas Melas, and Vrukalakos, the keeper of the Vale. She felt his unhuman, evil stare upon her and looked away. Surely *he* was not an influence of good.

As Milo rose to approach the altar, the Reverend Bandrocles came from a front pew, quickly, to occupy Milo's chair. It seemed to be important to them to keep a balance, to maintain four occupied chairs. Methodical, so methodical.

When Milo Traphonius lifted his arms, the two hundred people in the church subsided instantly into silence. He cleared his throat like the bearded toastmaster of an affable business party and smiled down on his town.

"My fellow *akousmatikoi*, the Synod of Thessaly," he began. "Brothers and sisters, all—and Mrs. Mary Graham. We have gathered together in part to remark upon our plans for March, and the most important Commemoration in Grecian history. As you all are aware, there was a time when we were worried about that upcoming occasion, deeply concerned for the safety of the group. But the wondrous, *Logos*-inspired arrival here of the child, Joseph Graham, has given us firm hope and confidence of our continued survival." That word again, Mary mused: *survival*. What could he mean?

"It seems to me," Milo proceeded, "that we need to explain certain matters to young Joey's earth-mother, Mrs. Graham. Please feel free to comment whenever you desire to do so. Mary," he peered down at her paternally, "our history begins beyond the mere dozen years that this little town has been in existence. I imagine you have surmised that much. Ours is, in point of fact, an ancient heritage, one which *precedes* your Christ, the great Buddha, the boy King Tut, even many of the Olympian gods of our own motherland, Greece."

The tiny Aristides waggled a hand, urgently, smiling almost mysteriously from his seat. "Why not begin with the story of Pythagoras?"

"Very well, George, I shall." Milo peered reflectively upward. "Once there was a man named Pythagoras who interpreted and put into concrete practice the essential, germinating genius of a man whom he himself knew slightly— an old man. The result was a rare mingling of great minds, the one aged and dying, the other just beginning his finest contributions. Soon, it was rumored everywhere in that old world that the mathematician Pythagoras had taught his own group of followers the most intensely vital secrets of life itself." He paused for emphasis. "They are summed up, in the usual inadequate way of summation, in the single term *metempsychosis.*"

Since he'd often addressed her personally, his expression professional but mild, Mary looked cautiously up at Milo to inquire, "Isn't that the same thing as reincarnation?"

His expression now was pitying. "Scarcely. Reincarnation is a doctrine showing that human beings, at death, go first to Paradise and thence to a new birth, in a fresh infant form. Much, even all, of that past life is forgotten. Virtually wasted. It has nothing to do with *freedom of choice.*" He shook his head. "We do not really wish to question the Almighty's motives, but from an earthbound, pragmatic view, it is hard to condone reincarnation. Why, the giants of mankind tend to die when their intellectual powers are at their greatest! Viewed so, death becomes an unpardonable intrusion. But *metempsychosis* is the gift of man to men. It is the word chosen to describe the passing of the soul from one body into another body—at death *or* before—with the memory intact. Pythagoras was able to demonstrate that all material existence represented punishment for sins from a former existence. Since he believed absolutely in the basic freedom of all wise, thinking, or contributory men, because he loathed the waste when great men or women died with his rebirth scheduled at unguessable distances in time—the memory destroyed—he proposed something elegantly simple, Mary: He suggested the substitution of one body for another body, *ahead of death*, when one's anatomy was ill and growing decadent."

Mary nodded slowly, beginning to remember what she'd learned years before. "I do recall now that there were various societies which subscribed to the concept of metempsychosis."

"Yes, in one manner or another," Milo agreed, pleased by her knowledge. "Ancient Egyptians, the Brahmins, certain Buddhists, even savage tribes in Africa, and the Hebrew Kabbalists. Does it not make sense to you, my dear, that when one's mortal body has plainly outlived its existence yet the mind itself is richly valuable, the body should be cast aside? *Replaced?*"

"Perhaps. If no one is killed to *get* a new body."

Milo didn't seem to hear her. "Why, I can now recall my own experiences as a hare, a bird, a brown bear—the adventures are absolutely delightful." He was growing rhapsodic, his blue eyes frosting over. "When I was a lion I sensed a sheerly physical power under my command that was sweetly heartening. My finely attuned nose, the sensitive pads of my great feet as they readied to leap, the feeling of being equal to any physical task—for those tasks were simple—are some of my most cherished recollections. The long grass whipping at my tawny flanks as I prowled, in quest of food—the sense of excitement when at last I spotted my prey—well, it was all highly instructive."

Mary stared at the old man. She was amazed; he was claiming that he had literally occupied animal bodies. She feared now that he might lapse into some mad revery.

"You are saying, Milo," she interrupted, "that Pythagoras claimed to know the secrets of immortality through metempsychosis, and taught them to all his followers?"

"Not 'claiming,' child: telling. He *was* able to do so, and did." Milo drew himself erect. "But great as he was, Pythagoras was not the originator, as I already indicated. As Aries creates, ramming his way ahead with fresh concepts, Taurus gives those views substance, a practical foothold. Taurus was Pythagoras's role in history. That of Aries belonged to the fine man of rare, uncanny knowledge—a true god cut from the Olympian cloth: the genius, Empedocles."

"Is the Greek 'E' in this church in his honor?" Mary inquired.

He nodded. "It is. Our church is dedicated to Empedocles, our entire way of life is. Perhaps you'd like to know why, to learn more of him?"

It was probably best to humor the old man. "Yes, Milo, I would."

"He was born at Agrigentum, in Sicily, before the Peloponnesian War. Although he was born wealthy, Empedocles fought manfully against the injustices of the aristocracy. At one point he was like a young Franklin, a youthful Jefferson of centuries later. Eventually Empedocles became a philosopher, a stirring poet, an incisive statesman, a heuristician, and a healer. He was a man who possessed a touch, a mere *look*, which brought health." Milo's eyes misted over, almost as though he'd known the poet. "Empedocles was the first man in history to adduce and address the subject of evolution, knowing far more than that fool Darwin—because Empedocles *experienced* the reality of having *been* lower life. He *lived* as lesser creatures, and remembered."

Mary thought of the werewolf legend, a part of her mind still amused—was that how it began then, with people who believed they entered wolves' bodies? It was incredible that here was a man, in the late twentieth century, who *still* believed it was possible!

"In time," the Patriarch continued, "Empedocles combined his knowledge of science and nature—of politics and medicine—with his unique expertise in magic. *Enoi,* he was incalculably brilliant! He became the greatest seer, or sage, who ever trod this earthen ground, although this was kept from most historians—the same imbeciles who began rumors that his work was recorded, committed to paper. Only part of his poetry endures, in the literature that most men know. He was extensively quoted by Cleomenes before the start of the revived Olympic Games. He taught Pythagoras all he knew about the harmony of the spheres, enabled that mathematician to learn the secrets of life-eternal, through transmigration. It is still an incredible tragedy that his sensitive soul was tortured until he was obliged to die, by leaping into Mount Aetna." Milo's eyes frosted. "It was the only way he *could* be slain, could be removed from this planet—by being forced to suicide.

"But not," Milo progressed, his eyes glinting with pleasure, "not before he had created his finest work. The most valuable work ever achieved by man. Its existence, as I say, has been rumored—rumors of a legitimate *grimoire,* or sorcerer's book. And yet it is a book which is much more than that."

"Much more," Melas cried from his chair, bobbing his head with passion. "Much, *much* more!"

"Why?" Mary Graham whispered.

"Because it is said to contain prophecy telling of every important development in mankind, for two thousand years, including man's destiny. At the end. It is said to contain curers for every one of man's illnesses, even perfect, logical replies to *any* crucial query man might dare pose. The nucleus of every faith, every invention or discovery for countless centuries is said to reside in that book.

"And my dear child Mary," the Patriarch concluded with a deep breath, "all that is *true.* The book—the fantastic *Logos*—exists!"

She stared at the old man in wonderment. She heard a rumbling sound and turned her head. A cart, covered by a drapery of shimmering gold emblazoned with numbers and ornate Greek letters, was pushed gently to Milo's side by Reverend Bandrocles. The minister stepped back, awed. On the cart there rested a glassed-in, thickly huge and heavy unbound manuscript of great antiquity. From where Mary sat she could see the yellowing, crack-paged condition of the parchment. Somehow, even for her, it exuded an aura of incredible age that seemed almost to reverberate in the stunned church. It sat before them emanating a silent power, the repository of weeks, and months, years and decades—of *centuries*—during all of which men and women dropped in death while yet the *Logos* lived on.

Around her, on every side, there had been an instant murmuring of bursting excitement. Just as quickly as it had begun, then, the silence descended cathedrallike, and the people of Thessaly rose from their chairs to slip to their knees in hushed reverence and awe. For in the sense that a thousand years meant an eternity to mankind, the presence of this venerable manuscript from *three* thousand ago seemed almost to have been a part of man's history, *always*.

Chuck, beside Mary, whispered enthusiastically from his knees: "Only the Syndic has ever been allowed to witness *Logos* before! Oh, Mom, the Patriarch has bestowed a wonderful tribute in order to earn your cooperation! How marvelous!"

Despite herself, Mary realized that she did feel flattered. Now she wondered, for the first time, if it was possible that there was any scrap of truth to what they claimed for the manuscript from eternity—any shred of evidence that it might really be so old, that it might actually contain . . . *miracles*.

Milo rested his aging hands with respect and something approaching love upon the top of the protective glass. His voice, low and meaningful, echoing off the far walls of the *megaron*, grew urgent. All who looked at the old man waited for him with an intensity that was electrifying. Mary trembled.

"My people, I have protected *Logos* my entire life, and *with* my life," he spoke at last. His voice was subdued, almost as if a raised note might damage the book in the case. "Until now, it has been seen by fewer than fifty people during the entire twentieth century. Not only must it be guarded because of its age and delicacy but because the mathematical formulae contained in it indicate the means of warfare for which mankind may never be prepared." He paused, finally looking directly down at Mary. "We have no other central object of faith in our church, my dear. No other object of adoration. There are no towering figures, Mary, such as Christ or Buddha, for us to revere, other than Empedocles. To us, all others are recent incarnations of God's best. But *this*"—an index finger gently touched the book container with reverence—"*this*, my child, *is* God's word incarnate from the inception of civilization."

She took a deep breath before speaking, knowing her question was bald outrage: "Has it been carbon dated?"

The silence falling then was not born of awe, but shock, dismay, resentment. She had spoken with a courage she never knew she possessed; she had, in effect, cross-examined the Pope right in the heart of the Vatican. Now the old man was startled; he seemed puzzled, he seemed not to follow her reasoning.

"I mean," she went on, defiant of the staring, furious eyes around her, "how can you *know* it is really three thousand years old? Think, Milo! How can you be so sure?"

His gaze then was one of open antipathy for the first time. And during that dreadful moment, flinching from his fierce stare, she feared for her life.

Then his chest rose and dropped with a deep sigh. He appeared tired, even wan; perhaps, Mary sensed, he was truly disappointed in her. *"Dios Kodion!"* he exclaimed. "I accept these rude interrogations before the *panegyreis*, before the entire Synod—only because I have been obliged to act as your *syndikos*, young woman. Your advocate here. It has been my duty."

"But still," she pressed, persistently, "you have not answered me."

Milo stepped to the edge of the platform, towering above her, a strong old man whose dignity no one would question. "I could reply to you, my child," he began, "that it is because of the information in the *Logos* which I have studied and passed to the Syndic. That our own knowledge proves, simply enough, the volume's antiquity and greatness. But you might then question the intrinsic value of our knowledge, possibly demand a cheap exposition of our powers—as if the Word itself could be utilized for mere chicanery, mortal magic, for mundane entertainment. I will not demean *Logos* in such a way."

· Her lips parted and the Patriarch raised a silencing, commanding arm, his deep voice crackling with compressed fury and outrage. Mary, fearing an explosion of anger, gripped the arms of her chair tightly.

But once again, somehow, he gathered his massive control and inhaled. "Instead, my dear Mrs. Graham, I will reveal somewhat *more* of the truth to you, in order to answer your wholly impertinent queries. How do *I* know that this is, in point of fact, the *Logos*—that this is Empedocles's own vanished writing, the communication to him of God's word? *HOW?*" He appeared literally to grow in immense dignity before her, his gray beard bristling, his dark eyes challenging and vivid. "Because . . . Empedocles *gave it to me before he died.*" The old man's face almost glowed, incandescent with a truth he had experienced and would never doubt.

Mary stared, owl-eyed, when the Patriarch finished, his words echoing like thunder through the *megaron: "Because, my child—I am Pythagoras!"*

XIII

Such empty treasures, myriad and vile,
As men be after, which forevermore
Blunt soul and keen desire—O then shalt these
Most swiftly leave thee as the seasons roll;
For all their yearning is a quick return
Unto their own primeval stock.

—Empedocles

The one-room church on the outskirts of contemporary Indianapolis was as silent as an uninhabited, distant planet of roiling gases when the old man completed his incredible announcement. Eyes—dozens of pairs of them, the clear, undistilled vision and confidence of a town—turned to stare at Mary.

She had felt almost on the verge of fainting when the *pater familias* stopped speaking; and

now, her heart throbbing irregularly, dangerously, she realized with further deadening surprise that none of the others in the *megaron* had
expressed even in the slightest way the astonishment she felt. They gaped at her only to see *her*
incredulity, to see how *she* took the news.

They knew.

Not even Ellen or Chuck looked back to the
Patriarch in amazement. Their hot gazes, turned
to her now, were dispassionate, not even intent in
curiosity for her reaction.

Because *they, knew, too.*

Everyone, indeed, had known but her. *Known,
a miracle.*

Before she could gather her thoughts and
attempt to express them, the bass voice of the
incredible old man at the altar of Empedocles
alerted her again.

"Mary, child, kindly glance around you.
People, my people, yes. But more than that you
see with your modern eyes, much more. You are
looking at my *phrateres*, my brothers of ancient
Thessaly."

Slowly, wonderingly, Mary turned back to him,
her eyes blinking.

"Don't you begin to intuit, dear lady, or to
realize by now, that these kind and gentle people
are truly the people of Thessaly and of other
momentous Greek cities and states of old? You
peer, Mary Graham, at history. These are the
citizens of Attica and Corinth, Laconia, Athens,
and Alexandria and Acharnae." He laughed,
gently; the sound did not scold but was used,

instead, as an educational tool. She was being explained to—alerted, persuaded—by a great teacher born nearly three thousand years before. "All of us have undergone metemorphosis dozens, even hundreds of times, you see. To stay alive, to *keep* alive, a fabled tradition of excellence. And to maintain life for the finest minds—scholars, artists and artisans, scientists, poets—this little world has ever known."

Abruptly Mary felt small, shrinking away before their aged gazes into a condition of little-girlness. It was her schoolteacher Mom up there, lecturing from a platform of experience, wisdom, knowledge—an unassailable, impregnable platform before which the child Mary was rendered puerile, insignificant, futile and unfinished. Her eyes blinked; her head and balance rocked.

"Of course, these are not our original bodies. Those, alas, are dust, lo, these many centuries. Mary, almost everyone in this church, except you and your children—born *minutes* ago—is more than twenty centuries old." He saw her eyes widen in further shock. "You may now believe I look rather like the sketches and busts you have seen of my original form, but this serviceable body was chosen merely for its resemblance. Try, please, to forgive an old man a moment of vanity and nostalgia."

"B-But Andruss," Mary blurted, trying to pull herself together. She glanced at the fair-haired youth near her. "He—"

"Quite perceptive, my dear," he praised. "Yes, Andruss is younger." He pointed. "Your daughter knows the truth."

Ellen, prompt and obedient, spoke quickly to Mary after looking fondly at Andruss. "He became one of us just recently, Mom. In 1885. Wasn't that the year, Andy?"

He gave her a boyish grin, patting Ellen's hand. "This is just my third body, Mrs. Graham. You see, I was dying of smallpox in '85, at a very early age. It was deemed fit that I should continue to seem a boy until I was truly integrated and educated in the Greek way."

"Does that have something to do with why there are so few young children in Thessaly?" inquired Mary, barely above a whisper.

"It's part of the tale." George Aristides, his bald head glowing from the overhead lighting, turned to her. "In most cases—in the case of all original Greeks—one has free choice about the form in which he will incarnate. No one cares to be a helpless and awkward child; the incongruity, with the mature and civilized mind inside it, is unpleasant. Many of us choose a new, aging form as a matter of rank—in order to remind *all* of our experience, our station at the feet of Pythagoras. But few of us care to endure the bodily changes, the general inconvenience, of middle age. If no bodies are available, when the present ones begin to deteriorate, we settle for awhile in the frame of an animal."

"In this century," said Nicholas Melas from his seat behind the Patriarch, "Einstein showed that Time was truly, literally relative. Even unreal, at base. Other people have confessed that they do not even pretend to understand the complex nature of time. For example, if one can indeed predict the future unerringly, if one can *envision* it, then surely the future must already exist in some distant dimension. *Our* people knew the secrets of Time thousands of years before there was an Einstein." He smiled. "Before his native Germany existed."

"M-My husband," Mary began with sudden fear and intensity, eyes darting from face to face. "Barry. Was it j-just one of you, *using* his body— some kind of temporary occupation taught you by the *Logos?*"

The Patriarch looked down from the platform. "I regret to say there was no thinking or sentient being dwelling in your husband's corpse the night before last. Vrukalakos here— the keeper of the Vale of Aphaca—has the knowledge of *reanimation* and guards it zealously. He is unique. It is part of his contribution to our general welfare, but it is not the same thing we do, at all. Vrukalakos has the ancient power of . . . *tasting*, then reviving the dead, who must then feast upon the living for sustenance." The old man, in front of the aging and evil vampire, made a sickened, regretful expression. "Our friend is the father of vampires, the *original* vampire—but only young Andruss shares his gift. Customarily, the keeper's prey are . . . used . . . for purposes diametrically opposed to the high morality of our Church of Mycone. Indeed, it was Vrukalakos who animated Andruss after his first death in 1885. So he does both good and bad."

Mary stared at Andruss, dismayed and finding him repugnant, shrinking from him. Her fingers involuntarily fumbled, tugging Ellen closer to her.

Seeing the confusion, the Patriarch spoke rapidly, palm up: "Do not be alarmed, Mary. Andruss was never an evil soul. He uses his talents exclusively for a swift means of introduction to our ways—and of immediate purification." Pythagoras paused and beyond the church building wintry winds howled at the doors, threatening to burst through. "Your daughter Ellen has been purified by Andruss. She will always be one of us."

"No," Mary whispered, shocked, staring at her only daughter.

"No, no, Mary," the old man said with a laugh, "she will never turn into a bat to fly the night skies seeking victims. No one here but Vrukalakos would select the decaying *demetreioi* or use the properly honored dead in such a disturbing fashion."

"But Vrukalakos *does* turn into horrid beasts," Mary demanded, some of her old spunk surfacing. "Isn't that true? Wasn't he a—a dog, a bat? A bird? A deer who tried to wreck my car?"

The creature's dark eyes widened in fierce animosity as he stared horribly at her. "I wish I had killed you," he whispered. "I'd have enjoyed devouring your entrails. I'd have adored making you move, making you do—terrible things."

"Why?" Mary demanded bravely. "Why do you tolerate him?"

"For good reason. We must. When I lived first," the old man rumbled, his eyes downcast, "I introduced the theory of *antipathies*. Opposites. The Chinese picked it up, called it *yin* and *yang*. Even science tends to accept it nowadays. Opposites which attract, inescapably: man/woman, day/night, black/white."

"I've heard of such things," Mary admitted.

"It was not merely theoretical, I found," said the Patriarch a trifle sharply. "It was absolute fact. One cannot exist without his complement." Now he focused his full attention on her. "Because there is God, there is—an evil one. As there is the good done by me and by my *group* of *akousmatikoi*, there must be the terror achieved by the *individual*, Vrukalakos. Again, if you will, day and night, good and bad. They *balance*, you see, as nature must. Evil cannot be forever destroyed or eliminated. It can only be . . . countered."

"But what do you do with him?" Mary asked, biting her lip to keep from returning the vampire's fervid stare.

"Vrukalakos provides us with . . . services, such as we regretfully require. For example, those needed to procure your own cooperation. In return, he enjoys the gift of eternal life with us. Now, this may not be an arrangement entirely harmonious with your convenient modern or conventional morality. That morality seeks perfection from a simplistic, unrealistic foundation in a real world. But I am no dreamer, my child. I've always employed magic for practical purposes, quite methodically. And the method of antipathies *works*."

"That's not an iota better than the hypocrisy we see around us today," Mary argued, adding with a shudder, "and I find it appalling. How can good people have a partnership with such a repulsive creature?"

Vrukalakos arose from his seat, looming ominously. Before Mary's gaze his face began to alter, to dissolve, as if some vile acid had been spread over its length—and *another* face, that of a fanged and drooling vampire bat, blood in its mad eye, took its place. But then the man regained control with a twist of his cruel, lean body and plunged back into his chair, the face gradually resuming its customary saturnine demeanor.

"This is no partnership," George Aristides reassured the frightened Mary, half-standing. "It is a truce of considerable practical value for both sides. An accommo*da*tion, that is all it is. We know where Vrukalakos is, he knows what we're doing. One hand washing the other . . ." He drifted off uncertainly.

Nicholas Melas cleared this throat. "We require a periodic change of body when our present one shows signs of becoming run down," he said in nasal tones. "Earthly corruption arouses Vrukalakos to action. He procures a replacement, now and again, undefiled by his bite and before its own deterioration has become too advanced. Without this arrangement of ours, Vrukalakos would run rampant on society— uncontrolled—murdering and revivifying as he saw fit."

The man who was Pythagoras saw Mary's unwilted expression and lifted his large hand quickly. "No, my dear, your husband's body will not be employed by any of us. Not any of us. It is, again, at rest. As you saw yourself, in the photographs, it has been merely moved to the Vale of Aphaca."

"I want to go there," she declared, bluntly. "To see that it is properly and decently buried."

A shocked silence descended on the *megaron*. Had she asked so much? Mary wondered. But the old man smiled. "In March, my dear, we shall *all* visit that underground land we call Antipodes. Try not to continue taking all this so very personally."

"I must!" she cried. "Barry and I do not have the luxury of constant bodily replacements. And an awful prophecy Ellen made seems to be true. Now you tell me that my own daughter belongs to you. What did you *do* to get her entirely on your side? What hold do you have over Chuck? Only the, ah, affection he gets from Lythia?"

"It's the same damned hold we will have on you!" Vrukalakos shouted, his lunatic face twisted in a sneering, maniacal grimace.

The *pater familias* frowned angrily at the creature. "Be still, you bloodsucker!" He turned back to Mary. "He makes everything sound terrible," he said, apologetically. "But he is correct, often enough. My dear Mary, we offered your children certainty and safety in an insecure, uncertain world. We offered them friendship, a

241

massive family, the prospects of love, release from the obligation to make constant adult decisions—and . . . *eternal life.*" Seeing her stunned expression, he gave her a gentle smile. "The secrets of metempsychosis are being shared with them, generously. We are now officially offering them to *you*, as well. To you *and* your unborn infant, who can be raised as one of us right from birth. The opportunity, Mary child," he concluded persistently, compassionately, "to *live, safely—forever.*"

She leaned back in her chair, Ellen and Chuck smiling at her. She was astounded, unable to speak. She realized with shock that this was no idle conversation, that they were serious. That these extraordinary people believed it possible to accomplish immortality.

And they wanted her to share in it.

No wonder they went to such lengths, she realized, believing such a miraculous thing and somehow thinking it might be placed in jeopardy.

Could there by *any* truth to this? To *any* of what she'd heard?

For awhile the topics were then changed, and the Patriarch—was he *really* Pythagoras, a legend who had existed nearly three thousand years ago?—discussed with his Synod the coming March.

The Commemoration, he assured them, would be momentous, a unique event in all their lives— one that would forever change them. Preparations were being secretly made by the Syndic with examination of the *Logos* whenever required.

There was some comment from the Synod, which perplexed Mary, concerning the extent that personal belongings might be "taken along."

She felt puzzled anew and felt her headache returning with full force. What were they saying, that they were literally *leaving* wooded Thessaly in March—an entire townspeople—at this occasion called Commemoration? Or was it a collective visit somewhere? *Why* was this happening; *how* did it connect with such a blunt and alarming word as "survival?"

More importantly to her personally, if they were breaking up the town, why did they need her—or, for that matter, her children?

"Sir," she called, raising her hand. She couldn't decide whether to address the Patriarch as "Milo" anymore or not. "Where is the town going in March? Please tell me. What *is* the Commemoration you've been discussing?"

"Commemoration is an annual observation of our people, my dear," replied the old man promptly. "It has undeniably special significance next time. We learned that from the *Logos*. However, I cannot tell you just yet *where* we are going, or precisely why. These, indeed, must be the most important secrets in our history—with the existence of the *Logos* itself excepted. Naturally, such secrets are zealously guarded."

Mary looked around. "Does everyone here know but me?" she asked softly.

"No, no," he chuckled, "you aren't being left out again, child. But my people have a faith you lack. Only the Syndic, our council, knows the full story. We have been doing the necessary computations for more than one hundred years now. This could not be accomplished, however crucial, until your modern America finally produced the computer—which *Logos* predicted almost three thousand years ago, by the by. At last, we became able both to pinpoint the, ah, crucial day next March—and a special way to escape its hideous consequences.''

Her head throbbing, Mary tried to appraise his amiable, dignified and bearded face. Finally she ventured another question. ''Well, can you tell me under normal circumstances what the purpose of the Commemoration anniversary would be?''

The *pater familias* hesitated, reflecting. He touched the *Logos* protective container again, thoughtfully. ''It is the day when spirits are able to rise from their graves and wander familiar avenues, seeking both to haunt and to possess those who are, *um*, presently employing their bodies. A most dangerous period in any year, of course. The occasion is mentioned in most books about ancient Greece and in those writings which concern the supernatural. The spirits, you see, resent our use of their forms because, in life, they were unacquainted with our skillful interpretation and development of metempsychosis. Hence, they expired needlessly; now their souls are jealous and bitter.''

''We are obliged to restrain them from our bodies and our homes on Commemoration,'' said Aristides, ''with branches of whitethorn—such as you used to prevent your late husband's entry—

and ropes knotted in a specific, mathematically precise fashion, then smeared with a blend of pitch."

"In ancient Greece, my dear," the Patriarch concluded ruminatively, "this occasion was called, in full, the Commemoration of the Dead, for they have special powers then. But we shall be utilizing the occasion, in March, for a very *different* kind of uprising." He paused. "And if you simply, sanely, choose to go with us in living forever, I believe that you'll find that this will be your next step."

Part Three

*

The Changed

These monsters attacked men, sucked their blood, and ate their entrails. . . . A generic name for such beings was *lamia,* and whereas the great gods are forgotten, the *lamia* still lives on among the Greek people. The *lamia* is mentioned in the Middle Ages, and nowadays it is customary to frighten children with the name. If a child dies suddenly, it is said that the *lamia* strangled it. An ugly or insatiable woman is called a *lamia.* Such ghosts seemed to be *immortal.* The gods were not so.
　　　　　—Martin R. Nilsson, *Greek Folk Religion*
　　　　　　　　　Harper Torch, Mass., 1961

XIV

His vesture was changed into hair, his limbs
    became crooked;
A wolf, —he retains yet large trace of his ancient
    expression,
Hoary he is as afore, his countenance rabid,
His eyes glitter savagely still, the picture of fury.
                —Ovid, *Metemorphoses*

The patient is in a state of trance, his body is
watched, and it remains motionless, but *his soul
has migrated* into the carcase of a wolf, which
it vivifies, and in which it runs its course.
                —Sabine Baring-Gould,
                Book of Werewolves

That which remained partly human in him,
alive in the most grisly sense, still reacted with
terror each time he descended. Vrukalakos could

not begin to guess what Aether might do to him, since he could not die; yet always, when he stood before the enormous beast, it was his task to avoid an impulse toward trembling.

It was not the creature's size alone that terrified Vrukalakos, though that would have been enough—coupled with its grotesque face, the mouth lined with pointed teeth more than a foot in length—for an ordinary man. Often, in those rare moments when the vampire was reflective, he tried to figure out what it was about Aether that chilled him to his ancient bones. Recently he had abandoned the notion that it was its lifeless, gray skin that lay in sodden folds that, when Aether was angry, grew taut as it stretched out to kill. It was not even the spiny spikes lining its rubbery back. It was, quite simply, the intelligent eyes that, baleful and lined by blood, appraised him so coldly. Aether had no fear at all for what Vrukalakos could do. Aether could do the same, and much worse.

Now the creature accepted the newly purified corpse of Barry Graham with a disdainful, almost regal air. Watching it, Vrukalakos felt himself growing ill. Clearly, he thought, it is not enough.

At last he dared speak to it, his tones honeyed and placating, ever-watchful for one of the clawed things to reach out for him, breaking their perpetual contract. "When next I come," said Vrukalakos, perspiring, "it will be with something *special* for you, my pretty. Something rare, indeed, because it will signify that the compact with the Patriarch is at an end—and we have won, you and I, achieved our glorious triumph at last."

Aether, using one of its eyes, regarded the vampire meditatively. *More*, it seemed to say; tell me *more*.

"Here, great Aether," said Vrukalakos, reaching in his tattered coat pocket for the photograph, holding it high so that Aether might see. "*This* shall soon be yours! You shall again dine on living flesh, flesh that yet contains the mortal soul. His agony, his horror, will be splendid—will sate your appetite for weeks!"

The eyes of the massive beast scanned the photograph of Joey Graham. Aether blinked, appreciatively. Aether belched, and cavern walls rocked.

The old man who called himself Pythagoras was not only as good as his word, spending hours that Thursday night in explanation of many secrets of Thessaly to Mary Graham, but he also spent hours each day with her over the subsequent week.

There was no doubt that he intended to capitalize upon his initial impetus with her. She had planned to consider joining them and knew, now, that he was undeniably using subtle skills of brainwashing to buttress his efforts.

Yet there was, about the old man, as well, a great deal of the kindly, old-fashioned schoolmaster, a rich zeal for his subject, for his history, which injected in his every comment an unquestionable attractiveness.

While privately guarding against these subtle tactics, Mary had gone quietly along with these little learning sessions for several reasons. She realized that the Patriarch would, indeed, ask her children to commit her to an institution if she took the story to Indianapolis authorities. And even though the kids were minors, the first reaction of the police was bound to be that she was palpably mad, so the risk of going to them was too great.

Simply departing—slipping into her Granada and driving away—was unthinkable without her children. Besides, there always seemed to be someone in the house these days, or passing by— cheerful, friendly, and *watchful*—if not the *pater familias* himself. Mormo, for example, who turned out to be not so much a nurse as one of the parents of modern medicine, a full-fledged, experienced physician.

There was also the plain fact that, having learned as much as she had, Mary was filled with curiosity. Her reasoning continued to assure her that there was nothing literal about the "truth" they'd explained to her so laboriously. Despite the fact that more than two hundred people supported Milo Traphonius, adored him, she felt there had to be some other explanation. Something that made more sense than human beings who'd never died in more than two thousand years.

Yet, *those eyes*, she thought. Brilliance, not insanity, shone in every pair of eyes in Thessaly— and clearly, now, great age.

While December winds raged outside her cozy cottage, Indiana snow dumping generous dollops on the houses of the forest town, Mary asked numerous questions and received apparently direct answers—answers that were generally fantastic, but urged upon her in the most immediate, forthright, and convincing of ways.

The death-coach, she was told, had been used for centuries both to bring new "bodily temples" to the Greeks and to remove bodies that were to be discarded. It rode at midnight partly from tradition and partly because, wherever they had lived through the years, people tended to be sleeping then.

As Mary asked her questions, however, often feeling like her old self, there were moments of dull lethargy, leaden feeling, that came over her. A slight, hammering sensation that caused her to forget *other* questions she might ask. Trying as hard as she could to remember them, these queries always escaped her.

She learned that Lamia Zacharius had been only using that present identity, as they all looked upon their current forms as temporary, and willingly exchanged that "temple" for the one of young Lythia. The purpose was to get the quick cooperation of impressionable Chuck, just as Andruss had captivated Ellen. "We knew there would be some subtle pressure upon you to follow your children," the old man told her frankly. "The more we made you feel pressured but isolated, alone with your questions, the more we felt you would one day be adequately frightened as well as curious. In a sense, I guess, we are *all* lamia."

Milo confessed, too, that Mary had been watched by Vrukalakos in the transmigrated form of a yellow dog and that she'd been "wined and dined" at the services honoring Lamia's change, and at the Olympi-Inn. It was as if the old fellow sensed that, by making a clean breast now, his own credibility would be strengthened. And with it, of course, her willingness to join them.

She learned they had come to Thessaly twelve years ago because he, Pythagoras, summoned the faithful from many places. It was necessary to gather and prepare them "for that very Commemoration confronting us now in March."

On the Monday after the town hall meeting, Mary was assured by the Patriarch—who said he rather liked the name "Milo" and found it useful for plain, modern converse—that she was a logical woman who soon would choose to accompany them during their March exodus. For that reason, he explained, the Syndic had decided now to support her and her family financially. They had their own treasury, an ample one built over the centuries, successful in part because of *Logos* and because of astrological timing provided by *Bauernpraktik*—ancient Greek textbooks on astrology. "It could be said," Milo added, "that we are quite wealthy."

At first Mary argued that she couldn't let them support her. She wanted her independence to some degree. Yet it was true, she felt gradually, that these people owed her a lot. At the last moment, she telephoned Greta Bailess at Dutch-Touch Cleaners and announced her resignation.

Overwrought and filled with second thoughts afterward, Mary realized that there was a vital question to ask—one that had been eluding her. It seemed, now, perhaps because of her mother love, to slip through the leaden torpor, almost as if mere phone contact with the outside world loosened Thessaly's hold on her.

"It's because of Joey, isn't it?" she demanded. "If it wasn't for him, you really would not care whether I was with you or not in March. Isn't that so?"

Milo was clearly startled. Obviously, he'd believed her to be incapable of such reasoning just now. "He *is* essential to our plans," the old man conceded. "But—"

"*Why?*" she pressed him, alarmed. "What is there about my Joey that you all need so desperately?"

Suddenly Milo's eyes, his face, seemed to grow before her, though he had not left his chair. He grew, expanded in her consciousness; and there was a quick loss of attentiveness—a decrease in her powers of observation, in her attention span—so that, when it passed, the old man was simply chatting, jovially:

"There was a Scythian high priest named Abaris who worked for Apollo. The god was grateful for his help, presented Abaris with a golden arrow containing magical properties. Because his friends felt he was sacreligiously imitating a god, Abaris sold the arrow to me." He chuckled. "Those were interesting days, Mary. I used that arrow to predict the future, do minor healings, calm storms and even to fast indefinitely. But I seldom did that," he finished with that absurd boyish twinkle, "for I inordinately enjoy a good dinner."

The topic . . . *changed*, Mary thought, wincing. What had it *been*?

"Oh, I also used that bizarre arrow to take the discarded bones of Pelops and create a novel statue of Minerva. Now get this: The Trojans thought it was sent from Olympus directly and called it the Palladium. Ever hear of that?" He chuckled appreciatively, hands linked across his paunch. "It made the entire town absolutely *impregnable*, child. A rather superstitious lot, some of those old cronies."

She smiled, fascinated despite herself. When he spoke like that, people who had been dead *thirty centuries* flickered to life through his clearheaded reminiscences. It made Time shrink; death was democratic; each was equally dead.

She grew increasingly intrigued and drawn to these likeable people, began thinking of them just as "special folks," particularly Pythagoras himself. There was a vitality to him that lent credence to his stories. And the tales she heard only enhanced, despite herself, a growing involvement.

After all, only the counterbalancing Vrukalakos had ever behaved violently and he was largely kept in tow by the eternal compact with the Patriarch. None of the *akousmatikoi* had even used *grimmarye*—magic—for criminal purposes, she felt; none had seized or injured a living body.

They even did their utmost to obtain the "bodily temples" of those without families, those who had led empty, ill, or even corrupt lives. They were then purified through secret services presided over by the Reverend Bandrocles, a most moral man, and, rather than having a zombielike demeanor, the "shells" positively glowed with good health, due to the incisive, time-tested mentalities which were motivated by a peculiar but certainly disciplined morality.

The few discrepancies Mary saw would always be minor, easily attributable to a custom both foreign and ancient.

Just as importantly—as the days slid by toward Christmas—Mary realized dimly that her own natural fear of extinction, disintegration, and loss of personality was becoming more and more distasteful to contemplate. Having confessed to herself, one day, that it was lovely knowing Ellen and Chuck would live forever, it was merely a short step toward admitting that she found the idea tempting for herself.

Yet she still had not actually taken the final step as December twenty-fifth, and Joey's birthday, drew near. She could not have explained even to herself why she hadn't made the commitment, why a measure of her still resisted Thessaly.

Ellen and Chuck dated their Greek friends. Mary found it hard to conceive of Andruss and Lythia as people whose minds were created in other centuries. Now, their behavior around Mary was circumspect, American, even supportive. At length Lythia apologized for having snapped at Mary the evening that the four of them had been playing nude games.

That big lug Chuck even went into the woods of Thessaly on December twenty-third and brought back a huge, handsome evergreen he'd chopped down for Christmas. He bore it back to the cottage proudly, delighting her. Like old times, except for Barry. Just the four of them decorated it: Mary, Ellen, Chuck, and little Joe. She made eggnog, and when Milo and Velda Traphonius dropped by, all six sang Christmas carols as if there was nothing unusual about the origin of two of them hundreds of years before Christ. While they were not Christian, Velda explained, Christmas was a time of joy and gaiety to all of them.

But the following day, Christmas Eve, Mary drove into Indianapolis to buy Joey his birthday gifts. She was both distressed and oddly hurt to realize, midway through her one-woman parade through Washington Square shopping center, that she was watched assiduously by a persistent black tabby. Once she even paused to address the cat, telling it loudly that "you have no right to pry into all my affairs, and I'll thank you not to follow my every move." Mary was terribly embarrassed and not in the least amused when she realized that a number of Indianapolis people had overheard her one-sided conversation with the cat.

And that turned the tone of the afternoon of the twenty-fourth all wrong. Now she was shocked to see the differences between the society where she had lived and her new one, which, much more than she had realized, was altering and absorbing her with nearly magical alacrity.

These busy shoppers, sometimes rude as they collided with her and sometimes Christmassy-cheery and full of jovial salutations, were noticeable, she saw, for their glaring *individuality*. The clear-cut, unmistakable distinctions between each of them. No two Hoosier shoppers, store-keepers, or sales clerks were alike—not even the Santas. She saw, dimly, that in the absolute commitment they had made, Thessaly's Greeks all appeared to have been cut from the same obsessive cloth.

The great, green trees on the mall and glittering in individual stores made Mary nostalgic, causing her to recall parading the same route on so many occasions with Barry. Memories she had unconsciously shelved came flowing back. It was all, suddenly, such a painful wrench. She felt torn by ties of the past, of roots that were firmly planted in American, Irish, and French good earth, where Greek gods and sorcerers and mathematicians were subjects only for film spectacle.

She bought a single gift for Joey, at last: a shiny red dumptruck almost large enough to drive. Then she went out of the center to locate her car. She found herself shortly driving into a snowfall that acted as a symbolic ending to Indianapolis; and she grieved for her loss.

The last thing she saw before confronting U.S. 40 and the short trip eastward to Thessaly, was a tiny Catholic church atop a hill, the cross on the outside shimmering in the snow, the old building a warm shelter which part of her longed for more than anything she could remember in her life. . . .

On Saturday, December twenty-fifth, millions of people celebrated the birth of Jesus Christ.

Mary, Ellen, and Chuck Graham—in company with what seemed to be the Syndic and three-quarters of the vaster Synod—celebrated the birth of Joey Graham.

Joe was so inundated with presents that Mary found a stray, sane thought in her head: *What,* no frankincense and myrrh?

Joey was his old self again, and more. She had never seen him so ecstatically happy. Like a pale young prince, he accepted each gift graciously, and after ripping the bright wrappings away, even managed to mumble his thanks before moving on to the next in an endless assortment. She realized that they'd come close to *filling* the boy's bedroom. The fancy wrapping paper, ribbons, and cards—one tastelessly was captioned "Honoring Our Savior"—were scattered all over the downstairs of the Graham cottage like autumn leaves before a storm.

Midway through the festivities, the Patriarch himself arrived and presented to the new ten-year-old an ornate, hand-carved chair perfect for his small body. Joey seized it with tearful gratitude, showering the old man with kisses. He then used it as a miniature throne for the remainder of his package-inspections.

Things began to change, gradually. While she smiled, oohed and ahhed with Joey and the others over each present, Mary understood that the boy was being terribly spoiled. Even corrupted. Eventually, in fact, his performance became absolutely loathsome. Occasionally he followed a grunt of curt thanks with a request that the gift be exchanged for "somethin' better." When he happened to break a toy, he tossed the pieces aside with a grand gesture, muttering something that might have been "goddamn ole cheapskate."

Worse, when he reminded Milo of his promise to allow him to shovel snow, and the Patriarch replied that it "shouldn't be *you*, lad, under the circumstances," Joey rose from his chair and kicked it halfway across the room.

About four in the afternoon, Mary succeeded in putting the sated and weary little boy down for a nap. He'd been up half the night before in his anxiety and hunger for what he termed "loot," and now he was exhausted. "Poor little Joey," she said, beside his bed. "What are we doing to you?"

She, too, was weary, she realized as she sat down at a table bearing the crumbs of Joey's huge birthday cake. She was joined by the Patriarch, her other children, and Reverend Bandrocles. They beamed on her—*damn, I feel like the Virgin Mary*, she mused—but it was also their appreciation for her own efforts.

Much of the nagging, sonorous sound that had been plaguing her every time she'd sought to ask certain questions, had subsided now. Imploringly, Mary looked to the old man, the leader.

"Well, it's happened," she sighed. "The prince has had his birthday. He's ten. Can you tell me now, please, why you and the others have such abnormal interest in my son?"

The Patriarch nodded somberly. "Yes, I can. And I thank you, Mary, for your patience." He clasped his large hands together almost prayerfully and hunched forward, his gray beard narrowly escaping a plate with chocolate ice cream puddles. "It begins in legend, my dear. One as old as civilization. It was prophesied by *Logos*." He paused. "We were, *ah*, expecting Joe all along. Before you got here, we'd begun to wonder if the unthinkable had happened and our calculations were in error."

She stared, surprised. "How could you possibly be expecting my boy?"

"Among my people, my first *phrateres*, Mary Graham, there has always existed the legend of a fair-skinned, blue-eyed boy who would be born at a time symbolically *co-ruled* by Saturn and Jupiter. December twenty-fifth, a cuspal period in many years, astrologically speaking. I might add," he continued, "the boy whom our legend anticipated was to be born . . . *with a harelip*."

Mary gaped at him, astonished. "What's really the truth, Milo? You really have . . . anticipated . . . such a child for centuries?"

The old man's nod worked with a deeply sincere expression. "For quite a long while. We'd have been certain at once, had Joey been, as well, the seventh son of the family. But our research informed us of something you may not know: For seven generations of the Graham family there *has* been a boy-child. A blue-eyed boy, at that." His expression was solemn. "Consequently, we knew that Joey was the child predicted: Our spiritual leader, and that rarity: *a born vampire.*"

"Oh, my God!" Mary covered her mouth with her hands. "Joey is . . . like Vrukalakos?"

"Not in terms of what awful things he does, not at all." The Patriarch touched her hand sympathetically. "Allow me to put it differently. Joey will become the replacement for Vrukalakos, but a *good* vampire. That despicable keeper of the Vale doesn't know this yet"—his eyes burned into hers—"and clearly he must never know it. With Vrukalakos, we've known only the balance of legend. The elements of which I still may not speak." His sigh was heavy. "We cannot go on living with that monster another millenium. You were correct, Mary, for he even practices anthropomancy."

"He practices *what?*"

"Divination by studying the entrails of human beings, a practice begun with Monelaus in Egypt. Heliogabalus also practiced the filthy art. So did the slain Julian, the Apostate." He snorted. "All, as today, in the name of scientific progress. Fortunately, the others did not have immortality, which Vrukalakos possesses. Until, that is, we revoke it."

Chuck, fascinated, leaned forward. "How can that work?"

"Just leave it to me," Reverend Bandrocles put in, eyes shining. "You should not have to deal with the evil fostered by him."

Mary drummed her fingers nervously. "What

of the element of danger to my son?" She paused to look searchingly in Pythagoras's ancient, wise eyes. "I still don't understand why Joey can replace Vrukalakos, or how. What is special about him?"

The *pater familias* reached into his suit jacket and withdrew a photograph of the famed Eleusinian relief. Picturing the goddess Demeter regally raising a sceptre aloft, if also showed Kore—a buxom woman with her right hand resting on the head of a ten-year-old child. The boy, nude, had a harelip. "This sculpture was done four hundred and forty years *before Christ*," Milo explained.

"The child," said Bandrocles, "is Triptolemus."

"And he is, as well," added the Patriarch, "our young friend Joey."

"How . . . ?" Mary asked limply. "Who is—was—Triptolemus?"

"You have seen him in sculptures and paintings, many times," Pythagoras continued, "often bearing with him a cornucopia. Remember? A horn of plenty. Of wealth, symbolically of life itself. Sometimes he is called Ploutos, but no matter. Today there is little known accurately of Triptolemus, but Homer spoke of him being content who had seen the lad, even his blessed image."

"That sure don't sound like ole Joe!" exclaimed Chuck. Ellen smiled.

"Silence!" the Patriarch snapped. "Triptolemus was, in personality, a rambunctious, hyperkinetic youth. But to those who could see through, to the heart, there was great joy—and health. Sophocles said much the same. Aristophanes celebrated Triptolemus and the Eleusinian Mysteries alike as divine."

"Tell her why," suggested Ellen in low tones, her gaze evaluating her mother's face.

"For the first time there was a concept of the underworld as a happy place," Pythagoras explained. "So long as one knew *how*, and *where*, to go beneath the earth. We know, now—aided by *Logos*—that Paradise and Hades occupy the same general geographic realm in the earth, but on different psychological levels. Indeed, dear Mary, some psychologists intuit that the underworld was the unconscious mind, with all its potential for both good and evil." He lifted a pointed index finger. "And young Triptolemus symbolizes a guide for Greek initiates. A little child leading his elders, as your Christian teachings have it. Just as *your Joey*," his gaze held Mary's firmly, "is the *reincarnation* of Triptolemus and will become *our guide* to Antipodes, at Commemoration time. Our spiritual guide."

Mary hesitated, remembering Ellen's somnambulistic prophecy of doom in Antipodes. "Do you mean that you are all going to—to Paradise? *Heaven?*"

"Not," replied Pythagoras levelly, "in the literal sense of the word. Our goal remains, unalterably, that of ongoing life. And its continued means remain that of sweeping change."

For a long moment it was silent except, outside the cottage, for the *drip-drip* of slowly melting snow. The sun was out and shone with a dull, hot glare on the woods beyond the french doors.

Mary lifted her chin, searching the old man's lined, strong features. "You don't really *believe* any of this stuff, do you?" She covered his veined hand gently. "You don't actually think Joey is a literal incarnation of Triptolemus, do you?"

"It is a shame your thoughts must ever be clouded, for you are perceptive." He uncrossed his thick legs with a great sigh and arose, beginning to pace round the dining room. "I am a man torn not only between eras of historical time—*epochs*—but between the practical realities of this planet, and the universal enigma of God the Almighty, and His puzzling nature." Milo was agitated now. "I no longer know what one is to believe—what *should* be believed—or if *anything* should be believed. I am too old for all that, Mary—or too young," he confessed, turning back to those at the table. He leaned forcefully upon his hairy knuckles. "But I am realist enough to know that *your* faith, with an actual embodiment of God, has had incalculable spiritual appeal. My people, you see, are human. They require confidence, inspiration, in the presence of social trauma. Your Jesus leads many troubled people through periods of dark crises in the corridors of life and that must be reckoned to the good.

"Yet we of Thessaly," he sighed, "have no such embodiment. We 'buried' all our old Olympians. Tomorrow, however, we shall again have an embodiment to save us: Joseph Hadley Graham, the living reincarnation of Triptolemus."

Reverend Bandrocles's eyes blinked in solemn support and understanding. "Just as the coming of the Messiah was predicted—*expected*, mark you—for thousands of years, and still is, by many faiths, so it has been with our Triptolemus. We *need* him," he continued, "we *require* him for *hybris:* the conviction of our certain success under great trial."

"I still don't get it fully," Mary argued softly, her eyes moving from face to face. "For *what* time of trial must my little son be your embodiment of good, your cornucopia of success, of life itself? *What* crisis?"

For some while Pythagoras regarded her quietly, his expression as blank as that of Nicholas Melas. "We cannot tell you much of that, as yet. Perhaps you have the right to know a measure of it now." He nodded with appreciation. "You are a brilliant and perceptive woman, my dear. It will be pleasant knowing you at a moment when I have selected a less aged and gross body." She flushed and smiled. "Part of our ritual in the Syndic calls for a waiting period of 'seven times seven days.' Forty-nine. We knew that Triptolemus would have his birthday on December twenty-fifth, your Christmas, our starting point."

"And forty-nine days from that date is February twentieth," Chuck put in, proud of what he knew, "the beginning of the Pisces zodiacal period next year. The period including, as the Patriarch pointed out, the Commemoration of the Dead."

"And at that point," the old man picked up the

thread, "the Syndic and I must take the *entire* Synod—all Thessaly—through the Vale of Aphaca to Antipodes. In order to continue our eternal survival as living human beings."

"But where does Joey fit into that?" Mary demanded. "You don't think a ten-year-old boy can literally be your guide beneath the earth, in that terrible graveyard, where he's never even been!"

"Allow me to finish," Pythagoras urged politely. "There, we shall surely be confronted with something . . . quite *monstrous*. A challenging problem. One that only Vrukalakos has ever dealt with, and it is part of his hold on us. Its name, my child, is *Aether*. But I can tell you no more of our plans now. When the creature Vrukalakos dies, your Joey will be able to deal with Aether."

"But what is Antipodes?" Mary persisted, touching his arm. "Where are you going— beneath the earth?"

"Awhile longer, that is our secret." The Patriarch took a deep breath. "But I can say that your Joey Graham—*our* Triptolemus—will provide us with the spiritual strength and moral endurance to enable the good citizens of Thessaly to survive forever." He covered her hand on his arm, squeezing it gently. "And I have endeavored to make it clear to you, Mary, that if *you* choose, you too may survive with us. Forever."

XV

And then we came unto a roofed cave.
A joyless land,
Where Slaughter and Grudge, and troops of
    Dooms besides,
Where shriveled Diseases and obscene Decays,
And Labors, burdened with the water-jars,
Do wander down the dismal meads of Bane.
                  —Empedocles

The ceremony to introduce and enshrine young Joey Graham as the living Triptolemus was a simple, unremarkable religious service at the Church of Mycone. Everyone in Thessaly squeezed reverently into the *megaron* to watch the ancient rites, taught by the *Logos* and enacted by the Patriarch called Milo Traphonius and by Reverend Bandrocles. When at last it was done, and Joey was hoisted to the old man's broad shoulders as they walked outside to pause for commemorative pictures, a jubilant shout went up from every throat. Joey beamed down on them in a mood of ugly sublime pleasure. From the top of his blond towhead to his new tennis shoes, Joey had never been more arrant, more irritatingly grand.

Mary bit her tongue, lapsing into further inaction and indecision. This mood stayed with her as the new year began and as January turned into February. The days crept by, and with their passage, a sluggishness spread over the pregnant woman that she could no longer seem to combat. Everything was done for her; she seemed to have little free will. It was pointless to fight city hall.

Much of her time she spent studying and trying to help her newly accepted Thessaly companions prepare for March's Commemoration, ignoring whenever possible the changes occurring now in all three of her youngsters. Choices had to be made about the possessions to be taken when their exodus from the small town was made. The Patriarch had declared that everyone would be allowed to bring anything that he or she could carry that *wasn't dated* specifically—such as magazines, calendars, clothing of marked style, and the like. Milo issued to each man, woman, and child new, special clothing to be donned at a given moment in March.

Mary was dimly aware that she'd been under no further pressure, and she was glad of it. Apparently they considered her unprotestingly out of the way. Now she examined the clothing for a clue to the destination of the entire Synod. She'd come to have such admiration, even awe, for the old man that she half-expected clothing that gave an impression of manufacture for another planet. Something gossamer and sheer, with a shining helmet and bizarre laser gun. Instead, these clothes were not unlike maternity garments from her own mid-1960s. Only her fingertips and nose told her that there was a distinct difference in fabric. When she asked the Patriarch, one morning in early February, as she met him at Nick's general store, the old fellow smiled and offered a single, monosyllabic reply: "Fruit."

At home, smelling the maternity dresses again, she thought now that she did detect a faint fragrance of oranges. Was that the sly Milo's power of suggestion? She was really too muddle-headed these days to think it through.

The children had never been happier, Mary decided, watching their willing efforts on behalf of the community. It dawned on her that they seemed to have no traces left now of the United States of the 1980s, except the language itself. They were only eleven miles from Indianapolis, yet more than twenty centuries away. They had stopped going to school, and strangely, she had heard nothing from the offices of attendance in Indianapolis about their absences.

Young Joey was being accorded every courtesy. He was allowed to come and go as he pleased at every home in Thessaly, without knocking. A good-luck charm, she supposed. She wanted to thwart his move to the Thessaly side in a *remembered* kind of way, and to thwart his further spoiling; but she was practically one of them now herself and nagging hammers again began to pound when she tried to reason her way to a logical conclusion.

Besides, she found herself continually drinking a marvelous light wine brought to her daily by charming old Velda Traphonius. It was "so good for your baby and you," Mary was reassured; and with every sip, her will slipped farther away. Now she was often troubled with generally unfit feelings and more preoccupied with the prospect of first holding her new child. If it was a boy, his name would be Barry, Jr. And whenever she *did* feel uneasy, Mary recalled what the Patriarch had said—that wherever they went, there would always be a place for her baby. Quite literally *always*. Could she forsake such lifelong security for little Barry? Soon, she came to believe Pythagoras's every word and to depend on each of them.

Where the other children were concerned, Ellen and Chuck strove to be themselves around her, El being sweetly feminine and Chuck making his little jokes. Just when she needed them. In an odd way, she felt increasingly like a person living unfairly on welfare. One of the teenagers would repeat to Milo a glum or dubious mood of hers, and within an hour, the old man was stopping by with a tray of thick porterhouse steaks or a basket of fruit. His kindnesses were so plentiful that Mary could not see them as blackmail. Wasn't it petty, really, to cavil when her whole family was being treated so wonderfully by the Patriarch?

Joey's arrogance grew as time passed. She found it hard, in her sober moments, to avoid concluding that he was a permanently ruined ten-year-old. She would watch him perching on his hand-carved chair, a tiny blond god on his throne, and her heart ached for what was happening to him. No longer could the sleepy-eyed Mary reach Joey at all. He only tolerated her, at best, with a grand manner she was coming to detest—and fear.

At last, the first of March came and Thessaly's snow lay in shreds of limpid pale memory on an uncaring breast of earth. The town was decorated and protected, against emerging spirits, by white-thorn and pitch-smeared rope hanging everywhere. On the second, a meeting was called at the *megaron.* "Now we'll find out *where we're going!*" cried Chuck with enthusiasm.

"Yes," Mary answerd him softly, going for her coat and finding it heavy. "Soon it will be over. One way or the other, an end to this." She yawned.

The crowd, composed of the entire citizenry of Thessaly, subsided into silence instantly when the man who called himself Pythagoras stood before the church altar. He seemed, this day, younger and stronger if anything, his confidence and sense of leadership almost something you could touch. His cool gaze swept their eager faces, and he beamed on them.

"Empedocles first predicted in the *Logos* what

hundreds, even thousands, of psychics and astrologers have been prophesying for a considerable period of time: that the planet Earth is soon to confront its final days, as an outcome of the final war." A murmur of anxiety arose and he lifted a palm against it, casually. "All the best minds of Thessaly's scholars have, without knowing always what they were doing, checked it many ways with our own mathematical formulae and the IBM computer." He paused, raising his bass voice. "We have discovered that on March twentieth, the start of the Aries period, this world—*will be decimated!*"

The silence was deafening. "Who will survive, Patriarch?" Nicholas Melas asked finally, speaking for them all.

"Only a handful of life, of any kind, will survive. And no one can tell what proportion of that shall be *human* life—or where on this globe it will be found. There are too many details, too many absences of key data. As you all know, we are immortal so long as our normal human bodies survive. But no one," he advanced slowly, firmly, "*no one* survives on a planet with no vegetation. We cannot live long on a world without bodies to inhabit. And while there will be all too many of them left, after the bombs fall, the ones which remain will be uninhabitable, unclean, full of radiation beyond purification, just as the houses, buildings and cities themselves will be."

The feeling in the *megaron* was of having been betrayed by the Patriarch. Wasn't this to be a special, a celebrant day? Weren't they to learn how they would survive forever?

"That is why, my *phrateres*," intoned Pythagoras, "we must leave. All of us must go elsewhere, and continue to live."

George Aristides squeezed his wife's hand and looked anxiously up at the old man. "Then we *do* have a chance to survive, with Joey's assistance?"

The Patriarch caressed *Logos* lightly. He nodded slowly. "In Empedocles's great *Fragments*, he wrote: '*When down the Vortex to the last abyss Had foundered Hate, and Lovingness had reached The eddying center of the Mass, behold Around her into Oneness gathered ALL.*' And in our sacred work, he spoke often of that ghastly Vortex—a rift, in the wall of space and time. Students have puzzled over it, some postulating its existence, for two thousand years and more. For Empedocles spoke always as if he knew *where* the frightening Vortex lay, and *how* to use it. To use it in order to *escape* this space, *this* planet, *this* time.*" The old man shut his eyes, prayerfully. "And blessedly, my people, he *did* know. Empedocles told me the secret even as he was dying, lo, those centuries ago. And how to interpret his law, his direction, in that lost masterwork of his called *Logos*."

"Then where *are* we going, Pythagoras?" Vrukalakos demanded, his hot eyes gleaming madly. "*Tell us!*"

They were full of questions now. "To another planet?" asked Reverend Bandrocles excitedly.

The old man shook his maned head.

"*Forward*, then—to the future?" inquired

young Chuck Graham.

"*Backward*, to our great past?" pleaded Melas.

Pythagoras shook his great, bearded head and raised a broad palm. "Patience, *phrateres*, and I shall tell you. There is no future for this earth," he said bluntly, as silence fell. "We cannot return in time. That is a paradox and nature does not permit them. We have no spaceship with which to make uncertain travel to another planet."

"*Where*, then?" It was Mary, startling herself, her voice quietly intense. She hugged her unborn child. "*Where are we going?*"

"Beneath our feet, my children," the Patriarch rumbled, "to what we have called Antipodes—led by our reborn Triptolemus. The *Logos* instructed me to come to this town, in this state, in a nation not then dreamed of by anyone else, anywhere, but the genius Empedocles. He cited the longitude and latitude. He sent us to this place we call Thessaly, its ley lines foretold, its rates of vibration perceived, nearly thirty centuries ago." He spread his wide palms. "Beneath us, in a land of myth and proper Grecian fable, a land I once imagined was populated by god-men, lies . . . *the Vortex.*" His sober eyes, as he hesitated, reached every face beneath him. "There are no god-men there, perhaps the reverse of that. I was not wrong, however, about the existence of that place we seek: *counter-earth*, predicted during my first lifetime—a whirling, swirling mass vivified by the four elements: the water of Thales, the air of Anaimenes, the fire of Heraclitus, and the earth of my own original interpretation—that earth *below* us. There, we shall find a nebula suspended, free of *all* elements, the perpetually enigmatic Vortex into which no man has dared step before."

While all of them tried to absorb and perceive the aged fellow's words and intuit his meaning, Pythagoras took a deep breath and then grasped the ancient manuscript—free of the protective case—lifting it high above him. Now his deep voice cannonaded at them, boomingly reverberated in every shadowed corner of the *megaron*. "We know, *now*, where that Vortex is, and how to accept its alteration in our own bioelectronic field of force—all that we've needed to know! Together, *phrateres*, we shall all step into that spinning nebula which alters our vibrational rate and thus escape—on March nineteenth, at 6:06 A.M.

"—To go," the old man finished with a roar of inspirational confidence, "to where the last, angry war of unprogressed mankind will *never occur!* To the *counter-earth* I've long anticipated! To *another dimension of the planet Earth!*"

XVI

There budded many a head without a neck,
And arms were roaming, shoulderless and dire,
And eyes that wanted foreheads drifted by. . . .

Creatures of countless hands and trailing feet,
Many were born with twofold brow and breast.
Some with the face of man on bovine stock,
Mixed shapes of being with shadowed, secret
    parts. . . .

—Empedocles

At last the long days of preparation were nearly
at a close. Within a week, the long-lived citizens
of little Thessaly, Indiana, planned to disappear
from the face of the earth. Within seven days they
intended to be on their way to a life that was only,
in most respects, microscopically different from

278

what they had known in their own dimension.

In fact, according to the Syndic's careful studies and computerized statements of probability—a printed booklet was distributed to everyone, including Mary Graham—it would be a world less advanced in only a few key, scientific ways. The most notable of these was that, in the alternate dimension (which fully accepted itself as the planet Earth and would have been as surprised by the alternate dimension from which Thessalonians came as ordinary earthlings would have been to know about counter-earth), atomic power had never been successfully unleashed. There had been fewer wars, partly due to a certain psychological inclination toward isolationism and a lessened psychological need for expansion and interventionism, and the pressing need to split the atom had never developed. Instead, the other dimension's people—in other ways at a state comparable to that of this world during the 1950s—were, according to Pythagorean and computer analysis, passionately involved in space exploration. Not only had men already been to the moon and a space platform successfully achieved, but several astronauts had already landed on both Mars and Venus. Pythagoras was anxious to learn, when they were safely esconced in counter-earth, whether the altered timing of achievements and the subtle distinctions in human psychology would mean that facts *exterior to* the planet Earth were rendered different as well. "What I wonder, Mary," he explained to the pregnant woman one afternoon, "is that if the qualities intrinsic to counter-earth are strikingly different, will the people there then find that the inner planets of the solar system are inhabited? Or were?"

It did not alarm any of them to consider starting over elsewhere. People were apt to remain people; besides, the citizens of Thessaly had spent centuries being "different" from others. From their standpoint, it would seem that they were merely stepping *back* a few decades in time—but guaranteeing themselves innumerable years of future life.

One of the most notable changes over the past weeks was, quite simply, that Mary herself was going along.

By now, the thirty-eight-year-old brunette was scarcely recognizable as the woman who had moved to Thessaly with her grieving family. Her flexible but principled mind had been tortured with personal loss, suspicion, terror, incessantly intense enigmas, altered realities, a feeling of isolation and alienation from her own children, with the obligation to assimilate shocking declarations for which she had little preparation. Without even realizing the exact moment when her decision to go was reached, Mary knew—with the kind of ill-defined, trusting certainty that a third grade student anticipates being a high school freshman—that she would simply, unprotestingly accompany all the others.

Really, there seemed to be literally nothing else to do. Her entire focus of attention was on her unborn child and wanting to remain close to and needed by her living children. Physically bulky and mentally sodden, her ties with Indianapolis cut, she could only leave the problems of reaching a new dimension—counter-earth—to wiser heads. Experts who promised that she would be cared for.

Mary no longer questioned whether the formidable old man she'd first known as Milo Traphonius was Pythagoras or just a brilliant psychotic whose obsessions were marvelously envisioned and projected. She no longer questioned whether the townsfolk were thousands of years old, or merely the Jonestown-like unthinking and neurotic followers of a man of great willpower and faith. She no longer questioned whether it was even possible to pass into another dimension, whether it could be done safely, or even whether another dimension existed. Mary no longer questioned whether the end of the world—*this* world, "her" world—was truly coming, or if, perhaps, the end lay ahead only for those sick people who believed in it. She no longer questioned such things as self-fulfilling prophecy, mass hypnosis, or the unique efficacy of absolute faith.

Mary no longer questioned anything.

Mary was now a perfect citizen of Thessaly, absorbed, fitted-in, routinized.

For days upon end she would sit obsequiously in the ill-kept, cluttered but safe living room of the Graham cottage, pouring glass after glass of the treated kykeon wine brought her regularly by the maternal Velda. The bottle was ever-present these days, fondled as often as she had once held the photograph of her husband Barry and looked to his dear image for guidance.

No one nagged her. The television set wasn't being turned on, except now and then by her son Chuck, because the activities, dramas, soaps, and laughs of the real world beyond Thessaly now seemed both confounding and foreign. The only reading she did was in the writings of the ancient Greeks; she used it, unnecessarily, to fall asleep at night. In truth she was sleeping very well these days.

On this particular evening, Mary burped gently and patted her large abdomen with foggy tenderness as Ellen burst through the front door. The girl's face was contorted in something approaching hysterics. Mary looked up, seeing the expression, and frowned. Was El going to ruin her fine mood, her medium-high?

It was so peaceful, so wonderfully mindless. Joey was deep in a huge coloring book depicting Olympian gods and goddesses doing magical things, industriously at work in his little throne-chair, and Chuck was out at Lythia's place, doing God-knows-what. She bit her lip, amending her thought: doing teenage things. Wasn't everything just fine? Why did Ellen have t'come in now and look so much like she wanted to spoil it all?

The girl sagged onto a couch near her mother, burying her face in her hands as her shoulders trembled with some inner emotion. When she was able—quite unprompted by Mary—she looked up, her face streaked with tears. "Mom, I've—I've done something awful. I—*did it*, with

282

Andruss." She swallowed hard. "I had sex with Andy."

Mary stared at Ellen uncomprehendingly. She'd thought Andruss was with Chuck, at Lythia's. Apparently not. That confused her; it meant, she saw vaguely, he had lied to her again. Fuzzily, she inquired, "Do you know where your brother is?"

"Mom! Did you hear what I said?" Ellen's shoulders quivered. "I'm so s-sorry I let you down, Mom, *really* sorry."

Mary nodded with an expression of bewildered maturity. "Well, these things happen, don't they?" It occurred to her she already had believed Ellen was doing it, as Ellen had put it, euphemistically. Nice that she waited this long.

Ellen didn't seem to hear. "We—messed around, back before Christmas. I did . . . some stuff . . . for him. But now it's a lot w-worse than just having real sex with him. It's *more* than giving myself to him." Her youthful face became a mask of shock, of dismay. "Mom, listen! When he went to sl-sleep afterward, the body he's using—well, he loses *control* of it. All those things his b-brain does, when he wills it—they don't *happen* when Andruss is asleep! It isn't involuntary, d'you *hear* me?" The tears began to pour. Ellen looked used, beaten, "Momma, Andruss's flesh got all . . . *saggy. Gray.* And it *cracked*, right in front of me! Oh God, it was just *awful!*" She gulped. "Finally I r-realized that Andy wasn't actually a b-boy at all, but *a very old man!*"

283

Well now, this was obviously important to Ellen, and Mary strove, hard, to focus on what the girl was saying. "Honey, you found out about it in time, then. Look at it that way." Her mind created an image of her beautiful, softly rounded daughter with her lovely complexion lying beside a naked grandfather—worse, an animated *corpse*—but she couldn't deal with it and it swam away. "I mean, don't be too concerned. You can just leave the lights out, next time."

"We had a fight! A terrible f-fight!" Ellen sobbed, leaning toward her mother, wanting the woman's arms around her. "He—heard me crying, woke up, and wanted to know why. I *t-told* him!"

Mary set the wine glass on the end table next to her. "You can stop dating him, if you want. Of course, he's a—a *nice* boy, honey. The Patriarch thinks highly of him, you know." Wandering, her mind was wandering. She squinted. "You might even have to make a public apology. I don't think they like having their real age insulted."

It was a long moment that Ellen stared at her mother in horror. The realization of what had happened to Mary Graham—in part because of her own actions—gradually dawned on the girl until a surge of guilt was added to her original emotion. "What have we *done* to you?" she cried, taking Mary's hands in hers. They felt cold, clammy, like Andruss's. "Momma, you're half out of your *mind* on this—this 'medicine' Velda brings you. Please, Momma—*listen* to me!"

Mary shook her dazed head. "I don't think we

should talk about our friends this way."

Desperately, Ellen took Mary's shoulders and shook them. Mary's head wobbled. "Mom, d'you realize that when you b-bought everything the Patriarch told you, *you never even* asked *how he condoned Vrukalakos* murdering *Aunt Jeanne?* Do you? You never even *asked!*"

Just slightly, the heavy, blurred mass that had become Mary's mind slipped. Startled, it began sluggishly to ponder. Yes, Ellen was right: *That* was the key question she'd meant to ask for the past few months, the one that was always sliding just out of reach. She experienced shame. "I guess I just f-forgot." She stared blankly at Ellen. "Milo must have had an awfully good reason."

"Mom, Jeanne was your *best friend!* Even Chuck and I thought it was bad." She paused. "Maybe, if you'd said something then—stood *up* to us—we might have swung round to your side."

"Well, damn it, don't yell at me!" Mary drew back from her daughter, her head clearing further. "I thought you and Chuck *wanted* me to follow you and your precious friends. I thought that was the only way we could keep the family together!"

Ellen sagged wearily into the sofa. "At first, yes. Later too, I guess. But kids . . . kids always want something new and different to use in challenging their folks." She peered again at her mother's ashen face and began to cry. "I never thought that *anything* they d-did would make *you* go against your standards!"

A long return stare. It took a supreme effort of

will. Mary's brain shook off the restraining ropes. As they fell, a terrible headache formed at the base of her skull; but this time, she let it come. "There's—something *else,* isn't there, Ellen? Something I should know but you haven't told me. What is it?"

A glitter of hope touched the girl's eyes. "Yes, Momma, I'll tell you. It—it's Joey." She barely saw him in his throne-chair across the room, and blurted it all out when she saw her mother's intelligence assume form. "I was so mad at Andruss that I told him what the Patriarch told *you.* Y'know, about Joey's task being to replace Vrukalakos. And Andy, well, he was saved from *death* by the vampire—remember?" Realizing the consequence of her words, Ellen spoke more swiftly. "Andy got so mad at me he's gone off t'tell Vrukalakos what the Patriarch is planning!"

Mary's light green eyes blinked several times. She leaned forward. "You let Andruss tell that— that hideous *monster?*" she demanded. "El, how *could* you! He'll—"

Her head spun. There'd been a flurry of noise. Both mother and daughter looked.

Joey, a terrified expression on his pale young face, his tousled blond hair askew, barely glanced at them. Then he was scurrying through the front room and dashing outdoors, running at top speed.

The clearheaded Ellen was on her feet first. "Mom, what do we *do?*"

Mary got to her own feet unsteadily, her hand trembling at her temple as she concentrated. "All right, dear," she said, dredging up her old poise, "here's what we will do. You run down the street to Milo's house. Tell him what's gone wrong. Tell him that I've followed Joey."

"Momma, you don't know where he went!" she cried.

"Oh, yes, give me credit for still knowing my children a little." Mary nodded, already throwing on a coat. "He doubled back, along the side of the house. He's headed for the woods."

"Y-You can't follow him there, Mom," Ellen argued; "not in your condition."

"I have no choice, I'm his mother," she said simply. She took a deep breath and hurried toward the french doors. "Go ahead, now! Tell the Patriarch everything, as fast as you can."

Ellen, casting a last desperate glance, ran to the front door. She saw Mary quietly opening the french doors and stepping out, and she thought it was the most valiant act she'd ever seen. Tears smarting, she dashed down the street to the Patriarch's house.

Spring was still, at best, a coming attraction. Patches of snow crackled beneath Mary's feet as she strode quickly toward the range of trees. She wanted to run but did not dare. The temperature was chilly at night, but not unbearable, and fear coated her forehead with perspiration. Thank God there was a full moon, Mary thought, seeing the measure of illumination it provided as she disappeared into the trees.

Happily, too, the brisk air was working with her own aroused maternal determination to push aside the months of cloudy, will-less befuddlement. Still, nearly seven months pregnant now, Mary could scarcely hurry. Once she tried to run, couldn't; it was just a time-wasting waddle. The deeper she moved into the forest—occasionally calling Joey's name, though she knew he would not answer—the less moonlight existed. Soon it became a nightmare odyssey; tree branches slapped, seemingly with willed malice, at her arms and legs, tearing her skin and bringing tears to her emerald eyes. Yet she pushed on, thinking hard, ever more clearly, moving slowly and trying desperately not to fall and injure the baby she carried.

Suddenly she knew, without a shadow of doubt, where an honest and direct boy clinging to his impenetrable magnificence would go: Straight *to Vrukalakos's post at the great stone* herma *in the Vale of Aphaca!* Joey would *tell* Vrukalakos, right to his terrifying face, either to explain that he did not choose to replace the monster, or that he simply knew nothing of the others' plans. Knowing Joey, he might even *boast* of how grand it was to be selected!

And the saturnine, moustached face of that bloody creature sprang alarmingly into Mary's mind, galvanizing her to even more concerted progress through the tangled woods.

The image of a dead Joey, not unlike the reanimated Barry, swam before her eyes. Rushing now, trying again to run, Mary fell heavily once and thought she felt some dreadful *shift* inside. She used tree branches to tug herself, tearfully, to her feet. Now she could think only of her little Joey—her awful problem child, that emotionally disturbed, hyperkinetic lad whom she had always secretly adored because no one else could tolerate his presence, not until Thessaly—the child whom she had always defended against attack, and always would.

Even if it cost her her own life.

Breathing in gasps, sobbing both from exhaustion and terror for Joey, Mary broke at last into the clearing.

The Vale of Aphaca spread before her like a hungry maw in the face of the hostile fairy's forest.

And the moonlight bathed the scene clearly, showered it in a ghastly off-white; it highlighted details of the nocturnal trees and bolts and clumps of weed and grass. It seemed an etching made in hell, bloodless and lifeless. Beside the pile of great stones stood the omnipresent death-coach, ready for another soul-searing midnight ride. She saw the huge dark horses pawing the fresh, early-spring dirt, their ears laid back at sound of her approach, their staring eyes enormous.

And, on their other side, similarly listening in a curiously frozen, vulpine way, was Vrukalakos.

Mary saw only him for a moment, and then, clutched in the vampire's clawed fingers, *she saw Joey* too. Her heart exulted! Apparently Andruss had thought better of betraying the Patriarch. If only Joey had said nothing yet to the vampire, if *only* he had kept still for this one time!

Mary froze in fear. It became quickly clear that Joey had told Vrukalakos everything. She lifted a hand as she saw the towering, swarthy figure scoop the small blond boy into his powerful arms in a falconlike swoop, like a hawk snatching an innocent rabbit. She saw him turn, to head into that place of the dead—the enigmatic home of nameless terrors undescribed even by Pythagoras, the home of things that crept and hungered for the living. Empedocles's words—"This *feeding's* monstrous crimes"—leapt to her mind as she realized that Vrukalakos meant to take her Joey *below*, to be devoured by—*something*—she'd heard moving there.

"*Vrukalakos!*" she screamed desperately. "*Please*, stop! He's only a *boy!*"

Now the creature turned back and the glistening eyes, the wide tooth-edged red mouth, spread in hideous, derisive amusement. "And what is that to me, madam?" he demanded, the voice floating ghostlike to her across the clearing. "Did I not promise you revenge for your disrespectful ways? All things have no age, no meaning for me, except as hearty blood to be drunk and bodies to be reanimated . . . or *inhabited.*" He grasped Joey tight in his strong, wiry arms. "If this small one is truly Triptolemus, as he told me, his entrails should allow me to prophesy a vastly better future for me than what you fools had planned—*after* Aether has his way with the lad!"

"Joey had nothing to do with any of that," Mary pleaded honestly, moving to within feet of the vampire now. "He didn't *know* what the

Patriarch intended. He told you the truth!"

His flaming eyes peered into hers. "Truth? And what is that?" Vrukalakos shrugged, almost elegant in his hell-born hate. "It is truly relative. The truth is that Pythagoras would breach our compact, our contract—that he would cast me aside, risk abandoning the eternal antipathies that have kept us both alive. Pythagoras is a bloody fool!"

"*You are correct, Vrukalakos. I am a fool.*"

Mary and the creature each turned to see the old man, the Patriarch, approaching them. Dressed in his formal tunic and robes, with moonlight lighting him from behind, the old man seemed cast from silver. "A fool ever to believe that one should compromise with such evil as you have always represented. A fool to be obliged to wait more than two thousand years to learn it from a simple mother and her son. My good, I fear, is not so grand as I considered it, and you see, for *that* reason, a mischievous child will suffice to complete the complement." He stopped pacing and said, with dignity, "Release the boy."

Vrukalakos laughed. "And what if I don't?" His vampire-jet eyes shone like crow's wings. "You cannot kill me, man. And if I choose, I can take another form and flee instantly. Then, however, I would not have the pleasure of placating Aether or of taking my vengeance."

Pythagoras did not reply. Instead, he knelt beside Mary in a patch of bare ground and quickly, using his fingernail, drew a design in the dirt. Touching the stones with a rhythmical gesture, he whispered a brief prayer. Then he looked up at the thing that had been his unwilling ally for so long, and their intent faces were frozen in moonlight gleam.

"It is true. I cannot kill you." He did not rise. "But I can *contain* you, Vrukalakos, and *I shall!*" He looked in every direction and intoned a word: *"Come!"*

From every direction, they came. The forest began sending forth its almost infinite variety of animal life, bursting toward the Vale in abnormally quiet cooperation: bear, huge wild dogs, foxes, maniac cats slowly began to encircle the site of Antipodes, things slithering and hopping in the grass. All the beasts and birds pressed Vrukalakos closer, and closer. Winged things, bats and others, darted soundlessly around his swarthy head, jabbing and nipping, drawing blood.

Now, Pythagoras stood. "They are wholly under my control," he said, watching the vampire lift his arms to protect his eyes. "And you cannot occupy them whilst I do. Again, Vrukalakos: *Release* the *boy.*"

What happened next was lightninglike. With a glare of mortal hatred so vicious it was like a literal electrical bolt, Vrukalakos hurled Joey Graham to the ground, hard.

But before Mary Graham could call for him to run to her, the boy—shocked and so terrified that he was thinking unclearly—turned and dashed into the awful opening between the stones. Instantly he was out of sight.

"Saboi!" the Patriarch growled his imprecation, starting forward. "We must get Joey out of there quickly!"

"But *you* do not know the way!" exclaimed Vrukalakos, jubilantly spinning to face them. "I do—and he is meat for Aether!"

Mary screamed in terror. Before her eyes the creature's face and form blurred, and he was scuttling at enormous speed into the mouth of the cave. He had used his powers to become a rat! She gaped sickly at the vacated entrance to the Vale, unable to move.

"Quickly, my child!" Pythagoras cried, rousing her from her astonishment by seizing and shaking her arm. "We *must* reach your son before he does!"

XVII

Nowadays we tend to associate Pythagoras with early science and mathematics; but this is a mistake. He was primarily a religious mystic who was interested in *everything*. . . . In all, he [traveled] from his homeland for thirty-four years, and . . . encountered sages from India or China, for there is a strong element of Oriental *mysticism* in his later philosophy, as well as a belief in *reincarnation* that he elaborated into *metempsychosis*, the belief that the soul may pass into the body of other creatures. . . . This (seeking secret laws of proportion) was the essence of Pythagoras' vision, and . . . it is fundamentally a *true vision*—truer, perhaps, than we shall encounter anywhere else in the realm of magic. Instinctively Pythagoras understood the *upward* evolutionary movement of life . . . towards *distance vision*, the ability to grasp *far horizons of reality*. . . . We may note, in passing, that the Greeks seem to have *lived to a greater age than most races*.

—Colin Wilson, *The Occult*,
Vintage, New York, 1971

"Touch nothing here, disturb nothing unfamiliar," commanded Pythagoras, "only seek the hand of your child. 'Shriveled diseases and obscene days' lurk on our path, according to my compatriot Empedocles."

It was so dark in the tunnel that Mary reached into her pocket for matches. She struck one and held it aloft.

"Use them sparingly," ordered the old man. "We know not how far we must advance into the earth."

Narrow at first, twisting like a madman's mind, the tunnel quickly widened to a slick cavern with ice-clammy walls. Deep shadows concealed segments of walling that lingered like mysterious closets beyond the range of matchlight, and Mary was glad the Patriarch accompanied her. The shadowed compartments almost magnetized her; something within urged her to step in. Each step led them gradually down, down, farther into the bowels of the cavern.

"Joey!" she whispered, the breathed word nearly extinguishing the light. She was startled by the way her voice carried into the endless pit and echoed back at her. "Joey, it's Mom!"

Only deadly silence replied—

—And a miniscule, scrabbling *hint* of noise, so close to nothing that she could not be sure it wasn't her imagination. Pythagoras's big hand closed on her elbow, steadying her.

They advanced, always down, and after some forty feet the match flickered and went out.

Mary gasped. She thought she'd felt hot breath

on the fingers gripping the match. Never had she imagined such total darkness, and it frightened her badly. More than like a nightmare, it was a glimpse of some tormented hell of the unconscious mind where merry madness carromed off ebon walls and unseen ghouls chittered a greeting, imminent and deadly. As swiftly as she could Mary lit another match with shaking fingers, and as its white-orange puny flame ate perhaps an inch of darkness, she glanced to her right—

—And leapt, breath indrawn, into the old man's stalwart arms.

Her gaze had directly dropped upon a terrible mark, rumored to exist for thousands of ghost-mired years.

For on the cave wall, imbedded four inches *deep, were* claw-prints—*in effect, fingerprints, carved in solid* stone, *as if the product of a single fierce and indescribably powerful grasp of the slablike wall.*

She looked away fearfully. "Wh-What are those?"

The Patriarch's eyes were sad and worried, anxious. "The monster who lives below must be served, even today. Once, it would appear from these marks, he became almost *too* hungry to devour civilization and actually drew near the land of men. But for it to step cleanly upon the surface of our earth would be the only way it can die." He paused, and said its name. "*Aether.*"

"What *is* Aether?" she asked, her own voice unfamiliar in her ears.

He looked deep into her eyes. "Once it was said that its name was a symbol of the essential breath of man, the spirit-presenting gift of animation at birth, of vivification. Later I believed that it was only the bleak and black breath given man, that vaporous kiss which brings with it the pledge of inevitable demise. Now"—Pythagoras peered deeper into the shadows, and shuddered—"*now* I have come to know that Aether is much more, but I shall tell no one, ever, what bestial horror may lie near the heart of life."

They pressed on and then, to the horror of both the young woman and the aged man, there was suddenly a blazing of what might have been light but was more akin to the atmospheric haze drifting above the lambent surface of a poisonous mire, or perhaps to the vision furnished by torches seen at a great distance, dimly illuminating the process of some lost and arcane funeral.

In the ebbing and convoluted whorl of the bizarre light Mary could make out, beneath the "roofed cave," a distant procession of once-human creatures toting upon their gnarled but massive shoulders great, teeming jars. At their sides several smaller, more grotesque beings carried ebon whips which they sometimes unfurled in a cracking *snap!* of sound and which left scarlet ribbons of blood oozing in the bearers' broad backs. Seated against the walls, humped and grimacing in agony, yellowed creatures covered with running pustules moaned dimly and sometimes thrashed in a paroxysm of collective pain.

Still farther down, Mary saw, some kind of

lurid dance was in progress, the Terpsichorean-struck participants constituting a maze of anthropomorphic antihumans with the bodies of beautiful women and the passion-wracked skulls of cattle, hyenas, black panthers, and immense rats.

Then, mercifully, the tunnel Pythagoras had chosen led them past the distant scene and into another valley of total silence—an almost conscious suppression of sound. Mingling with the reeking odors of purling pools and gagging waste, amongst other stenches Mary could mercifully not identify, was the unvoiceable suggestion that this stillness was *commanded*, or worse, effected by the far-off approach of things monstrous and corrupt. In the detached, faint tinkle of sound she now sometimes made out, distantly, in the stifled quick-breath hint of sensual things roused from stealthy endeavors, there was also something chokingly *sexual* in nature—as if perversions beyond description awaited her passing.

Abruptly all the awesome absence of noise was shattered as though bombed away. Tumultuous, luridly loud, hell broke loose in a dinning cacophony of violent annihilative sound. At first it was impossible to distinguish one noise from another; then, as their ears made the painful adjustment possible, they could at least conceive of massive bodies lurching forward, legless and deformed, propelled on weighty, determined arms—of other bodies even farther distant, keening to listen and summoning rasping chortles that rose from multiple filthy throats—of some central source of lumbering clamor, drawing near.

Then, *smell* burst upon them. Fetid. Hot as sex, yet so frigid in intent that one winced away from it. *Sticky* smell, so adhesive it stretched like a taut foreskin on the flinching nostrils and crawled with the droning-away sound along the offended spine.

"Now we must go back," Patriarch said softly in Mary's ear.

She barely heard him. "No," she paused, "*you* go. I'll stay." Her eyes pleaded with him. "What was that?"

"'*And Aether,*'" the old man quoted, "'*the Titan, who binds the globe about.*' He lives everywhere beneath the ground, but the Vale is his entrance. He has sensed us somehow—us, Joey, and Vrukalakos. And to enter the world of Antipodes without a suitable sacrifice is to risk the worst death it is possible for a mortal to conceive."

"*Joey,*" she breathed, horrified. "The vampire . . . means *Joey* . . . for Aether?"

"I fear that he does," the Patriarch sighed, nodding. "And no man may know the nature of that heinous death—demise in Aether's claws— and survive."

Then the short figure shot forth at them from behind the outjutting wall and they jumped in abject terror as it began pummeling them with valiant fists.

It was Joey Graham, his frightened blue eyes blinking rapidly, his tiny body wracked with violent tremors as Mary snatched him into her waiting, relieved arms. He hugged her, hard. "Oh, Mom!" he sobbed, unable to halt his spasming limbs. *"Mom-Mom-Mom!"*

Pythagoras reached down with a soft, merry laugh and scrubbed at the lad's golden mop of hair with his large, kind hand. "Let us remove ourselves from this vale of misery for good," he urged lightly.

They began to retrace their steps, Mary conscious of her almost total exhaustion, blinded by her headache. The uphill climb was treacherous, much harder than going the other way. Passing the corridor leading to the outer chamber of Hades propelled her and the others to go faster.

But then the terrible sounds again *exploded*, careening maniacally off the cavern walls. Obviously they were nearer; clearly they approached from just *yards* of where they stood.

Mary paused, half-carrying the ten-year-old, to touch Pythagoras's hairy arm. "Milo, you said that *no one* could approach Aether," she gasped, "without a sacrifice. Not try it and survive." She tilted her head. "Vrukalakos . . . ?"

The Patriarch nodded. "He lost your son, somehow could not find him, and encountered Aether. In his thirst for revenge upon Joey and me, he has gone too far even for the intercession of my people."

"B-But you said he could not be killed," she protested, as they resumed their upward toil.

"There is life," he replied, panting himself now, "and there is life. And there are truly things *worse* than death. I pray you will not have to see what Aether has done to Vrukalakos."

Ahead, at last, they saw a glimmer of light and

Mary cast the matchbook aside for a tighter grip on Joey. She saw the way he cast petrified glances of fear behind them and tried to hurry. As they reached the surface of the earth, stepping out onto the ground of the Vale of Aphaca and Thessaly, Mary looked back in time to see the strong body of the vampire from ancient Greece hoisted into the air by a series of immense, titanic-clawed hands.

Framed against the stygian darkness of the tunnel entrance as they stood in safety and turned to stare, it was impossible for them to see the face of what had unhesitatingly plucked Vrukalakos's head from his neck with a snapping sound and hurled it far into the woods. But they heard the giant claws rend the vampire's magical body, tearing it into pieces, and they saw the sections of Vrukalakos's corpse come flying after the rolling, spinning head.

Mary turned away, sickened in spite of her hatred of Vrukalakos. Joey clapped his hands in glee. But Pythagoras merely pointed.

The maimed hands and feet continued to clutch and paw at the earth, writhing in mute agony, impotent now of any destruction or harm but that of repugnance, and shock—but they were still, *they realized when they turned to look upon its silent and agonized face, quite hideously* . . . alive.

A sound midway between a great cat's roar and the whining shriek of a large bird issued from the mouth of the cave, and for a dreadful moment, Mary thought the monster Aether would follow the vampire. Even as she stared, paralyzed,

Aether's vast shadow spread along the inner wall, consuming every inch of the gigantic cavern—some thirty-five feet in height, sixty feet in length. A burst of steamlike exhalation exploded toward them, foul and fevered, the lasting stink of that which thrives on the unwilling living and the unforgiving dead. It fell short, burning smoky holes in the earth where, Mary thought, nothing could ever grow again.

Then the Patriarch was shoving Mary and Joey aside, away from the opening to the system of tunnels leading to Antipodes. With all his time-tested might Pythagoras pulled and tugged the great stone until it sealed its terrible lips over the orifice of certain and eternal death. Finally he leaned on the rock, weary and apparently defeated, breathing hard. Sweat curled in his great beard like the rivulets of a river heading for its source.

Even still, behind him, came the noises of enormous, fistlike appendages—dozens of them—thrumming, drumming on the solid rock.

"W-Will it hold?" Mary whispered.

"It has, for millenia." The old man gave her his best answer, thrusting himself away from the rockface to begin leading the way toward the woods, and Mary Graham's cottage.

Joey could walk now but he seemed to be in shock, docilely gripping his mother's hand as tightly as he could. Pythagoras found the path in the woods.

The thought dazzled Mary then. "You wanted us—and *your own people*—to go *down there?*" she asked, incapable of comprehending the Patriarch's purpose. "You *planned* such a terrible event? Milo, what did you have in mind, really—some kind of ritual death, something symbolic you considered suitable?"

"I did not lie, child," he murmured. "It would have succeeded, if I handled it properly, if Vrukalakos were dead and your son the new keeper. And if we had gone at the propitious moment, astrologically. I knew all the methods, the correct procedures. They were mathematically conceived, computer-tested, spiritually blessed. I ask you: What more can you ask?" He smiled despite how aged he now seemed. "But it is over, Mary Graham. You have won your triumph, for what value it will be to you in a world of the dead. It is over."

Her heartbeat accelerated. "I suppose I have. But I don't know what you mean by its being ended."

They stopped on the fringe of her yard, just away from the trees, flooded with the cool rays of the full moon. He looked at her with an expression of eloquence and of such utter dejection that her heart, despite herself, went out to him. It no longer mattered, really, whether he actually was Pythagoras or merely a magical old man with the gift of absolute belief in himself. "I mean that *everything* is over, Mary, in the literal sense of the word. Within hours, at any rate. To begin with, losing Vrukalakos has broken the antipathy improperly and most of my powers will fade swiftly. This body is old; it cannot exist much

303

longer—but that, in itself, is of little note. What is important is that all of us—my *phrateres* of three thousand years—must continue to follow their overrated and presumptive leader. Into the arms of a God who may well feel outraged by how we have tampered with His abiding rules."

He stopped speaking for a moment and Mary, her natural perceptions returning, felt that something the Patriarch had said had even more meaning for him than the words he uttered.

He urged them to perch, for a moment, on the fence at the back of the large yard, slipping his arm around Joey's shoulder and glancing down tenderly at him. "Poor little Triptolemus, his reign was brief." He sighed, and drew his voluminous cape around him, shivering. "Aether, my dear Mary, draws this close to the surface of the earth only infrequently. In hunger he lurks, hoping someone will move the stone. Even evil, you see, may be pitied. It too has its yens, its precious hungers and desires. While Aether is below, he is served the bony cadavers of time past and time present, goes back to sleep, and must wait another hundred years for his chance. My plan was to divert Aether as we entered the secret tunnels by using Vrukalakos, whom Aether trusted in mutual malice. The vampire, you see, did not know that the monster's closest entry to humankind was scheduled. Aether would turn upon Vrukalakos as we, protected by Triptolemus's spiritual substitution for the vampire, slipped by and made our way to that fabulous nebula of which I spoke. Ah, I was eloquent," he exclaimed, striking his bare thigh, "an eloquent fool!"

"Never a fool," Mary said gently, "Pythagoras."

He swiveled his hirsute head to peer at her, pleased that she had finally addressed his antiquity by name. "Alas, my child, we do not now dare enter the doorway to hell with such a ravening beast clawing at the stone. Even with our Joey's brave assistance."

They resumed the walk to Mary's french doors and the Patriarch reached down to pick the boy up and hug him with cordial, grandfatherly affection.

When at last he replaced the weary boy on his feet again, Pythagoras's face and physical bearing suggested that all his miraculous, uncounted years were gathering like sneaking assassins, merging with the wounded and dispirited man who had spoken to her so recently.

But his *eyes*, Mary saw, were another proposition. For a moment they were aflame again with the old confidence, the almost arrogant resolve to do what he considered best. He raised a wide palm to rest it on her shoulder and she felt, in that instant, almost that she was being comforted by her own father.

"Do not grieve for us, child," he advised her, leaving the palm where it was. "Grieve instead for the people of the late twentieth century, the only ones with whom we could not merge and retain our ways intact. Grieve for the greater darkness that even now moves in twisted shadows in the computerized night sky."

She did not believe such danger for a moment, now that she was herself again. When she spoke, she referred to him and to his people, and knew that he knew it. "Is there anything we can do, sir?"

"There is nothing *you* can do, or your children," he responded with a sad shake of his massive head. "Perhaps I asked too much of you all; perhaps I may even remain a villain in your lovely eyes, but I hope that shall not be true. It appears that the long lives and priceless labors of the Synod are simply at a close. Believe me when I say that I take no solace in the end of your race on March twentieth. And try to believe me when I say that I strove to operate from a proven, enduring body of principle—a part of which is my conviction that a known, established civilization is preferable to a theoretical existence after life. I must question my wisdom now, at last—a query postponed far too long. The answer frightens me." He drew himself erect, withdrawing his hand from her shoulder and lifting his head. "Still and all, I have tried to celebrate God's greatest gift of life as it was never celebrated anywhere else in the world, and that, I suppose, must be my only laurel when I am summoned to a *different* kind of eternity."

"What will you do now?" she asked. "Or does it matter to you?"

"Of course, it matters!" he said hotly. "Am I not still alive, child?" Then he laughed heartily and bent forward to press his lips against her

306

forehead in a kiss of forgiving, fatherly farewell. They felt cold. "I go now to plan how best to break this dreadful news to the Syndic and thence to the Synod at large. We know, now, that our days too are numbered and must begin learning what all you others have intuitively known all your lives." He gave her a brisk, youthful salute. "Take heart, Mary Graham—and love life while you have it!"

She stared after him. Instead of reentering the woods, the Patriarch passed beside her cottage to the street and doggedly moved, in trudging steps, toward his own house. Suddenly the man she'd called Milo Traphonius appeared incongruous, an aging Shriner tottering away from his last parade, an overweight and overaged *gallant* caught in his cape beneath a modern streetlight like some lunatic Durante soon to bid Mrs. Calabash goodbye.

Yet she went on looking, because human dignity is lovely to see, because whether he was insane or not he was beautiful in his courage, memorable in having always been himself.

Mary took Joey by the hand and went inside. She told Ellen and Chuck only a part of the story, and began wondering what the Patriarch would do when March 20th came, and went, and he and his people were still alive.

Immediately her concerns were with getting the ten-year-old Joey settled beneath the covers, taking his temperature and soothing him with motherly reassurances until he dropped into what seemed to be a deep, natural sleep. With the justifiably famous resiliency of the very young,

Mary prayed, he should awaken, and in time, be all right. When he slipped his thumb in his mouth, however, she withdrew it—barely able to avoid the temptation to yank it from his lips. Would they ever be themselves again, she wondered?

And was the baby inside her all right, or had she hurt it, perhaps irreparably hurt herself? She did not know, as she moved around the house, fending off Chuck's demands for more detail; there was no way to be sure. She took the rest of the tainted kykeon wine from the end table in the front room where she'd left it, went upstairs, and poured it into the toilet. She found the aspirin bottle in the medicine cabinet, took three of them with a glass of welcome cold water, went in to sit in Joey's room, and looked out the window.

It was a chilly night, but a rebirth awaited them in a spring that wasn't far ahead. Perhaps, at least; but wasn't "perhaps" all any of them—except possibly Milo's people—had to depend upon? She tried not to think about Chuck and Ellen because she could not, just yet, trust them again. They had committed perhaps the only unforgivable sins possible for American children at a certain age; rape, robbery, even treason might be more readily forgotten. Besides, being a human mother, Mary wanted to punish them awhile with that dignity permitted her kind: silence.

She looked at her wristwatch, saw that it still worked, saw that it was midnight, and inhaled in a little gesture of joy. There would be no death-coach thundering across the short streets of tiny

Thessaly for the first time in a dozen years. Its horrid coachman lay in anguished pieces in the woods.

Joy seeped away. Somehow that didn't seem so important anymore, nor did much of what had happened. Dreams might endure a lifetime, but the nice thing about a nightmare was that it ended. It occurred to her that she would be free to leave now, to tell the children the entire story if she pleased, and, sadder but wiser, take them back to the civilization she knew best. With the Patriarch defeated, possibly ostracized, Chuck and Ellen and Joey would accompany her. And, if they all survived their trauma, it would be possible to pick up the pieces and start anew. They would learn that Lythia and Andruss were only living shades, fleshy scraps of retooled garbage no better—no more worthwhile—than their poor father. They would seek, in time, loves who would, for awhile, live.

But even that didn't seem as important as once it had been, although surely *real* life—however temporary and bound to be cut short—was preferable to the faded memory of life. Her gaze had fallen upon the house down the block and other matters of moment occupied Mary Graham.

In those four dark walls was a very old man who was virtually alone and believed it to be with the full and enormous weight of an almost three-thousand-year-old failure on his ancient shoulders. He was right, of course. It was all over now, and with its end, came their release—Mary's and her family's—from a strange, foreign way of life.

Yet without wondering why, sensing that she would never be able to put a label on it other than that she had periodically been exposed to ideas of genius, Mary felt tears start in her eyes and her heart go out into the silent Thessaly night to the man who called himself Pythagoras, and who, she suddenly knew, *was*.

What *wasn't* over came to a head a few days later.

Without having informed the Syndic of what had happened to him in company with Mary Graham and her son Joey, or even of what had happened to Vrukalakos and why he had vanished, the Patriarch arose in the early morning hours of March nineteenth and walked alone to the Church of Mycone.

There in the *megaron* he withdrew the *Logos* from its protective container, pored over it awhile, sighed, and carried it in his strong but aging arms to the Vale of Aphaca. There he found the writhing, agonized pieces of his mortal enemy and buried them. He whispered a few ancient prayers and hoped, privately, that the time would come when the ground in this spot would stop rising and falling.

Gripping the immortal book tightly against his bosom, he again summoned the animal life of the Thessaly forest. Together, Pythagoras and his beasts approached the gigantic stone, and with the utmost difficulty, pushed it aside. He paused at its entrance and set fire to the particular pages near the end of the *Logos*, ignoring the smouldering

310

heat searing his breast, and paused for a last look at a world he had known for almost three thousand years.

It was the final, desperate hope of the Patriarch that he might succeed in clearing the path for his *akousmatikoi* to enter the tunnel safely and escape worldwide Armageddon through the Vortex to the nebula and thence to his counter-earth. He had left the directions, the last instructions he would give, at the *megaron*, beneath the giant Greek letter E. He had set fire to the *Logos* because he believed such a stupendous event and the presence of the theological marvel might give him a few moments of protection against Aether. It was important, too, that no one should ever gain possession of the book.

When he stepped into the cave, followed by his directed assortment of animals and birds, ready to die for him even as his people had been prepared, there was—beneath them—a scrambling sound, as if something had got clumsily to its many feet and rumbled upward toward them. . . .

Later in the day, when Pythagoras was missed and young Andruss discovered the gaping aperture remaining in the Vale of Aphaca, they began coming to Mary for an explanation. She had been the last one with whom the Patriarch had spent much time and they knew, now, that she had been with him on the journey to Antipodes.

She gave them the explanation they sought, haltingly, with tears in her eyes. With the information the old man had left in the *megaron*, it was enough.

"Pythagoras has obeyed the ancient injunction," Nicholas Melas grunted without changing his expression beyond the glint of respect in his eyes.

George Aristides had tears in his eyes, too, as Mary did. "The tradition," he explained to her and the children, "saying that a Greek leader must always be obligated to take the *ultimate* step. Even eager to do so. And now, of course, we must follow the Patriarch."

Mary's lips parted in amazement. He had said it so simply that she wasn't sure, for an instant, that he meant what she had thought.

Melas looked past her. This was a Thessaly issue now. "You are correct, of course," he agreed. "I will gather the entire Synod at the *megaron* within the hour."

Suddenly Mary jumped to her feet and stood in front of Joey. "You can't take Joey!" she declared, shielding him. "I told you what terrible creatures lurk down in that God-forsaken hole of a place, and it's certain death without either Pythagoras or Vrukalakos. I won't let you take him!"

"You are quite right in all you say. Of course it is certain death," Melas agreed. "Myths are of no assistance now. But the Patriarch may have paved the way for us with his last breath."

"A good leader is always followed by good people," Aristides agreed, nodding, and both of them left without a single backward glance.

She saw no one but her own children for the

312

remainder of the day. At a distance she could hear busy sounds, murmurings of conversation, low calls. That evening of March 19th she stood in the backyard behind her cottage, watching with ambivalent feelings as the two hundred citizens of Thessaly walked in the new spring twilight toward the forest and an incredible destiny predicted nearly three thousand years before.

It was, of course, a brisk and ordered pace they set, not military in the sense of pacing columns, but precise and brave. They wore the costumes Pythagoras had given them; they were a town full of people from the riotous 1960s, it seemed, their arms clutching the few possessions that, in some cases, went all the way back to ancient Greece. Their olive complexions and their newly found Hoosier faces were Indian-stoic; they looked straight ahead to the future, as they always had. One of them, who had clearly cheated, carried beneath her arm a *Good Housekeeping* cookbook.

Chuck and Ellen stood at Mary's side, Joey hiding, speechlessly, behind her. They had not asked to go. Youthful, unable as yet to summon adequate compassion and feeling for something they felt betrayed by, they seemed—at a glance— the three children who had come to Thessaly months ago. Andruss and Lythia, passing them, turned fleetingly to bestow parting smiles, but neither Ellen nor Chuck altered expression or lifted a hand to wave.

Yet when the last citizen of Thessaly had passed into the woods forever, Chuck and Ellen gave their mother a fond hug, and going back into the house, had tears gleaming in their eyes. Suddenly in pain, Mary went upstairs and rummaged around until she found the long-discarded photograph of Barry Graham; then she pressed her lips against it, and fainted.

She was in labor all evening and much of the night, with Ellen obliged, because of fat Mormo's departure, to serve as doctor and midwife. Chuck and Joey waited downstairs in the living room, the teenager pondering his guilt and terribly worried, the younger boy adrift on a sea of frightening fantasies.

Shortly after three A.M., Ellen came wearily to the head of the stairs to call down to them. A premature but apparently healthy baby boy was delivered. He did not have a harelip; he was not blond. He was to be named Barry Traphonius Graham and, Ellen said with a grateful laugh, her mother said she'd hit anyone who objected.

Moments later it was an ultimately happy moment for all of them, a family that had strayed out of Time but had found its way home again.

Gathered in Mary's room with tiny Barry, Jr., they paused when she raised a hushing finger to her lips.

For many hours they had been aware of the fact that Thessaly had gone mute. There was not a single creature left anywhere in town—to growl or threaten, to chitter or sing. No wings had flapped, no scurrying field mice darted defensively through the long green grass, no insects buzzed and lived out their miniscule moments, no gallumphing dog bounced forth to utter his amiable rough song. Like a family dwelling in a darkened prehistoric cave in a universe without farms and buildings, without horse-drawn carts or roaring automobiles, they had listened to the silence of what seemed to them the most deserted town in the history of the civilized world.

It had washed over and through and around them, that bizarre derelection of the familiar, reminding Mary of something she had read in an occult book when she had been struggling to learn about Thessaly: the theory that if one could hear *well enough*—if one could cut through all the clamor of life—one might hear the sound of the planet Earth itself, *breathing*. Talking to itself. It had drawn them psychically together like the prehistoric family around its superstition-budding fire, faces painted crimson in the warpaint of flaming ignorance, hands grasped seancelike to mumble and ward off the awesome advance of knowledge, of progress.

Moments ago Chuck had found his nerves shrieking and gone over to switch on the television set. A young man who might have been retarded was cavorting around a long-haired blonde with geometrically improbable breasts.

But now he, Ellen, and Joey heard Mary's indrawn gasp, and somehow, when their eyes met hers, they knew what she knew:

Today was Commemoration Day. They remembered what Pythagoras had said, about the dead rising from their graves, the past haunting the life-stolen present. And they remembered, with considerably more pain and terror, the final

315

prophecy of Pythagoras: That *this* Commemoration Day would mark the end of the world.

Because, as Mary touched a trembling finger to her lips, they heard distinctly, above them, the sound in the dark night sky almost regretful in its whining drone, the clear sound of progress, of knowledge.

The sound of the planet Earth, breathing. Talking to itself. Possibly, praying.

The television screen went blank. For just a moment the words appeared, "Due to conditions beyond our control . . ."

The little family grasped hands.

The dead rose from their graves, to confront the newly dead.

> All things doth Nature change, enwrapping souls
> In unfamiliar tunics of the flesh.
>
> —Empedocles

AUTHOR'S NOTE

There is a need for me to tidy up before allowing you to go mumbling off into your nightmare.

First, but not most important, the Greek legends, terms, and events such as Commemoration Day described in *Death-Coach* are, to the best of my knowledge, authentic. Authentic, according to my considerable research, in terms of the ancient Pythagoreans.

Second, far more important to note, most of what you have read has little or no bearing upon the life of contemporary Greeks. Not even the slightest effort should be made by the reader toward assuming that the author is anti-Greek or is attempting to do a hatchet-job on one of the finest, most time-honored nationalities of this earth. Putting it honestly in terms that often have

317

a different and more unpleasant context, "I've never met a Greek I didn't like."

Third, however, some of the warnings implicit both in the words of Pythagoras—and the author—may be worthy of your attention. I know that many of the ideas expressed both by him and by me are outrageous and fascinating. That, you see, is what makes a book a book.

—J. N. Williamson,
Indianapolis, Indiana
March 1981

Empedocles of Agrigentum (d. 425 B.C.) spoke of two fundamental powers which set the universe in motion and continued to operate it thereafter—love and hate. These two principles drew things together or drove them apart. . . .

Every state of existence thus has a 'magical' element in it, for it is in that situation by reason of its pathemic response to its surroundings. . . . A strong feeling charges the whole body, energizes the mind and colors the soul. It can quite literally reinvigorate, renew, fortify, blight, damage and even cause death. . . . Each person creates and lives in his own pathemic atmosphere, and his love, serenity, compassion, jealousy, greed, lust, fear, anger, hatred, pride, all contribute to determine his fate. . . . The sufis say that if we do not resolve discord within ourselves on earth, paradise itself will not make us happy."

—Benjamin Walker, *Man and the Beasts Within*
Stein & Day, New York, 1977

ADVENTURE FOR TODAYS MAN

SOLDIER FOR HIRE #1: ZULU BLOOD   (777, $2.50)
by Robert Skimin
Killing is what J.C. Stonewall is paid for, and he'll go anywhere
and kill anybody if the price is right. In Zimbabwe, he must in-
filtrate the inaccessible mountain camp of a fierce warrior chief-
tain, and gets caught in the middle of a bloody revolution.
Stonewall's instinct for survival is as deep as the jungle itself; and
he must kill . . . or be killed!

SOLDIER FOR HIRE #2: TROJAN IN IRAN   (793, $2.50)
by Robert Skimin
Stonewall loathes Communists and terrorists, so he is particularly
eager for his next assignment—in Iran! He joins forces with the
anti-Ayatollah Kurds, and will stop at nothing to blow apart the
Iranian government!

THE SURVIVALIST #1: TOTAL WAR   (768, $2.25)
by Jerry Ahern
The first in the shocking series that follows the unrelenting search
for ex-CIA covert operations officer John Thomas Rourke to
locate his missing family—after the button is pressed, the missiles
launched and the multimegaton bombs unleashed . . .

THE SURVIVALIST #2: THE NIGHTMARE BEGINS
                                         (810, $2.50)
by Jerry Ahern
The United States is just a memory, and WWIII makes the 1940s
look like playstuff. While ex-CIA covert operations officer John
Thomas Rourke searches for his missing family, he must hide
from Soviet occupation forces. Is Rourke the cat or the mouse in
this deadly game?

*Available wherever paperbacks are sold, or order direct from the
Publisher. Send cover price plus 50¢ per copy for mailing and
handling to Zebra Books, 475 Park Avenue South, New York,
N.Y. 10016. DO NOT SEND CASH.*

WORLD WAR II—
FROM THE GERMAN POINT OF VIEW

SEA WOLF #1: STEEL SHARK   (755, $2.25)
by Bruno Krauss
The first in a gripping new WWII series about the U-boat war
waged in the bitter depths of the world's oceans! Hitler's crack
submarine, the U-42, stalks a British destroyer in a mission that
earns ruthless, ambitious Baldur Wolz the title of "Sea Wolf"!

SEA WOLF #2: SHARK NORTH   (782, $2.25)
by Bruno Krauss
The Fuhrer himself orders Baldur Wolz to land a civilian on the
deserted coast of Norway. It is winter, 1940, when the U-boat
prowls along a fjord in a mission that could be destroyed with
each passing moment!

SEA WOLF #3: SHARK PACK   (817, $2.25)
by Bruno Krauss
Britain is the next target for the Third Reich, and Baldur Wolz is
determined to claim that victory! The killing season opens and the
Sea Wolf vows to gain more sinkings than any other sub in the
Nazi navy . . .

*Available wherever paperbacks are sold, or order direct from the
Publisher. Send cover price plus 50¢ per copy for mailing and
handling to Zebra Books, 475 Park Avenue South, New York,
N.Y. 10016. DO NOT SEND CASH.*